Cynthia Hickey

A LOVE FOR DELICIOUS

Cynthia Hickey

DEDICATION

To all my readers who wanted to see Delly's story in print.

ACKNOWLEDGMENTS

Thank you to God for the unending story ideas,
Thank you to my husband, Tom for his unfailing
support, thank you to my family for their patience when
the house needs cleaned.

1

Delicious Williams released the handles of the hand cart and glanced at the dusty faces of her five stepchildren, ranging in age from two to twelve. A two-day walk on foot had left them all disheveled and exhausted. "Y'all stay here. I'm going to look for your uncle." She put a hand to her bodice where the deed to land in Oregon, wrapped tight in oiled paper, crackled with promise.

"We're most likely too late," Ezra Junior said as he reached to the back of their mule, Old Blue, and helped down his youngest siblings. "Uncle Zeke is probably across the river by now and on the trail."

"We won't know unless I ask." On tip-toes, she surveyed the throng of people converged in the town and spotted the sign to a blacksmith. As good a place as any to inquire about one Ezekiel Williams.

With their father not buried a full two days yet, Delly hated leaving the young'uns behind, even for a minute, but at the age of twelve, Junior was more than capable of keeping an eye on them while she asked some questions.

"Are we going to walk all the way to Oregon?" Ten-year-old Dorcas asked. "Because, we just got to Independence, and the bottoms of my feet are almost wore through. Mabel's about to keel over dead, not to mention her kid, and Old Blue sounds like he's been smoking tobacco for too many years."

"The goat and mule are fine. We'll walk if we have to." Delly sympathized with the child, but she'd promised their pa she'd get to Oregon. She never backed down from a promise.

Her feet hurt too, not to mention her back. The blisters on her hands from the cart handles were as big as the Ozark Mountains and not near as pretty. Well, lily white hands were for ladies, something Delly definitely was not. Orphanages weren't known for making ladies out of the children housed there. "I'll return shortly."

She hefted her skirts and dashed into the melee of Main Street. *Please, Lord, keep an eye on my babies.* So intent was she on her prayer for safety, she didn't spot the massive horse until almost too late. When it reared, flailing massive hooves, Delly shrieked and jumped back. Her foot caught on the sidewalk, sending her spiraling backward and landing with a splash in a horse trough. Murky water closed over her head, before she came up sputtering.

A large hand engulfed hers and pulled her to her feet. "Are you all right, Ma'am? The road's a dangerous enough place when someone's paying attention, much less when they're off in daydreams."

"Daydreams!" Delly shoved her wet hair out of her face. "You should control that … that beast."

Hazel eyes narrowed beneath the brim of a floppy hat. "You frightened Cyclone. He's as tame as a puppy."

"Hardly." Delly wrung out her hair then struggled to repin the wet mass. "But I do thank you for your aide in getting me out of the trough."

"You're welcome." He tipped his hat. "Exercise more caution crossing the street, Ma'am. Good afternoon."

"Certainly, sir." With as much of a swish as she could get out of wet cotton, she whirled and traversed down the sidewalk toward her destination. The nerve of the man! The deed! She pulled it from her bodice and unwrapped the paper. Water marks stained the edges. Delly shot a prayer of thanksgiving toward heaven that the words on the paper were still legible.

She stepped through the open door of the blacksmith. Humidity and heat slammed into her. "Excuse me. I'm looking for Ezekiel Williams. He's a wagon master."

A man, bent over a fire, turned and spit a wad of tobacco, barely missing the hem of her skirt. His gaze traveled from the toes of her soaked boots to her dripping form. He raised his eyebrows. "Last train left day before yesterday. Won't be any more this year."

"Was it Mr. Williams's train?" Delly kept her aching hands hidden in the folds of her faded calico.

"Can't tell ya. Only that they're gone. Check at

the mercantile. Might know more over there." He motioned his head to the west.

"Thank you." She turned, glanced in the direction the children waited, then marched down the sidewalk and across the street. With a deep breath, she pushed open the mercantile door.

The aroma of pickles and baked bread greeted her. Dust motes danced on sunbeams radiating through a sparkling window. Rows of colorful fabric lined one wall, tools another. Behind a long counter were stacked piles of food stuffs. A plump woman leaned against the counter, elbows propped on the polished wood. She glanced up with a smile. "I'm Mrs. Avery, owner of this fine establishment. You look like you've come a fair piece and ended up half drowned."

"I have." Delly squared her shoulders. "I'm looking for wagon boss, Ezekiel Williams."

"You just missed him. He led his train out yesterday, but came back today for some forgotten supplies."

Delly grinned. They'd catch up with him after all.

The woman straightened. "Most likely they're still right across the river waiting for the congestion to clear. If you hail the ferry quick, you might catch 'em. A pretty little thing like you, the ferryman might let cut in front of the wagons." She peered over Delly's shoulder. "Got a wagon? Provisions? Where's your man?"

"I have none of those."

"Then most likely the wagon train won't let you join. Single women aren't exactly welcome."

Delly rubbed her aching temples. She'd worry about that when the time came. Besides, Mr. Williams couldn't turn away family. "I'll take my chances, thank you."

"Them yours?"

Hands flat against the glass, seven-year-old Ruth and four-year-old Daniel peered through the window. Delly sighed and nodded. Why couldn't children follow orders? "Two of my five children, anyway. Is there a place I can fill our water jugs?"

"Sure. Well's out back." The storekeeper stuck her hand in a jar of licorice sticks and pulled out five pieces of the candy. "Treat the little ones."

Delly smiled. "I've not much money to speak of."

"No bother. My treat." The woman cocked her head. "You plan on taking all five to Oregon?"

"Yes, ma'am."

"By yourself?"

"If need be."

"Wait here." Mrs. Avery ducked behind a curtain.

Delly slid the candy across the counter then opened the door. "Hand these out to your brothers and sisters. Make 'em last, and go wait where I told you." With her heart in her throat, she watched as they scampered back to where she'd asked them to stay, dodging horses and wagons like nimble goats.

"Here you go." Mrs. Avery set a crate on the counter. "It ain't much, but a gentleman ordered a few supplies and never returned. They're bought and paid for. You might as well use them. Just a few crackers, a jar of pickles, sewing kit, some medical things, a guidebook for the trail, stuff like that."

Delly took a step back. "I don't cotton to charity, ma'am."

"No such thing. I'll just put 'em back on the shelf. Doesn't seem right since they were paid for a week ago. If not for yourself, take 'em for the children." The woman pushed the crate closer.

Delly nodded, knowing she couldn't deny the woman meant well. The small crate likely held a week's worth of supplies, and the sewing kit would come in handy, too. She'd worry about what to do next when the time came. With tears in her eyes, and a whispered "thank you", she hefted the box and headed back to the cart, uncertain how she'd manage to squeeze in one more thing, and yet grateful she had something to add to their meager possessions.

"Dorcas, help me fill these jugs, then we'll head for the river. Your uncle's on the other side." Delly grabbed one jug and handed the other to the girl.

"Does he know about Pa?" Dorcas's chin quivered.

"No, I'm afraid not." Guess she'd be the bearer of bad news along with the deed to the land. Why was it in Ezra's care anyway? Anybody who knew her husband knew he was a carefree soul who would lose his head if it weren't attached. And what did Ezra's warning about a man trying to take control of the precious slip of paper actually mean? Delly glanced around the throng of people. Were she and the children in danger?

She led the way to the offered well, filled the jugs, stored them in the cart, then turned toward the river. By the time they reached the bank, exhaustion weighed her limbs. Fatigue showed on every line of the children's faces. Across the water a sea of canvas topped wagons crowded the bank. They'd made it. The wagons hadn't left yet.

Delly handed the ferryman some of their precious coins then, taking a deep breath against the nausea rising in her stomach, pushed the cart onto the wooden ferry. Junior tugged against a reluctant Old Blue who brayed like a bee stung his flanks. Mabel, their goat, followed suit, planting her tiny hooves against the wood. Delly sympathized with the animals. She had no desire to step on the ferry either.

The two youngest children, sitting on top of the mule, let out shrieks of alarm. Delly's heart thudded. "Dorcas, tie Mabel and her kid to the back of the cart."

Delly went to Junior's aide. With quick movements against the fighting mule, she removed the smaller children from the animal's back and situated them close to the cart. "Now, ya'll sit real still and enjoy the ride. Hold on tight." She caressed the baby's chubby cheek, then straightened.

She grabbed the mule's halter and inwardly cheered when he stepped onto the softly swaying ferry. "Good boy."

With the use of a long pole, the ferry man pushed them slowly away from the bank of the Missouri river. "Hold on, folks. It's a mite bumpy today."

Delly turned and glued her gaze to the opposite shore rather than the churning water. There was a reason she was a mountain girl. Babbling brooks were more her style. As long as the water didn't get deeper than her knees, she didn't worry about losing her breakfast. She preferred anything other than the brown water swirling around their wooden raft. She tilted her chin to the sun, catching a small fishy smelling breeze as it swept over the river.

A man yelled from behind them. Delly glanced back to see a tall man in city clothes slap his hat against his thigh. A few minutes earlier, and he'd have shared their ride.

Something about the way his gaze seemed glued to her sent shivers down her spine despite the heat of the day, and she gave thanks he'd missed the ferry. He waved his fist and shouted something she couldn't decipher. Delly shrugged and grasped the taut rope beside her hand.

Halfway across the river, the ferry bucked against a floating log. Sarah screeched. Blue tossed back his head, ripping the reins from Junior's hand. The boy flailed and fell backward into the rushing water, disappearing into its depths.

Delly turned to the ferryman. "Stop!"

With her heart threatening to burst free from her ribcage, Delly studied the water. Junior's head broke the surface, his mouth open in a silent scream; unlike his siblings who screeched like a flock of crows. He waved his arms and sunk again, appearing a few yards farther down river.

The ferryman stepped to the edge of the raft, causing it to tilt dangerously. The children's wails increased. The man stretched his pole as far as possible. With his free hand, he gripped the rope circling the ferry. Another lurch, and his feet slipped on the wet wood.

Delly reached forward and grabbed the back of his shirt. "Please. We need to go back. Maybe he'll wash ashore down river."

"No stopping now, miss. Must be rain in the mountains. River's rising as we speak." The man pulled his pole back in and leaned heavily on it. "I'll be lucky to make it back myself."

"Please. Oh, God, help him." Delly bent, reached between her legs and pulled her skirt forward, tucking it into her waistband. Ignoring the wide-eyed stare of the ferryman, she turned to the children. She couldn't lose Junior. The children couldn't lose Junior. Not after the death of their pa. "Dorcas, watch the babies."

"No, Ma." She clutched Delly's arm. "You can't leave us."

Delly peered into her daughter's face. The child was right. Without Delly, they'd have no one. But Junior. Delly squelched her fear and leaned over the rope, searching the water for another sign, while the babies continued to scream.

"Look, Miss. That feller's gonna help." The ferry man pointed to the bank they approached. "God bless his soul. He needs to be part fish to dive into this river."

A light-haired man tugged off his boots, tossed his hat on the ground, and dove into the rushing water. He reappeared after several seconds and swam with mighty strokes to where Junior's head broke the surface.

Delly swallowed against the sobs rising in her throat. She kept her gaze glued to the two bobbing heads in the river and prayed while untucking the skirt of her dress.

~

Zeke spat out the dirty water and shook his head, flinging his long hair out of his face. The boy, about twenty feet down river, continued to bob up and down like a cork. Thank the good Lord, the boy could swim. Zeke increased his efforts and fought to close the distance between them.

"Help, Uncle Zeke!"

Zeke squinted. Junior? He glanced back at the ferry. Where's Ezra? "Hold on, Junior." He put his head down and fought harder. When he got close enough, he grabbed the collar of Junior's shirt and pulled until the boy was close enough to hang onto Zeke's back.

His muscles screamed in protest as he fought to gain access to the bank. With the added weight of his nephew, he went under several times, gulping in more of the mud-filled river. By the time he got close to shore, several men reached out long sticks for him to grab onto. He gripped a branch, only to have his hand slide free. A long splinter buried itself in his palm. Another man threw a rope to him and Junior. Zeke grabbed hold and the man reeled them in like a big mouthed bass. Exactly what Zeke felt like, gasping for air the way he was.

When they finally reached the bank, Zeke turned Junior over to one of the men, then flopped onto his back. He couldn't remember the last time breathing felt so good. He'd never take it for granted again. He turned his head to see Junior sprint to the ferry where passengers disembarked.

With a grunt, Zeke pushed to his knees and accepted the help of two men who grabbed his arms. "Thank you, men. Didn't think we'd make it for a minute there."

"You've got guts, that's for sure." One man handed Zeke his hat and boots, then clapped him on the shoulder, before jogging to his wagon.

Guts? Maybe. Zeke hopped on one foot then the other as he tugged on his boots, being careful of the splinter in his hand. He hadn't thought twice when he heard the screams. What else could a God-fearing man do? He'd want the same done for him.

By the time Zeke made it back to the wagons, his nieces and nephews crowded around, chattering like a flock of chickens. Zeke glanced over their heads, looking for Ezra, and laid eyes on the prettiest gal he'd ever seen. She was also the one he'd pulled out of the horse's trough earlier.

The sun shone off hair the color of a raven's wings. Eyes as stormy as rain clouds, and filled with a world of pain, stared back. Zeke tipped his hat. "Ma'am."

"Seems you're a rescuer twice today. Thank you." She paled and stepped forward. "Are you Ezekiel Williams?"

"Yes, ma'am." He studied her face, noting a scattering of freckles across otherwise blemish free skin. "What are you doing with my brother's children? Where's Ezra?"

"She's our ma, Uncle Zeke." Dorcas slipped

her hand into the woman's. "Pa's dead."

Dead? The blood drained to Zeke's feet leaving him colder than the dunk in the river. He gaze flicked back to the woman who blinked back tears. "How? When?"

"Two days ago. Shot for cheating at cards earlier in the week. He took a fever and died." The woman picked up baby Sarah from where the child sat on the grass. "I'm sorry. I'm Delicious Williams, your brother's widow. Seems we've met. And again, I owe you my thanks. If you hadn't jumped into the river after Junior …"

Zeke rubbed his hands up and down his face. Widow? Heaven help him. When did Ezra get hitched? Must've been recent. He hadn't seen him in over a year. He eyed the hand cart and mule. "Where you headed?"

The corners of her mouth tilted upward. "Why, to Oregon of course."

2

"No, you aren't." Zeke's brows drew together. He pulled some coins from his pocket and thrust them at her. "Take these and go back to the ferry. I don't allow unescorted women and children on my train."

"If you don't let us go with you, we'll walk all the way alone if we have to." Delly handed the baby to Junior then planted her fists on her hips, refusing the money. She blinked against the tears stinging her eyes. He couldn't send them back. They had nowhere else to go.

He shook his head, glancing at their piled cart. "It's too dangerous for a woman and children without a man. When others pay for me to take them, I have no choice but to do so. You have no wagon and not enough provisions. The list goes on."

"I'm a man, Uncle Zeke." Junior glared up at him. "Or close enough to it. Besides, we're family."

Delly squared her shoulders and stood as tall as her petite frame would allow. "We have you, and you, Mr. Williams, seem to be stuck with us."

She studied the tall man. Dripping hair just brushed his shoulder. Hazel eyes that changed with the light and his emotions. A cleft in a strong chin. Handsome, better looking than Ezra. If only he looked less dismayed at the thought of them following him. "Ezra sent us to you. He said you'd look out for us."

"This is plumb loco." He slapped his hat against his thigh. Marching a few feet farther away, he growled, then turned to stare at Delly and the children. Tension lines radiated from his mouth. He sighed, obviously resigned. "You're right. I can't leave family. Follow me."

He marched toward the cluster of wagons. "Bring the mule, that noisy goat, and the hand cart, too."

Delly grinned at Junior and hefted the handles of the cart.

"I knew he couldn't leave us, Ma. Uncle Zeke's one of the toughest, but nicest men out there." Junior grabbed the reins to Old Blue. "Maybe he'll let me work with the oxen. Do you think?"

"I don't know, Junior. First thing is to get you into dry clothes and food in your belly."

"Aw shucks. I'm almost dry, but I am mighty hungry. Almost drowning is hard work." He bounced Sarah on his hip. "Hope Uncle Zeke's got a wagon for us to use. I don't cotton to carrying a baby all the way to Oregon."

Delly reached over and ruffled his hair. "Neither do I or Old Blue, but with God's help, we'll do what we have to."

Delly and the children followed Zeke through a

crowd of wagons. The scent of frying bacon and brewing coffee filled the air along with the lowing of oxen and the bray of a mule. Tall grass tickled Delly's feet and calves. A butterfly fluttered around the hem of her dress. If Oregon was anything like this, Delly would be a happy woman. Surely, the stories Ezra had told were the truth. Oregon was a land of milk, honey, and the fulfillment of dreams.

Several women glanced up from their cook fires. Some smiled shyly while others stared with open interest. One blonde shot daggers from icy blue eyes. Despite her sore hands, Delly tried to appear pleasant. After all, she'd spend a lot of time with these fellow travelers.

Zeke led them to a wagon. A grizzled man hunched on a three-legged stool and whittled a piece of wood into a sharp point. His gaze scanned Delly and the children, then slid to Zeke. "Boss?"

"Clear them a spot in the smaller wagon, Melvin, then take care of the mule. This is my brother's widow and young'uns. Seems they're going to Oregon with us."

Delly let go of the hand cart. "We can pack away our own things. We don't want to be a bother."

Melvin jumped to his feet, knocking over his seat. "No bother atall, Mrs. Williams."

Rolling her eyes, Delly forced a smile. If the rapturous look on the man's face was any indication, he was already smitten with her, and her husband's body barely cold. She'd married for security, and lost that very thing within a matter of days. Now, it was up to her to provide that same security for her stepchildren. She couldn't rely on someone else. She'd have to find a gentle way to let him know she wasn't interested. Caring for the children and getting to Oregon were her only concerns. Nothing could deter her from that goal. "Thank you, sir."

"Close your mouth, Melvin." Zeke clapped him on the shoulder. "A fly might get in." He turned to Delly. "You've been through enough today. Let Mel help. And I'm sorry, but the hand cart will have to stay. We've no way to transport it and don't need the extra weight." With long strides, he headed toward the opposite side of the wagon circle. With each step, his shoulders seemed to sag more.

With a smile at Delly, Melvin followed after his boss.

Delly collapsed against the cart. Silly girl. It was only planks of wood and two wheels, but the cart was one of the remaining remnants of home. She felt sick leaving it behind, but saw the wisdom in the wagon master's decision.

Her gaze shifted to him again. Was it grief over his brother's death that dragged him down—or the fact he got saddled with Delly and the children? If it were the later, he'd be no cause for concern. She'd manage. She only needed him for protection and guidance. The rest was on her shoulders.

Which contrasted sharply with everything she'd ever been taught. The head mistress of the orphanage drilled into the girls' heads that men had the ultimate last word and authority over women. Even more so if they were married. Ezra gave Delly a request. As his wife, didn't that mean she needed to satisfy that request if at all possible? Did Zeke as wagon master overrule the demands of Delly's dead husband? Her head hurt with all the questions.

Zeke hadn't asked about the deed. She watched his broad back as he stopped beside the animals gathered in the middle of the wagon circle. Should she tell him Ezra gave it to her? She fingered the buttons of her white bodice. Maybe she'd wait and see whether he broached the subject.

The scent of cook fires continued to tempt Delly's stomach. What could she fix the children to give them full bellies? With her meager supplies, there wouldn't be much. What was she thinking, traveling to Oregon with what she could fit in a hand cart? She mentally checked off their provisions. Maybe she could trade services for supplies, at least until they reached Fort Laramie where she'd spend the last of Ezra's coins.

"Delicious." Zeke approached with long strides, his shadow stretching across the ground. "Feel free to use any supplies you may need."

"It's Delly, and I've brought a few things." Her name might be unique, but she'd never cared for her mother's strange choice of name.

He raised an eyebrow. "I'm looking forward to a good cooked meal and not the slop Hiram, my guide, or Melvin serve. In exchange for meals and laundry, you have the use of the wagon and any supplies. I noticed you brought a tent so sleeping accommodations are taken care of."

"Yes." Although it would be a tight fit. "Could the older two bunk in the wagon? Or the girls in the wagon and the boys in the tent?"

"Whatever you prefer." Zeke glanced around them, his gaze lighting on Junior. "My nephew can be used tending livestock, since you've contributed one mule and a goat." He grinned, revealing a dimple. Delly's breath hitched. "Maybe you can do some rearranging and fit all of you inside, including Daniel." He nodded toward a ring of rocks. "Best light the fire for our dinner. We leave shortly after daybreak." He tipped his hat, motioned for Junior to follow him, and ate up the distance back to the corral with his long stride.

Bunching her skirt in one hand, Delly climbed into the first wagon and stopped at the sight of wooden crates and sacks stacked clear to the top of the canvas. *Thank you, Lord.* Zeke had labeled the crates with their contents. His supplies looked like more than three men could possibly need. Had he expected them? Had Ezra planned on taking them to Oregon all along? She wracked her mind for clues and slumped against a stack of flour bags.

Ezra had sold off the milk cow and chickens. Said they'd need the money but hadn't said for what. He'd built the hand cart. She slapped her palm against her forehead. How stupid could she have been? Well, no sense dwelling on the past. She was here now.

She grabbed flour, coffee, and bacon. Tomorrow, if they stopped in time, she'd fix beans and corn pone. She climbed out and glanced toward the larger wagon where the children played, drawing pictures in the dirt. Melvin rolled their cart toward the smaller wagon.

When he offered to help, she waved him away.

It wouldn't do to get used to someone helping her do something she'd be doing three times a day. She set the supplies next to the fire ring, and then coaxed a flame to life. She set water to boil and biscuits to bake before examining the second, smaller wagon.

Besides her trunk and the family's bedding and clothes, it contained a tightly rolled corn husk mattress, another larger chest, a rocking chair, and crates of ammunition. Delly smiled and scooted things closer together before reaching for the mattress. Unfurled, it filled the floor space, providing room for her and the children to stretch out sideways. Sleeping off the ground was a blessing Delly didn't expect and one she intended to enjoy to its fullness.

"Good evening!"

Delly poked her head through the slit in the canvas. A pretty blonde woman, the same woman who glared at her earlier, stood with a toddler on her hip and swayed from side-to-side.

"Hello."

"I'm Sophia Miller." The willowy woman thrust out a hand. "This is Josiah. My father is Mr. Oglesby. I've two scoundrel brothers Joseph and Samuel."

"I'm Delly Williams." Delly climbed down. "Zeke's widowed sister-in-law."

"I'm a widow, also." Relief washed over the woman's face. "Thought you were his wife for a moment. You seem awfully young to have a passel of children, though."

Delly laughed. "Stepchildren." She moved the

biscuits farther from the fire and laid bacon in a cast iron skillet. Cooking over an open fire on the plain would require some trial and error. "And there are a lot of them. While on his deathbed, my husband requested I hunt up his brother, and here we are." Strips of bacon sizzled in a hot iron skillet.

"I could introduce you to the rest of the folks, if you've a mind to get acquainted." Sophia set Josiah down and handed him a piece of hardtack from her apron pocket. "I only know a few so far, though. There's a young couple, the Sorenson's who've got a newborn little girl. Josiah, get away from the fire! Oh, the boy will be the death of me. Plus, there's other families, some around our age, several older."

"How long have you been a widow?" Delly poured boiling water over the coffee grounds.

"About a year." She sighed. "It was real hard until Pa came to St. Louis and fetched me to head west. I wasn't taken with the idea, but hated being alone even more. You?"

"Less than two days." Delly blinked against the burning in her eyes. "And married a week, although Ezra courted me for a couple of months." And kept his love of cards from her. She knelt in the dirt and poured coffee into mugs. If only a cup of coffee could soothe her hurts. Make her feel loved. Give her the strength and wisdom to take five children across half a continent to a strange place.

Help her discover where she fit in the world.

Sophia gasped and clutched a hand at her throat. "You poor thing. Did you love him dearly?"

Delly expelled her breath roughly. "As well as most, I suppose. We didn't know each other well."

She lifted the lid on the Dutch oven to check the biscuits.

The other woman stood and grasped Josiah's hand. "It was nice meeting you. Pa most likely has supper done so I'd best get back." She chuckled. "I never took much to cooking." With a swish of her skirt to avoid the fire, Sophia pranced back to her wagon.

Delly shook her head. How could the girl not know how to cook having been married and all? She stood and searched the area for her family. The three girls had switched to playing with rag dolls under the larger wagon, while Daniel made faces at the baby. "Dorcas, run and fetch the menfolk, would you?"

By the time the bacon was fried crisp and the biscuits brown and flaky, Zeke and his hired hands sat across the fire from Delly and the children. All three of the men, dug into the food heaped on their plates like they hadn't eaten in days. Junior rattled on and on about the day's exciting events, hardly stopping long enough to partake of the meager meal. It wasn't much, but Delly would do better tomorrow. Not for a moment would she give Zeke a reason to doubt his decision to allow them to head west with him.

She watched him from the corner of her eye. The fire cast shadows on his strong chin and jaw. Now that his hair dried, she could tell it was dark blond and, even tied back from his face, brushed the collar of his chambray shirt. A rough looking man chiseled by God's own hammer, appearing all the world like Delly always imagined Adam to have looked.

A toddler let out a cry from across the way. Delly glanced over to see Sophia scoop up her son. Zeke didn't bother glancing over his shoulder. Delly sipped her coffee. Maybe she'd misunderstood the relieved look on the young woman's face. But she would've testified that the woman released a pent up breath at knowing Delly wasn't Zeke's wife. From what Delly could tell, Zeke didn't share the admiration. A smitten man would've cast a look back, right?

~

It took all Zeke's control not to squirm under the studious gaze of his sister-in-law. What could she possibly have to dwell on for so long? He'd washed his face and combed his hair before coming to supper. Even took time to swipe the trail dust from his clothes. The children ate like silent ghosts, their gaze never leaving his face. It made his flesh crawl to be watched like a bug under glass.

Hiram and Melvin must've felt the same way because they ate faster than starving men and rushed back to tend the corral animals. Zeke had no idea how to talk to a woman and children. Nor was there time to process the news of Ezra's death. Something he sorely needed to do. Maybe tonight while he bedded down under the main wagon he could put his thoughts in some sort of order.

Zeke met Delly's gaze across the fire and heat stronger than any flame shot through him. He could see how his brother fell for the woman, but she barely looked out of short dresses herself!

"Children, help me put these things away and

then prepare for bed." With the gracefulness of a swan, Delly stood and reached for the Dutch oven.

Fatigue lined her face, yet not once did she ask him for help. Did he frighten her? Repulse her? He shrugged. Why should he care? Today was not the day to become infatuated. Nor anytime soon. After he settled in his verdant valley, then he would have the luxury of pondering marriage.

"Are you sure about this, Delicious? The trail ahead is difficult at the best of times."

She stiffened. "I'm an orphan and a widow, Mr. Williams. There is nothing left for me in Missouri." Although her voice was soft, her words were like a rod of steel. Only a fool wouldn't know to step away. With a swish of her skirts, she climbed into the wagon.

Zeke prayed his new responsibilities would survive the arduous journey. He couldn't take losing another family member on the trail. Not after losing Becky and the baby. After tossing the dregs of his coffee into the sputtering fire, he stood and stretched the kinks out of his back as Junior grabbed a bedroll and dashed toward the corral. Zeke shot out a hand to stop him.

"Not so fast, pardner. You'll sleep under the wagon with me."

"But you said I could help with the livestock!"

"I did." Zeke nodded. "But you'll be with me, and it isn't our watch yet."

Junior huffed and switched directions. "Where are we bunking down?"

"Under the big wagon unless you want to listen to the others moving over your head all night."

"No, sir! Dorcas talks in her sleep."

Zeke put an arm around the boy's shoulders. "I'd like to talk to you a bit, Ezra, man-to-man if you've a mind to answer some of my questions."

"Sure, Uncle Zeke." Junior tossed his roll beside the wagon wheel and perched on a boulder.

Zeke pulled up a stool. "Tell me how your pa died and how he got hooked up with Delicious."

"She wants to be called Delly," Junior chuckled. "Said her mother couldn't possibly have been in her right mind to give her a name like Delicious. She's a good ma. Pa said she looked like an angel when he saw her crossing the street in a pink calico dress. They courted for a few weeks. Ma got booted out of the orphanage when she turned eighteen, escorted a family to Missouri where she met and married Pa. I think he loved her more than she loved him. At least he said it often enough, but she cares for the little ones." He stared toward the other wagon. "She's awful quiet, unless you get her riled, then boy howdy, a man can't win.

"Pa said she had the bite of a grizzly bear and the touch of a butterfly." He shrugged. "Not sure what the purty words mean, but Ma turned pink when he said 'em."

Zeke laughed, wondering how long it would take the mite of a woman to get mad at him. He seemed to have that kind of way with women. If she were as feisty as Junior made her sound, maybe she'd make it across the prairie after all. He pulled out his knife and picked at the splinter in his palm.

"Pa gambled a lot, though." Junior choked on his words. "Went to the saloon the morning after getting hitched, cheated at cards, and got shot. Ma tended him the best she could, but he died anyway." He sniffed and made his way to his bedroll.

Zeke let his hands dangle between his legs and hung his head. "Go to sleep, Junior. I'll be over in a bit." Knowing his brother died was hard enough, but knowing he died a painful, lingering death was almost torture. There hadn't been time to enjoy his new bride. Now, the girl was left with five children and no means to support them. Zeke sighed. He had a hard decision to make. His head told him to marry Delly and give her the security of a husband. His heart told him he didn't want to marry ever again.

The wagon creaked and the object of his thoughts climbed from the wagon bed, a shawl wrapped around her shoulders. She lifted her face to the sky. A slight breeze ruffled the hair fluttering loose from its bun, highlighting the strands with silver. Moonlight cast a heavenly glow, leaving Zeke feeling as if he dreamed. She looked every inch the angel Ezra had thought her to be.

He pushed to his feet and approached with slow steps lest she disappear like a vision. "Delly?"

Her hand flew to her throat. "Mr. Williams, you startled me."

"My apologies." He removed his hat and worried the brim with his fingers. Women being the foreign creatures they were, he'd never had cause to propose before. Should he get down on one knee like in the books? No, this was a business proposition, nothing more. A way to save reputations and insure safety. He hoped. He must've stared because she crossed her arms and tilted her head.

"What is it, Mr. Williams?"

"Um." He crumbled his hat. "I'm thinking we should get hitched."

"You think so?" Her eyes flashed lightening.

Zeke swallowed against the mountain in his throat.

3

"Have you fallen in love with me, Mr. Williams? Is that why you wish to marry?" Delly's blood turned to ice. She'd thought for sure Ezra's brother would be a gentleman. Not someone interested in a body to warm his bed. "Has my beauty struck you dumb?"

Zeke took a step back. "No, ma'am. I mean, it isn't that you're homely, far from it." His face paled, and he took a deep breath. "Since we are traveling in such close proximity, I thought you'd want to marry to protect your reputation."

If not for her outrage, Delly would've laughed at the mortified expression on his face and the way he worried his hat. "My reputation is just fine, Mr. Williams. I believe the children are sufficient chaperonage. If it bothers you, stay away."

Her heart fell with a thud to her feet.   It wasn't that she wanted to marry the man. She hardly knew him. But once again someone wanted her for what she could do for them rather than for herself. He'd said to save her reputation, but she didn't believe it for a moment. Years of riding the trail had left him lonely, plain and simple.

She took a deep breath. "Thank you for the consideration, Mr. Williams." She blinked away the gathering moisture in her eyes and climbed back into the wagon, the peace of the night shattered.

If only she hadn't promised Ezra to see the deed to his brother. If only there was somewhere for her to give the children a good life rather than take the difficult trail west, promises of a better life or not. She hung her shawl on a hook and crawled onto the small area of the mattress her sleeping children had left her.

The oiled canvas overhead shut out all of the starlight. From the direction of the corral a cow mooed and a cowboy's gentle lullaby hushed it. A peaceful place despite the many wagons, and yet as lonely as if Delly were the only person present. Tears welled and rolled down her face, soaking the flattened pillow beneath her head.

She'd thought marriage to the charismatic Ezra would cure her own loneliness and give her a feeling of self-worth and love. Instead, she was worse off than ever. Sure, the children cared for her. But was that out of necessity or the lack of anyone else to tend their needs? Her heart clenched. She did love them so, from Ezra Junior, who so wanted to be a man, to tiny Sarah and her pudgy cheeks. *Thank you, Lord that Zeke wasn't married and thus want to claim the children as his own.* The loss would crush her.

Sarah snuffled and threw a chubby arm over her sister. Delly ran a finger over the soft skin of Sarah's hand until the little one frowned and rolled over. What was she doing? Delly had no idea how to survive through Indian territory in a wagon.

God and sheer determination would have to be enough.

~

A loud voice jerked her awake. Delly blinked against the sleep in her eyes, grabbed her shawl, then parted the canvas of the wagon to peer out. Dawn peeked above the horizon, casting the morning in a rosy glow. Women crawled from tents and wagon beds to start breakfast.

A red-faced man, and a woman about Delly's size, with skin the color of creamed coffee, stood in the shadows of a nearby oak tree. A red scarf covered the woman's hair. The brown dress she wore was only a shade darker than her skin.

The man towered over the woman who stood with head bowed while he screamed at her. Delly strained to hear the woman's quiet replies, and the inhabitants of nearby wagons stopped their morning preparations to stare.

"Where's your master, girl? We don't take to runaways here."

"I'm freed, sir." She flinched at the man's raised fist and clutched a calico-wrapped parcel to her chest.

"Ain't no such thing. There ain't nobody in Missouri gonna free the likes of you."

"I ain't from Missouri. I have papers, too." She reached inside her dress; her voice soft and lilting with a touch of drawl.

"You ain't nothing but a lying…" He struck her, landing a blow to the side of her face. She fell to the ground with a small cry and wrapped her arms around her head.

Anger as hot as a smoldering fire welled in Delly. No man had the right to strike someone who is defenseless. Especially with such a size difference. Before it registered what she was doing, Delly scurried from the wagon and stood before the huge man, her shawl wrapped tightly around her shoulders.

She pulled her frame as tall as she could. "Who gave you the right to strike my servant? You step back this instant or I'll have no choice but to call the sheriff. We haven't started on the trail yet. All it'll take is to send a rider back across the river."

Her knees shook beneath her nightgown, and her mouth filled with cotton. Could a simple mountain girl pull off such a daring stunt? Surely the man would see right through her drawl. She thanked God for the soft morning light and prayed it would hide the fear in her eyes and the trembling of her hands. She breathed through her mouth to block out the stench from the man's unwashed body.

"Yours?" He blinked down at her like an oversized owl. "If she's yours, why is she running around at this hour? Besides, she told me she was freed."

"I said servant, not slave. Our business is ours alone, and since it is no longer dark, and my servant has returned, you have no complaint here. I will personally deal with her wandering off." Delly stooped and helped the other woman to her feet then pulled her closer to the safety of the wagon. "You shouldn't have stayed so long helping dear Mrs. Miller care for her cough." The poor thing trembled against Delly with eyes as soft and wide as a doe, but Delly caught her nearly imperceptible nod. Good she understood.

The man took a step in their direction.

Delly stepped in front of the cowering woman and gritted her teeth. She lifted her chin and locked gazes with the stranger. "Are you going to strike me too? I may not be as easy to subdue."

The man laughed. Shivers skittered down Delly's spine as he reached for her. "A little bitty thing like you wants to tussel with me? This ought to be fun."

"What's going on here?" Zeke stepped from behind an oak tree. He'd heard the shouts during his morning rounds and it hadn't taken him long to assess the situation. Delly, not reaching the man's shoulder, stared down the stranger like a dog protecting its bone. The woman had grit, that was for sure.

Zeke ran his gaze over her in the thin dressing gown and shawl, then glanced away and frowned. What was the woman thinking coming out dressed like that? The rising sun illuminated shapes better left covered in mixed company. Especially with men like the stranger roaming around the wagons. Not to mention the cattle drovers and other single men headed west with Zeke's train.

"Mr. Williams." Delly's cheeks sported bright spots of crimson. "This man struck this woman and knocked her to the ground. Her lip is bleeding, and I believe he's threatened me."

"That right?" Zeke sauntered closer, keeping

his hand poised over the gun at his hip. He stood a couple inches taller, but the other man outweighed him by twenty pounds or more. Although he didn't cotton to fighting for the sport of it, Zeke wasn't the type to back down when things warranted a punch being thrown. He released his pent up breath when Hiram, clutching his rifle, stepped from behind the wagon.

"This is one of them runaway slaves." The man thrust out his massive chest. "I aim to get one of them rewards."

Zeke glanced at Delly. She shook her head. Her eyes pleaded.

He puffed out his cheeks then expelled a deep breath. What was he getting himself into? "Looks like you're mistaken, mister. Seems to me this woman belongs here. What train are you traveling with?"

"That ain't none of your business. I'm with God-fearing folk, and we don't hold to women wandering at night. Especially ones of color. They're either a slave or a harlot. Makes me wonder about the other one too, coming out dressed like that."

Delly sucked in her breath with a hiss. Zeke held up a hand to motion her to remain quiet.

"These women appear to be neither. Go on your way and there'll be no harm done." Zeke removed his hat and offered his hand. "We're heading out today. I'll watch over these two personally."

The stranger refused the hand and instead glared. "If you're sure she ain't no runaway." He shook his head, and with one last glower at the women, turned back to town.

"Thank you, Mr. Williams. My knees were shaking like wind-blown corn stalks." Delly placed a hand against the wagon to steady herself. "I declare, I thought my heart would bust right out of my chest."

"Might as well call me Zeke since it appears I'm going to get you out of one scrape or another." He slapped his hat on his head, then rubbed a hand over his chin. Drat the woman! "I don't ever want to see you facing down a drunken man in nothing but your nightclothes. Not ever again. Is that understood?" It took all his willpower not to shake the little minx. "Walking around without the proper clothing is a distraction I don't want the men on this train to have to deal with." Or himself. The picture she made with tousled curls and eyes still droopy with sleep would be an invitation not all men would turn down.

"Was he drunk? I didn't notice. The unwashed smell was strong enough to hide anything else." She smiled, a dimple winking in her cheek. "And, although I'm fully covered, I'll not venture out of my tent or wagon in such attire again. You have my word."

"Perfect." He sighed and turned to the stranger. "Are you a runaway?"

The woman clutched her parcel to her chest. "No, sir. I've got my papers right here." She pulled a folded slip of paper from her pocket. "My name is Sadie. My daddy was a poor white farmer, my momma a slave. Right before he died, he freed my momma and me. She died of a fever on the way to Independence."

Zeke read the paper before handing it back to her. "Why didn't you show this to that man?"

"I tried to. Don't think he can read. Said it was just words on paper. Something I made up. I can read, though. I'm not a liar, sir." Sadie bowed her head.

"Look at me." Zeke waited until her gaze met his. He didn't cotton to men beating on women. He sighed. He couldn't leave her here. "You're a free woman with papers to prove it. Act like one and people will treat you like one." Her eyes widened, and he turned back to Delly. "Can she ride with you? She might be a welcome help."

"Sure she can." Delly grabbed her hand. "If she wants."

"I'd be right proud to help you." Sadie tossed her parcel into the wagon. "My momma taught me some healing things, and I'm right handy when there's a birthing."

God preserve them from a birthing. "I'm getting everyone ready to leave in an hour." Although he swallowed hard against the topic of babies, Zeke's mood lightened with the thought of another person to help Delly and the children. Plus, the new addition ought to put a stop to any gossip about improper chaperonage. "Today, Thursday, May fifth, is the day we start traveling, ladies, just in case you want to keep a journal. Lots of folks do."

"That's a wonderful idea, Mr., uh, Zeke." Delly's cheeks brightened again. "I will consider it.

Thank you."

He knew she thanked him for more than the idea of journaling her travels. He tipped his hat. "Get the children up, feed 'em, and tie down everything you can." *Good Lord, what am I thinking taking on another lost lamb?*

"You're a mite touched in the head, ain't you?" Hiram lowered his rifle. "Taking on another woman?"

"I might be at that."

~

Delly rushed to the wagon and climbed up, calling over her shoulder. "I need to get dressed, Sadie. Would you mind fixing up some cornmeal mush if I hand down the ingredients?"

"No, ma'am."

She paused before swinging her leg over the wagon bed. "It's Delly Williams. Not ma'am." She couldn't help the leap of joy in her heart. Just the night before she'd cried out to God in loneliness and now He'd sent her a friend. She quickly gathered cornmeal, lard, salt and raisins and handed them to Sadie. "We need enough for us two, three men, and five children."

Five children!"

Delly didn't think it possible but Sadie's eyes grew even wider. "Yep. Ranging in age from two to twelve." She flashed a grin and withdrew, leaving the other woman to mutter to herself while fixing breakfast. "I'd best wake them."

She folded blankets and shook shoulders, all the while keeping an eye out for the guidebook. Where could Melvin had stashed it when he loaded their supplies? She wanted to make a habit of studying the pages since they were starting out.

The children grumbled at being woken so early, but did as they were told. Delly let out a cry of delight when she came across a notepad and small bundle of pencils stored in the gift crate from the mercantile. And the promised guidebook. She flipped through the pages, before something else caught her eye.

A corner of the deed stuck out from beneath the leather cover of her Bible, where she'd placed the night before after changing into her night clothes. She ought to give it to Zeke, but knowing the power that sheet of paper gave her, stayed her hand. No, she'd hold onto it until they reached Oregon and she stepped foot on Ezra's, her, land.

By the time she unburied her trunk, the children were dressed and outside waiting for nourishment. She dressed quickly and slipped the guidebook into her apron pocket.

Sadie had everyone served by the time Delly joined them around the fire, and most were scraping the last of the food into their mouths while they stared at the dark-skinned stranger serving them.

Delly smiled and accepted a tin plate of corn mush and a mug of coffee before settling on a three-legged stool. "This is Sadie, y'all. She's going to share our wagon." Five heads nodded as if used to Delly inviting folks to bed with them. By the time she finished eating, the oxen were harnessed and Sadie was cleaning up the dishes.

The camp broke out in raucous conversation, shouts of greeting, and whistles. Junior jumped up to tie Mabel to the tail of the wagon, leaving the kid to follow, then dashed away. Dorcas shooed the other children inside the wagon, while Delly sat feeling as useless as a splinter. She knew things moved fast once it was time to go, but figured there'd be a horn or something to signal folks. A whistle split the air. A little late in coming. She crammed the last of her breakfast into her mouth and jumped to her feet.

Zeke strolled by and tossed her a pair of leather gloves. "Hope you know how to drive a team. It's either that or walk, and I could use the men somewhere else besides driving."

"Of course I know how to drive a team." With a small farm wagon, of course, but she could learn.

He smiled. "Don't have the little ones ride in the wagon if we go over steep hills. Too many accidents happen that way. They can walk or ride your mule."

"Where's Junior?"

Zeke frowned. "I thought he was here." He shook his head. "We need to be moving within five minutes. There's another load of wagons getting ready to cross the river."

Delly glanced to the opposite bank that disappeared beneath a sea of rippling white canvas. "I'll find him." She couldn't expect the others to wait because a twelve-year-old decided to wander off. The guidebook quoted several incidents of lost children, and she wouldn't leave one of her own behind. Delly climbed to the wagon seat and stood so she could see the area surrounding the wagons.

Already the front of the line was pulling out of

the circle. Within minutes it would be her turn. She donned the gloves which were a size too large then climbed into the driver's seat.

The oxen's massive horns curled above their heads. Delly's heart lodged in her throat. Would they follow her commands or be as ornery as Old Blue? Four cantankerous animals of their size would be a match for a man, let alone a woman. She glanced over as Junior trotted to the wagon with a bulge in his shirt and a blue-tick hound loping behind him.

"Junior," she warned. The question in his eyes tugged at her heart.

"Please, Ma. Look how skinny she is. She's been following me all morning."

"What's in your shirt?"

"A pup!" He pulled out a miniature replica of the dog at his heels.

Delly shook her head, knowing what her answer would be before she spoke. She couldn't deny the look of longing on her son's face. If a couple of dogs brought him comfort in the wake of his pa's death, then so be it. "They are your responsibility. Now, git. Your uncle was looking for you." How was Zeke going to feel about two more strays?

Sadie joined her on the seat. "How you plan on feeding them dogs, Miss Delly?"

Delly shrugged. "No idea. I'll cross that bridge when we come to it. The mother can hunt for herself, I reckon. The pup can eat scraps." The wagon in front of them pulled forward, and she gripped the reins. *Here we go. Lord, be with us.*

4

The wagons rolled westward across timbered land surrounded by seas of tall grass and wildflowers. Ruts dug deep in the ground from earlier travelers. As each wheel rumbled through a hole it produced a bone-jarring thud that vibrated along Delly's spine. Sadie sat, silent beside her, hands folded in her lap.

Delly arched her back and glanced at the azure sky where a hawk danced on a windy current. Between the oxen's ears, the trail wound steadily westward, appearing to grow narrower until it disappeared over the horizon.

As the morning wore on, Delly had yet to see a sign of the hardships, other than boredom, outlined in the guidebook. She lifted her face to the warm sun and listened to her two youngest children chattering from the back of Old Blue, Mabel's and the smaller goats's bleating, and Dorcas's and Ruth's laughter as they skipped beside the wagon and picked a bouquet. Delly had made the right choice to do as her husband asked. Leave behind the poverty of a farm that barely eked out a living and go to a better land.

The wagon creaked beneath her as the oxen

trudged after the wagon ahead of them. A wooden bucket banged against the sideboards. A tattered checkered shirt fluttered from the opening in the canvas of the wagon in front of them. She needed to thank Zeke for putting them in the middle of the train. She felt sorry for those in the back, consigned to eating the dust of nineteen other wagons.

So docile did the oxen proceed, Delly let the reins lie in her lap. Occasionally, she spotted Junior darting alongside the herd of cattle, the hound at his heels and the puppy trying to follow. Delly laughed. The poor mutt would be exhausted by dinner. Maybe she could convince Junior to let it ride in the wagon for part of each day.

With the morning stretching before them, she decided getting to know her new friend might pass time. After all, they'd be living together for several months.

"What brings you out here, Sadie? Is someone waiting for you out west?" Delly asked.

Sadie jerked as if the sound of Delly's voice caught her by surprise. Her gaze landed everywhere but on Delly. "No, just me looking for freedom from bounty hunters and haters. My daddy inherited my momma when she was real young. Around sixteen. Fell in love with her. He was quite a few years older.

"When he found himself sick and dying, he freed us both. Momma said we ought to head west where there ain't no prejudice. She died from consumption a few weeks back. That's my story." She pulled at a loose thread on her sleeve. "They won't give me any of that free land, 'cause I'm colored, but I can find myself some honest work. Work that isn't based on the color of my skin."

Delly swallowed past the tears clogging her throat. "I'm sorry I told that man you were my servant. And I'll have plenty of land, if you want to stay with us. Lord knows I can use the help."

Sadie waved aside her apology. "Needed done at the time, and I'm mighty grateful for the offer."

"When folks start asking questions, you tell them what you want. I'll back you up."

Sadie's look brightened. "What about you? I don't reckon you birthed all these young'uns. Not at your age."

Delly gulped. "No, my husband, Mr. Williams's brother, died a couple of days ago. These are his children from a previous marriage. I promised to hunt up Mr. Williams and head west. Just hope I can make it with so much responsibility sitting on my shoulders."

Sadie folded her hands in her lap. "This trail is full of dreams. I reckon you got as good a chance as any of these other folks. 'Course the road's probably littered with a lot of them dreams that failed. You seem to have a good head on your shoulders, though. Easy to see with the way you care for the babies. You'll be all right, and I'm here to help."

"I pray so. Junior almost drowned crossing the river. Fell right off the ferry, and the guidebook says there are worse dangers ahead. Heading out, full of pride and ignorance, well, I'm wondering how much I really thought things through."

"You're fulfilling a promise." Sadie patted her

arm. "I'll help with the babies. We'll do all right."

"Thank you. I'm glad you're with me." Delly looked over her shoulder to count the wagons, thankful for the total of fifty or so that lumbered down the road. Not as large as some wagon trains she'd heard about, but hopefully enough to ward off trouble.

In the distance, a cloud of dust rose behind the last wagon. Delly squinted. "Somebody is riding hard," she noted.

Sadie twisted to see. "Someone wanting to join us, maybe?"

Zeke galloped past, headed for the dust cloud, and Delly stretched so far to follow him with her gaze, that if not for Sadie grabbing the back of her dress, she'd have fallen off the wagon.

"No man is worth taking a fall for," Sadie laughed. "Even one as handsome as our wagon master."

Delly's face burned as hot as the sun. "I'm merely curious as to our visitor. It could've been the guide galloping by for all I care."

"Sure, Miss Delly." Sadie laughed and slapped her leg. "That fine man would be the answer to all your problems."

Delly gripped the reins harder. "I can handle my own problems, thank you very much. And there are six hundred and forty acres of reward waiting for me in Oregon. I don't need another husband." Zeke looked at her and the children as an inconvenience. A burden. And Delly wouldn't be a burden to anyone.

~

"Looking for someone, stranger?" Zeke asked when the man stopped. Dust covered the man's fancy clothes. Zeke eyed the brightly colored brocade vest, then glanced down at his own well-worn buckskins. The man definitely didn't look like a traveler. Especially with two six shooters riding low on each hip.

"I'm Ira Bodine, and I'm looking for a Mr. Ezekiel Williams." Ira's dark eyes narrowed. Lifting his beaked nose, he sniffed then twisted his handlebar moustache around his index finger.

"You found him." Zeke held out his hand.

The stranger stared at Zeke's hand for a moment, then accepted the shake. "I'm looking to join up with your group."

"You'd need a few more provisions than you can stuff in a saddlebag. I can't let just anyone join up and take what the others have prepared."

"I've enough to get me to Fort Laramie, then I'll restock." His gaze flitted to the wagons.

Zeke stroked his chin. Something about the man's intense gaze that settled on Zeke then flittered toward the wagons didn't sit right. The man acted like he looked for something, or someone. Zeke didn't need more trouble on his train.

"I'm sorry, Mr. Bodine, but I'm going to pass on allowing you to travel with us. My advice would be for you to hook up with some cattle drovers. There's a group maybe half a day's ride ahead of us. You'll make better time, too." He nodded at the man's stony look, then turned Cyclone back to the line of wagons.

As he rode, he kept his shoulders tense, almost

expecting a bullet in the back. The farther he went, the more he relaxed, at least physically. A dandy like that didn't usually charge up on a wagon train, at least not in Zeke's experience.

Hopefully, Ezra gave Delly the deed to the land. Without it, they were all sunk. Ezra said he'd keep it safe. Maybe his young wife was the safest place he knew. Zeke needed to have a talk with the young widow, and fast. He glanced over his shoulder. Yep, the dandy wanted something and with Ezra's gambling, Zeke would eat his hat if the man wasn't after something as valuable as a little over twelve-hundred acres of prime Oregon Territory.

~

"Delic…uh, Delly…Where'd you get a name like Delicious, anyway?"

Delly glanced to where Zeke rode next to the wagon. His massive horse didn't seem to mind the miles. Its long legs ate up the distance like a child with a stick of molasses candy. Delly sighed. "When I was born, my mother said I was the most delicious thing she'd ever seen. Is there something I can help you with, Mr. Williams?"

Was she that frightening? The big, strapping man got tongue tied every time he had to say a word to her. She bit her lip to keep from smiling.

"Would you walk with me? I have something we need to discuss."

Delly glanced at Sadie, who nodded. She handed the other woman the reins. Once the wagon came to a halt, Delly climbed down, careful to sweep her skirt away from the wheel. What did he want to talk to her about? The deed, most likely. Well, she wouldn't give it to him. Not until he promised to give her Ezra's share of the land.

Zeke dismounted and led her, and his monster horse, in a diagonal direction away from the train. The horse snorted, shooting a puff of warm hair down Delly's neck. She jumped sideways, eliciting a chuckle from Zeke.

"Don't be afraid. He's very gentle."

"He's a beast." Delly shuddered. "What's his name again?"

"Cyclone."

She studied the ebony horse. Her head barely reached his back. "The name fits."

"Your hair looks as silky as his coat."

She spun to face Zeke. Did he just compare her to a horse? High spots of color dotted his cheeks. He looked as surprised as Delly at his comment. "Did you bring me out here to make advances?"

"No, ma'am." He sighed and stopped. "Did Ezra give you anything when he died? A deed to land, perhaps?"

Delly squared her jaw. "Why?"

"He had it for safekeeping. Too many things could've happened to it while I was on the trail." Zeke reached to scratch behind Cyclone's ears. "Now, there's a stranger following us. Could be nothing, but my gut tells me the man is looking for something. You told me Ezra took a liking to playing cards and that has me worried."

Delly stared across the sweeping plain, barely taking in the vastness now that the trees had thinned. "Was the man's name Ira?"

"How did you know?" Zeke's hand stilled.

"Ezra did give me the deed. He said to keep it away from somebody named Ira." Shivers danced down her spine despite the warmth of the day. "You don't think he lost the land in a poker game, do you?" She couldn't bear the thought. What would they do?

"No." Zeke shook his head. "Whatever else my brother might've been, a liar wasn't one of them. He promised to keep the deed safe. But that doesn't mean he didn't flap his gums and let some unsavory characters know about the land. Where is it?"

"Safe in the wagon. Unless someone gets a hankering to read the Bible, they won't find it." She took a deep breath and squared her shoulders. "I want my husband's half of the acreage."

Zeke's eyes widened. "Well, who else would get it?"

Her mouth opened and closed like a snapping turtle. No argument? No trying to talk her out of it with condescending remarks about how a woman couldn't handle land on her own?

"You thought I'd take it from you?" A muscle ticked in his jaw.

She shrugged.

"I can't believe…" He whipped off his hat. "Well, you don't know me, so I can excuse your believing I could be such a scoundrel." He banged his hat on his pants, sending a cloud of dust on the breeze. "But to think I'd steal from a widow and my brother's children, well, I just don't know what to make of that."

The man sure didn't seem to have trouble

talking when he was angry. Delly took a step back.

"What kind of husband was my brother? Obviously not a very good one if he left you thinking like that."

Delly opened her mouth to respond, but Zeke continued before she got a word out.

"Junior said you were only hitched a week. Guess my brother couldn't keep his temper in check for even that long." He speared her with a glance, his eyes the color of a spring meadow after a rain. Delly flinched. "You think I'm going to hit you? Did Ezra hit you?" Zeke's shoulders deflated. "I'd best get you back before you run screaming into the prairie."

"I am not a screamer."

"You sure like to think the worst of people, though."

She returned his glare and kept her hands tightly clinched under her apron. Biting her tongue in order not to say something she'd regret, she lifted her chin. No, Ezra never laid a hand on her, but his fits of anger often resulted in a broken dish or two. The same blood ran in this man's veins. The man who's family she'd traveled to Missouri with and struck her a time or two. Made advances she'd rather not had, also. She'd not let a man rule over her like that again.

"Tarnation!" Zeke grabbed her around the waist and hefted her into Cyclone's saddle. Then in one smooth motion, he swung up behind her. "Riding is faster, and I wouldn't want you to suffer my company any longer than necessary."

Cyclone took off like a bullet, throwing Delly

back into Zeke's chest. She couldn't deny she liked the sensation his hard chest and strong arms stirred, but she didn't need the distraction. Nothing could deter her from her goal of self-sufficiency. Not a handsome man or the fear of a stranger after something in her possession. But her feelings were no cause for her rude behavior. She'd need to apologize at first chance.

When they rejoined the wagons, the travelers had stopped for the lunch hour. Zeke put an arm around Delly and lowered her to the ground. With one hand on the saddle, she glanced up. "I'm sorry. I'll never doubt your intentions again. It's quite clear that you have only mine and the children's safety as your top concern."

"Thank you." With a jerk of the reins, he turned his horse toward the back of the wagon.

Seconds later, he poked his head around. "What's all this wood in the supply wagon?"

She planted her fists on her hips. "I'm not burning buffalo chips until I absolutely have to."

"So your squeamishness is causing my animals to work harder." Zeke marched to stand in front of her.

"If it appears they're struggling, which it doesn't on this flat prairie, then I'll dump it." She raised her chin.

"Tarnation!" He stomped away.

Delly joined Sadie at the fire where a pot of coffee boiled. She accepted a mug with thanks and set another on the hot stones for Zeke when he returned. At Sadie's questioning look, she turned away to search for the children.

"They're eating cold biscuits and bacon in the wagon," Sadie said. "I thought it best they rest before we head off again."

"Good idea." Delly smiled her thanks.

"Ruth cut her foot on a sharp stone, and I put salve and a wrap on it. She'll be fine. Do you think the oxen can carry her weight for a day?"

Delly frowned. "She can ride the mule with the little ones." One day out and one of them was hurt? They couldn't ride in the wagon. She'd read stories of children falling out and being crushed by the wheels.

Dust rose behind the line of travelers. Delly bolted to her feet. Sadie followed, eyes glued on five approaching wagons. Zeke stepped from around the other side and motioned for them to stay put.

Delly watched as he approached the first team of mules. A woman with a couple of small children, and judging by the roundness of her belly, another one on the way, waited beside the wagon with a man as thin as he was tall. Zeke conversed for several minutes then rejoined Delly and Sadie.

Their guide took sick outside Independence," he told them. "These folks will be joining us on the trek to Oregon." He didn't look happy as he stormed over to the coffee, lifted his mug, and took a deep gulp.

As they moved closer, it didn't take Delly long to figure out why. The woman by the first wagon looked like she'd give birth before they reached their destination.

5

Over the next few days, the newcomers quickly became Delly's friends. Big-hearted Ben and equally loveable Alice along with their young daughter, Abby, and son, Seth. No matter that Alice was ten years Delly's senior. They'd connected right off.

Occasionally, Delly let Sadie drive while she walked alongside with Alice. She'd rarely had friends before. Bonds weren't formed in the orphanage. Too many children came and went. Now, she had two dear ones, not counting the occasional conversation with the widow Miller who still seemed to have her cap set for Zeke, and resented the sight of Delly.

Delly bit her lower lip. Considering her resolve never to marry, she thought of Zeke more than she wanted. Of course she would. She drove the man's wagon every day. She was surrounded by his belongings. Washed his clothes and cooked his meals. That had to be why she sought out his tall form periodically as he rode up and down the line.

"You seem to be a long way off." Alice

smoothed damp hair from around her face. "Can't say I blame you. I'd like to be somewhere cooler."

"I'm sorry. Just lost in my thoughts."

"And tired, no doubt. I know I am." She rubbed her rounded stomach. "This baby came as a surprise. We'd already sold the farm when I found out. No turning back then."

"This trail does take a lot out of a body. When are you due?" Delly thanked God for Sadie, especially since she had no idea how to birth a child.

"Sometime in August, I reckon."

Delly wouldn't want to birth a baby on the trail. The constant worrying over the ones that could walk, including two-year-old Sarah was enough for her.

Three wagons plodded from the opposite direction. Delly and Alice stopped to watch them pass. A haze of dust lingered in the air painting the scene with a dreamlike quality, then settling like a fine powder on top of everything the wagons passed. Something about the slump of the man's shoulders in the lead wagon tugged at Delly's heart. "Why are they headed back?"

Alice shrugged. "If Mr. Williams hadn't taken us on we most likely would've too. We would've managed to survive somehow. Maybe try to rent land. It's better to head back three days out than half-way. Anything could've happened."

"I'm going to talk to Zeke about letting them join us." Delly hitched her skirt in preparation of dashing ahead.

Alice shot out a hand to stop her. "Don't. The

poor man had a hard enough time letting us come, with me in a family way. I heard him tell Ben last night that we'll be lucky to get over the mountains before snowfall. Plus, with Zeke being a godly man, he wants to stop half days on Sundays." A child's cry carried from the wagons behind them. "I'd best get back to my young'uns." She turned and strolled toward the end of the line.

Good. With the day being a Sunday, Delly could look forward to some rest and time to catch up on chores.

She and Zeke had barely spoken to each other outside formalities around the supper fire. Not since their walk into the prairie, anyway.

Why did she look for him so often? She told herself it was because he was Ezra's brother, but she knew different. She'd never met such an open man before, or heard of a wagon master so concerned about each person under his care. Not that she'd met many, but Ezra mentioned to her that a few years ago an elderly gentleman told him during a game of cards that wagon masters were only interested in the money they received. That description didn't fit Zeke.

During her thoughts, she hadn't realized her steps had slowed until the goat bleated. She reached over to pet Mabel, glad she'd agreed to bring her along. The milk helped keep the babies healthy, and Mabel's kid kept the little ones entertained with its frolicking. Delly smiled. And there was a jar of cream hanging from the wagon top jostling its way to butter as they bounced over ruts. She'd always been good at coming up with ways of making do, and they could use some of the butter to trade when they came across a trading post.

She pushed back her bonnet in an effort to catch a breeze. How could the nights be cool and the days so hot?

A young man rode by and it took a minute for Delly to recognize her oldest son beneath the scrap of fabric he wore on his face. "What is that, Junior?"

He jogged up to her and removed it from the lower half of his face then handed it to her. "It's called a ban-dan-a. The drovers wear 'em to keep from eating dirt. Hiram showed it to me. He's teaching me to scout some too. When I'm bigger, I might lead wagon trains from Missouri to Oregon too."

Delly turned the square fabric over in her hands. It mostly resembled a colored handkerchief. She could make these out of scrap fabric from her quilting stash and help keep her and Sadie from getting grit in their teeth. Wouldn't they be a sight in their bonnets and face rags? Maybe she'd make one for the children, too. They'd look like a family of bandits, sure enough. She handed it back to her son.

"Uncle Zeke said we're stopping for the day." Junior's eyes sparkled as he retied his bandana. "He's leading us a mile west to find grass to graze the cattle on. Do you want me to lead Blue?"

"Please. And keep an eye on the little ones. Sadie and I will catch up." Knowing a few hours of rest loomed before her put a skip in Delly's step as she scampered back to the wagon seat.

"Are we stopping?" Sadie handed over the reins.

"Yes. We'll have time to make bread and beat the dust out of our clothes." Maybe spare a little water to watch their faces. Delly swiped her arm across her forehead and grimaced at the grime. She'd been dirty before, but never like this. The dirt settled everywhere. Her teeth, her eyes, her hair, even managing to find its way down her dress to coat her body. What she wouldn't give for a bath.

Sure enough, Zeke circled the wagons in an area that, while not lushly covered with grass, had enough for the animals to graze. To Delly's delight, a small brook trickled through low-lying bushes. While she couldn't manage a full-fledged soak, at the very least she could indulge in a sponge bath.

She climbed down to start a fire, leaving the unhitching of the oxen to Zeke's hired help. She peeled the gloves from her hands and winced at the new blisters forming in spite of the protective leather. She'd need to nurse her hands while changing the bandage on Ruth's foot.

After helping the little girl from the wagon, Delly settled her on a three-legged stool beside the fire and set a pot of water to boil. Leaving Ruth to wait, she went to rummage through the wagon's contents in search of salve for her hands. When she returned, Mrs. Miller and two other women waited with crossed arms.

"Afternoon, ladies." Delly raised her eyebrows in question.

"Mrs. Williams." Mrs. Miller spat the words as if they left a bitter taste in her mouth. "We have some concerns that need to be addressed."

Delly dropped the salve into the pocket of her apron. Her hands, unfortunately, would have to wait. "The water's almost ready. Can I interest you in some coffee?"

"No, thank you." Mrs. Miller's ice-blue eyes glanced at her companions then back to Delly. "Being upright, God-fearing women, we have an issue with an unmarried woman, widowed or not, living in such close proximity with an unmarried man. Not to mention the colored girl with you. This men of this train don't need the temptation."

Delly sighed and scratched her eyebrow, then stared at the dirt under her fingernails. How did Mrs. Miller always look so fresh? Did the woman ride in the wagon all day? She sighed.

It wasn't Delly's unmarried state that bothered the woman, just Delly herself, cooking and cleaning for the man Mrs. Miller had set her sights on. Fine, she'd play the woman's childish game.

With a cool smile, she glanced up. "Well, Mr. Williams did propose to me. I said no, but maybe I should reconsider his offer if it bothers you women so badly. I thought Sadie would be sufficient chaperonage, but maybe I was wrong." Delly ducked her head to hide her smile. "I do need to think of the children, after all. Being a widowed mother, I can't care for them by myself." Lord, forgive her, but she enjoyed the draining of blood from Mrs. Miller's face. She'd never had time for small-minded people who couldn't keep their noses out of other people's business.

The woman's mouth gaped like a beached fish.

"He proposed?"

"Why, yes, just the other day." Delly scooped coffee grounds into the water then set a smaller pot to boil which she would use to clean Ruth's foot.

Ruth sat with wide eyes and glanced back and forth between Delly and Mrs. Miller. "Is Uncle Zeke going to be my new pa?"

"Possibly. Let's unwrap that dirty bandage, shall we?" She speared her visitors with a sharp glare. "Now, if there isn't anything else I can help you with, I need to tend to my daughter."

She watched them march away. "Of all the insufferable—"

"What was that all about?" Zeke asked from behind her.

~

"You heard?" Delly straightened, her face pale, dirty bandages fluttering from her hands like flags.

"I did." Zeke removed his hat and took his time hanging it on a hook in the wagon bed. Was it possible Delly was reconsidering his offer despite the heated discussion of a few days ago? He'd made a purpose to give her a wide berth unless absolutely necessary, but couldn't help seeking her out with his gaze when he passed.

Wasn't every day a man laid eyes on a woman with eyes the color of a stormy sky and hair as dark as a moonless night. No, Ezra struck gold when he married such a fetching woman. Especially one unafraid of hard work.

"Don't worry." She knelt in the dirt and took Ruth's foot in her lap. "I have no intentions of stepping on anyone's toes. Feel free to court Mrs.

Miller. She's quite lovely."

"Ha!"

Delly glanced up. "You don't think so?"

"I have no intentions of courting anyone." Zeke pulled up a stool. "There isn't time in my life right now for a family."

"You don't want us?" Tears welled in Ruth's eyes.

Zeke held up a hand. "Wait, that isn't what—"

"There's where you're wrong, Mr. Williams." Delly washed Ruth's foot then pulled the jar of salve from her pocket. "You have a family, for now at least, whether you want one or not."

"That isn't what I meant." Why couldn't he speak a coherent sentence around this woman? She barely reached his shoulder when they stood side-by-side, yet the very sight of her intimidated him.

"If it's a wife you don't have time for…" She spread salve on Ruth's foot then wrapped it with a clean bandage. "Then you might want to let the single ladies know. I don't think they have a clue." She cupped Ruth's cheek. "Let Uncle Zeke take you back to the wagon, all right? Your foot looks good. Healing real nice."

"We'll continue this discussion later." Zeke scooped his niece in his arms.

"There's nothing to discuss." Delly stood. "Neither of us is interested in getting hitched. I want to get my family to Oregon and get settled. Unfortunately, I need your help to do that."

"Then you'll send me on my way."

"Not too far, obviously. Our land juts against each other, I assume." She bent and lifted the blue-speckled tin pot. "Coffee?"

Zeke growled and stomped to the wagon. After settling his niece inside, he leaned his head against the rough wood.

"Uncle Zeke?"

He lifted his head and gazed into the hazel eyes of his oldest nephew. "Something wrong, Junior?"

"No, sir, but I'm wondering if I can put the pup in the wagon tomorrow. He don't weigh much and his little paws are getting bloody from trying to keep up."

Zeke couldn't resist Junior's imploring eyes. "Sure. His mother can too, since the little ones ride the mule. But your ma might get upset if they leave a mess."

"They won't. They're good dogs!" Junior stretched over the tail of the wagon and handed the puppy to Ruth before galloping away.

Zeke envied the boy his childishness. At the age of twelve, chances were good he'd be acting like a grown man by the time they reached Oregon. He glanced at the little family gathering around the lunch fire. Would he lose one of them on the way? Most likely. What if he lost Delly? How would he care for five children on his own?

If someone would've told him a year ago he'd be responsible for another family, he'd have told them to jump off the highest cliff. Since he'd lost his wife, he'd vowed never to be personally responsible for a woman and child again. At least not on the trail. No help for it. God saw fit to land Delly and the little ones in his lap.

He patted Ruth's cheek and smiled at the sight

of her nuzzling the pup. "I'll bring you something to eat. Stay off that foot as long as you can."

She nodded, and giggling, fell back onto the mattress with her new furry friend. Zeke watched for a minute, relishing in the childhood abandon of a child with a puppy. *Please, God, let my family make it through.*

"Mr. Williams. Zeke."

He closed his eyes and cringed before turning to face Mrs. Miller. "Is there a problem?"

"No." She glanced down, then coyly up, fluttering her lashes. "I came to invite you to eat at our fire."

"Thank you, Mrs. Miller, but that won't be necessary any longer." He grabbed his hat. "I have my own fire now." Not that the woman wasn't lovely; tall, slim, hair the color of corn silk and blue eyes that always looked wet, but she didn't compare to the petite, raven-haired Delly. Nor, he'd wager, would she feel as good in his arms as Delly had during their horse ride. Even angry, Delly fit as if God created her to be there. Too bad he wasn't prepared to take a wife. Obviously, something some women didn't understand.

Mrs. Miller's full lip quivered. "Can't you call me Sophia? I believe we know each other well enough."

Well enough? A lump the size of Missouri lodged in his throat. The woman counted a few suppers on the trail as knowing her well enough? "Okay, Sophia, but really, Sadie and Delly will have our own supper prepared soon enough. There's no need for me to eat your supplies. They need to last you for months."

She sashayed closer and toyed with the buttons on his shirt. "Money isn't an issue with the Oglesby family, Zeke. We can purchase more supplies."

"Please, Sophia." Sweat peppered his brow. He removed her hands and stepped back until the wagon wheel pressed against his spine, leaving him feeling like a bug caught in a Black Widow's web. "You need to transfer your attentions somewhere else." On some other poor unsuspecting fool.

She sighed. "If you say so. I'll speak with you tomorrow."

Zeke released a deep breath and turned toward his fire. Delly crossed her arms and glared after Sophia.

6

After washing in the shallow creek, Delly sat on a boulder a small distance from camp. A mild breeze teased at her wet hair, cooling her head. She stared across the prairie.

The sight of Sophia Miller cozying up to Zeke left a bitter taste in her mouth. With the way the blood drained from his face, Zeke obviously didn't return her feelings, so why didn't he make her stay away? Men were such easy creatures to manipulate. If Zeke weren't careful, he'd find himself with a bride whether he wanted one or not. One word from Sophia that Zeke toyed with her affections and Mr. Oglesby would most likely come visiting armed with a gun.

Muted conversation from the supper fire drifted her way. Zeke's laughter rang out, and she turned to see what was going on. Junior jumped up to pantomime something. His shadow danced on the ground. Delly should've joined them, but regardless of how much she loved the children, moments of peace and quiet were as precious as the gold foretold in California's streams.

Instead of the peace she craved, she focused on her feelings for someone she would never have. If only their land wouldn't sit next to each other. She wasn't foolish enough to think she wouldn't require Zeke's help in settling. She couldn't build a cabin by herself, after all. But once they had a home, a garden planted, and livestock, she'd rely on him no more.

The guidebook spouted pages of promises about fertile Oregon land. Anything could grow there. Delly wanted to plant an apple orchard and sell her produce. Stashed in her chest was a gourd set aside for that purpose. Surely there would be a market for the bounty from her garden as more and more people settled the area.

With sure steps, and a straight back, she moved to rejoin the others, taking a seat across the fire from Zeke. Seconds later, she rethought her decision.

The fire cast shadows across his face and danced in the reflection from his eyes. Delly grabbed a stick and poked at the embers. Anything so she wouldn't have to look at him. Sparks shot into the sky to join the stars.

"Tell us about your travels, Uncle Zeke." Junior sat cross-legged at his feet. "Pa said you dug for gold once upon a time. Found some too."

Zeke removed a blade of prairie grass from his teeth. "Not me. Your Uncle Rupert did. I lived in Arkansas at the time. Scraped out a modest living in the rich soil. When Uncle Rupert struck gold, he sent for me—" He cleared his throat. "I went to join him, then ended up in Oregon instead. Claimed land for your Pa and I."

"Is that where Pa disappeared to? Is that where he was when Ma died?"

"Yeah. He came back as quick as we got word. But it was a long journey." Zeke stretched his long legs in front of him. "He came home to tend to you youngsters."

Junior shoveled the last of the beans in the pot onto a plate. "We lived with the neighbors for six months."

"I'm real sorry about that." Zeke ruffled Junior's hair.

What kind of man left his wife and five children behind to hunt for gold? Delly tossed a handful of sticks on the fire. The man she married, that's who. The same man who went gambling the day after their wedding. She'd been a blind fool, wanting nothing more than a permanent roof over her head. Would anyone ever love her for her?

She transferred her gaze to Zeke. What would it be like to be married to someone honest and trustworthy? She'd probably never know. Because she'd never marry for anything less than love again. She didn't care if the man was poor and they lived in a tent.

"What made you become a wagon master?" Junior scraped his plate clean with the last biscuit.

"I found God in Oregon, heard how many people die with each journey, and figured I could help people by taking wagon trains west. So, I hired myself the best guide I could fine, and here I am." He glanced at Delly. "But I'm thinking this will be my last trip." He winked.

Her face heated. Why must he torment her? Hadn't she made her intentions clear? And not just her, but those of the widow Miller left little doubt as to what she wanted.

The sound of a fiddle being tuned drifted across the circle. Zeke glanced that way. "There'll be dancing once in a while. When folks have cause to celebrate. Do you dance, Delly?"

"Never had the opportunity." She choked on the words. There hadn't even been dancing at their wedding. Instead, Ezra held her hand in front of a preacher, the five children in a line behind them. No sense dwelling on things she couldn't change. She'd gotten hitched with her eyes open. Ezra needed a ma for his kids, she wanted a permanent roof over her head. Her mouth twisted. Instead, she got stars in her eyes that quickly faded.

~

As one-by-one, Hiram and Melvin headed to the stock, and Sadie ushered the children into the wagon, Zeke licked his lips, digging up courage from deep within. He locked gazes with Delly. "Since neither of us is looking to be hitched, do you think we could be friends? Like we would be if Ezra were still alive?"

"I suppose we could." She glanced toward Sadie and the children. "It would make life easier on everyone. The young'uns like having their uncle around, and Junior needs a father figure."

Zeke almost changed his mind right then and there. He was the furthest thing from a father figure as anyone he knew. What kind of example was a man that traveled back and forth across the country each year? Children needed stability. Structure. Sure, he had plans to stay and set down roots, but what if he couldn't? What if the life of a rancher bored him? He forced a smile. "Good night, Delly." He watched her until she climbed into the wagon and disappeared.

With camp sounds quieting, Zeke spread his bedroll beneath the wagon and stretched out. He glanced to the one where Delly and the children slept. Father figure, huh? He snorted. Maybe someday, but this wasn't the day.

7

"**Why are we** stopping now?" Delly's shoulders slumped. Seemed every time she turned around they stopped for some reason. "We just got started today. We'll never reach Laramie by June at this rate." She handed the reins to Sadie and leaned over the side of the wagon. "Junior! Run up ahead and see what the hold up is, would you?" She wrapped her shawl tighter around her.

"It's cold for May, isn't it? I'm glad we had the foresight to stock up on wood. There wasn't any around this morning. No buffalo chips either." Not that Delly wanted to use any. "I look forward to a hot meal when the temperature drops like this."

"Goodness, Miss Delly." Sadie let the reins droop across her lap. "You sure are out of sorts this morning."

"I'm sorry. I woke up cold, and I've been grouchy ever since." She ducked her chin into her chest. "Don't you think it's time you dropped the Miss?"

"Wouldn't be proper. Folks'll frown, and that might cause problems for you. And don't worry.

It'll warm up. In a few weeks, you'll be boiling hot and grumbling about something else."

Junior dashed back to the wagon. "There's a narrow bridge up ahead that's owned by Indians. They're demanding a toll."

Dorcas jumped up and down beside the wagon. "I want to see the Indians."

"Not now. You can see them when we cross." Delly leaned over the side and tried to see for herself. "How much do they want?"

"Seventy-five cents."

She bit her bottom lip. "That seems like a lot of money. It's not like they're ferrying us across the river. Is there any other way?"

"No, Uncle Zeke said it's best to pay. Tomorrow we hit another dangerous river that we'll have to ford. It's called the Elkhorn. Here's the money. I'll have to pay to cross the mule and goat too."

"Nonsense. Just tie them to the back of the wagon and give your uncle back his money."

"I don't know…"

"Just do as I say!" Delly slammed back against the seat. The impact took her breath away, sent a stab of pain through her back, and increased her irritation. She ought to be glad for the distraction the Indians provided. It'd been the same view every day. The back of the oxens' heads, and the wagon in front of them had a tear in the bonnet that Delly's fingers itched to fix. The incessant buzzing of flies attracted to the animal's sweat was enough to make her want to scream.

Junior marched off to fetch the animals. They'd

only moved a few feet by the time he returned and tied them to the back. When they finally reached the bridge, Zeke stood ready to translate. Next to him stood two male Indians, dressed in buckskin britches and flannel shirts.

Dorcas frowned. "They don't look much like Indians to me, 'cept for the long hair and dark skin."

"Mornin'." Zeke tipped his hat, his gaze settling on Delly. "Seventy-five cents for the wagon and another for the mule and goat."

"I won't pay but one fee." Delly stared straight ahead, not making eye contact. She refused to use Zeke's coins and she had precious little money left. She wouldn't squander it on greedy Indians. "They're attached to the wagon."

The corner of Zeke's mouth twitched. The Indians made wild gestures with their hands. "They say seventy-five cents twice. They think you're trying to rob them."

"That's silly." She turned her head to glare at them. "Tell them I wouldn't rob anyone. It's the other way around, the way I see it." She crossed her arms. Sadie glanced from her to Zeke, her smooth brow creased with worry. "Stop fretting, Sadie. I know what I'm doing." She hoped.

The Indians laughed and slapped each other on the back. They pointed at Delly and guffawed.

Zeke shook his head. "They admire your spunk. One of them is interested in buying the pale faced woman with hair the color of a raven and eyes like a thunderstorm. Interested? He says he'll trade me two ponies for you." The corner of his mouth twitched again. "I could probably use them for my ranch."

Her mouth dropped. "No! Tell them I'm taken or something."

He clapped one of the Indians on the shoulders and whispered something. The three men guffawed, and he turned back to Delly. "One toll it is."

"What did you tell him?"

"That you were more trouble than seventy-five cents would buy."

Neck heating hot enough to challenge the sun, Delly paid the toll, nodding at the Indians as they passed. She took a deep breath and willed her heart rate to return to normal. When had she acquired her stubbornness? She'd never balked at rules before. And how dare Zeke ridicule her in front of the savages.

"I don't know how you stayed so calm." Sadie handed back the reins. "My hands are shaking. I thought for sure they'd scalp us. And for them to want to buy you, mercy, I couldn't hardly breathe."

"They didn't look very dangerous to me." Quite the opposite, in fact. Delly was beginning to suspect the guidebook wasn't entirely true about what the emigrants would encounter on their journey.

Sadie sat back and removed the kerchief covering her head. Ebony curls fell to her shoulders. "They did to me. How did you know they'd compromise?"

"Their toll was robbery, and they knew it." Delly removed her glove from her right hand and fingered Sadie's hair. "You have the most gorgeous hair. I wish mine was as thick. Yours is as soft as down."

"The blessing of having a white daddy. Besides, yours is as fine as silk and as dark as those Indians'. Makes you look like a fairy tale creature. Seeing as how the Indians like it so much, I'd keep it covered if I were you."

Delly laughed. "Best we appreciate what we possess then, huh?" She shook her head. "I'm going to have a fit if we have to pay a toll every time we cross a bridge or a river. I didn't know anyone owned this land out here."

"And I wasn't aware you had such a temper."

"You have no idea," Dorcas shouted from behind them. "It just takes a while to rile her, then watch out!"

~

They rode into the late afternoon before stopping on the bank of the Elkhon River. Delly despaired. The scene reminded her of Independence. Everywhere she looked wagons waited to cross. A sea of white rippled as far as she could see. The breeze whipped the canvas and filled the air with the sound of buffeting sails. The wagons must have counted in the hundreds.

"I don't believe it." She climbed from her seat. "This is ridiculous. Dorcas, help me get dinner started." She stomped around the camp like a caged animal, grumbling about yet another delay.

"I'm driving tomorrow, Miss Delly." Sadie glared at her. "You're unpleasant to be around. Maybe you need to lie in the back like a lady of leisure and rest. Must be the strain of sitting on your bottom all day that has you so riled." She took the kettle from Dorcas. "Go get us some of those fine biscuits from yesterday, Miss Dorcas. Maybe gnawing on one of those will settle your ma's temper."

Delly stretched, placing her hands on the small of her back, and laughed. "You're right. My whole body aches." She glanced around them. Her moods changed with each minute it seemed. And she hadn't set eyes on Zeke all day. That couldn't be the reason for her behavior, could it? If it was, she'd have to get over the notion right quick! They'd both made it more than plain that romance, and marriage, weren't in the picture for either of them.

Trees lined the banks of the river and overlooked shallow bluffs. "This might be a pretty place if there weren't so many wagons. But it's cold again. The weather is as unpredictable as my deceased husband's chance of winning at poker. There are so many people there's nowhere to go for…any privacy."

"Looks like we'll have to be inventive. We'll walk a ways with some of the other women and form a circle. I heard some folks saying that one person gets in the middle to do her business while the others shield her with their skirts." She demonstrated by picking up her skirt and holding it out on both sides.

Delly frowned, picturing it, and not liking what she saw. "I guess it'll work. Still doesn't give us much, but it's better than nothing."

Sophia Miller sashayed around the wagon. "Uncouth, if you ask me. Everyone will know what you're doing."

"As if they don't when you disappear behind a bush?" Delly rolled her eyes. How the woman did put on airs. They'd see if she still acted so fine by the time they reached Oregon.

Sophia snorted and crossed her arms.

Ben and Alice strolled up. "We've got to dismantle the wagons. Take off the wheels and float the beds across," Ben told them. "According to Mr. Williams, we'll take the women and children first then come back for the supplies. Leave behind anything that isn't necessary." He glanced at the small pile of firewood Delly had piled.

Her wood? "But what if we can't come by any more for a while?"

"Then you'll burn something else. The boys and I will be by soon to help you dismantle."

Junior ran up, his hat in hand. "You women should see this! It's sheer pandemonium. They're floating the wagons like big rafts, using long poles to steer. The poles keep falling into the water, and the wagons start floating down the river and run into each other. Those that don't have wagons are crossing on the backs of their horses or trying to swim. One man already drowned." He stopped to take a breath.

"Uncle Zeke told me to come get the mule. He's got a better idea about crossing. He's bound and determined to do this orderly. He's really smart, ain't he? He said he's never seen this much commotion just for crossing a river. Said you'd think the west was going to disappear the way people are in such a rush. Wants to get ahead of them if we can. We'll be crossing first thing in the morning. Pile up your stuff."

Sadie's mouth fell open when he dashed away. "Land sakes, that boy was running at the mouth."

Delly wondered if she looked as surprised. She'd never heard Junior spout off so much as he did on the trail. If you asked him, he'd probably say his uncle walked on water. And there was only one man Delly knew of that could do that, and he didn't walk with a physical form anymore. She ducked her head to hide a smile, although Zeke did seem more than mortal at times. Especially the way he worked without ceasing as if physical tiredness was something that didn't dare touch him.

They worked well into the dark unloading the wagons so the men could take off the wheels, then loaded everything back on with the wheels laid flat on the wagon bed. She'd even had to take off the canvas covering so the wind couldn't catch it and sail them down river. Perspiration soaked her skin and ran in rivulets down her back. Exhaustion weighed her limbs and left her feeling sixty years old.

~

With her heart in her throat, Delly watched as Zeke swam his horse across with the end of a rope tied around his waist. Cyclone never faltered in the current, putting one massive hoof in front of the other. Zeke rode hunched low over the horse's ears, his muscles rippling through the red plaid shirt he wore under a buckskin vest. He was the epitome of the western hero in every novel Delly had ever spent time with. She shook herself free of purposeless wonderings and moved to help the others.

With the help of Hiram and Melvin, Ben stayed on their side and secured the other end to a sturdy tree. When Zeke reached the opposite shore, he tied the rope to another tree and whistled for Ben to begin.

Because of the way the wagons had stopped the night before, Ben would go first with the bulk of his supplies. Melvin would take the women and children across on Delly's wagon.

Ben and Hiram shoved the first of their heavy wagons into the river. The bed settled just above the water line, made waterproof because of the oil Zeke had the foresight to paint over the wood before setting out. The men pulled themselves hand over hand using the rope, until the wagon bed hit the opposite bank. He cupped his hands around his mouth, and yelled. "We'll swim back over on the rope once you women are across. Shove her off, Melvin."

Alice grinned. "He's some kind of man, my Ben."

Delly smiled back. "Him and Zeke are both made from a rare cloth, that's for sure." Some woman would be very lucky to get a man such as Zeke for a husband.

The men shoved together, sliding Delly's wagon into the water. The river splashed up and over, soaking Delly's precious stockpile of wood. She should have listened and disposed of it. She groaned and tossed the sticks into the water, watching the current swirl them away. While Junior held the raft steady, they finished loading the supplies. Delly and Sadie grabbed the rope, along with Melvin, and Junior jumped off.

"Get back on here!" What did her son have planned now?

He shook his head. "Can't. Got to swim the stock across. Uncle Zeke's coming back to help me." He slapped his hat on his head and dashed to where the stock clustered behind a makeshift corral.

Melvin ordered the children into the center of the bed, nodded for Delly and Sadie to grab hold, and started pulling them across. The river ran swift, tugging the wagon bed away from the rope. "Pull harder," he yelled.

They strained against the fast moving water. Delly glanced down. Her stomach heaved. The river roared over rocks, causing the bed to pitch and roll. Several times one of them would slip and almost lose their footing. How many of these nightmares would they have to face?

They heaved in unison to pull the wagon across the river. Alice's daughter, Abby, wailed every time the water splashed over the edge, threatening to drench her. If she'd had time, Delly would've plopped down and cried with her.

Sadie tripped over a sack of flour and tottered toward the edge of the wagon bed. She flung her arms over the rope. Her legs thrashed as she struggled to gain a foothold. Delly watched in horror as the other woman slid out of the wagon.

"I'm losing my grip!" Sadie kicked frantically. "Heaven have mercy, I can't swim."

"Grab her, Mrs. Williams," Melvin shouted. "I'll try to hold the wagon steady."

Delly let loose of the rope and scrambled across the piles of dry goods. *Lord, please don't let her drown in front of my eyes.* She grabbed her friend around the waist, heaved, and pulled her to safety. "You okay?"

Sadie nodded, her chest heaving. "Just got to catch my breath. I'll help pull in a minute."

Delly grasped the rope and, hand over hand, continued the pull across the water. How she wished Zeke stood on the opposite shore. Something solid for her to focus on. Her mind filled with the urgent need to set both feet on land. She struggled to keep her own footing on the slippery wagon bottom. The extra weight of her drenched dress made her movements slow and clumsy. By the time they reached the shore, her nerves were on edge and nausea soured her stomach.

Her hands burned, her clothes clung to her body, soaked with water or sweat, she couldn't tell and didn't care. There was no strength left in her. Her chest heaved with the effort to breath.

Sadie held out her hands. Bleeding welts covered her palms. Alice dug through her supplies to find the medicine kit.

A shadow fell over Delly, and she stared up at Zeke. He grinned. "You women did good. Once the wagons are back together, you can rest. We start again early in the morning."

Delly slumped to the ground. Where'd the man get his energy? "I can't move."

"You'll feel better with some hot coffee in you, and make a habit of wearing gloves every day." Zeke tipped his hat.

"Thank you for that bit of information." He most likely brought up the subject of coffee so she'd make a pot for him.

He frowned. "Are your hands as bad as Sadie's?"

Delly held them up, palm out. "They've been better, but no, not as bad." The skin stung like hornets.

Zeke took them in his, warming her even through the leather he wore over his own hands. "If not taken care of, these blisters could get infected. Then you won't be able to do much at all."

Did he only care about how much work she could do? "I'm putting salve on them nightly."

His features softened as his gaze met hers. "Just don't want anything to happen to you, that's all." He nodded and strolled away.

Delly watched him go, his long strides carrying him to other emigrants who might need his help. She wanted him to go, yet at the same time, wanted him to stay until the fear of the river crossing became nothing but a memory.

"My momma would be horrified. My hands look like they belong to a common field worker," Sadie moaned.

Alice tossed her a jar of salve. She laughed. "Now you'll smell like one."

Delly pushed to her feet. Her arms felt like they weighed fifty pounds each. Her stomach rolled. If she felt this way after only a few weeks, how would she ever set up a home in Oregon before winter set in?

8

The aroma of brewing coffee drifted through the canvas, teasing Delly awake. She burrowed further into the quilts. Her nose felt like the snout of a calf left out in the snow. She poked her hand free of her cocoon and tucked it back beneath the covers. Freezing! The weather in this new land couldn't make up its mind. Hotter than blazes one day and as cold as the darkest winter the next.

As quickly as possible, she tossed the blankets aside, pulled on her dress and shawl, then glanced toward the children's and Sadie's vacant spots.

"I thought I heard someone rustling around in here." Sadie parted the tent flap. "Coffee's ready, lady of leisure."

"Thank you. I need something to warm me." Delly shivered and stepped outside.

"Someone thought to bring a thermometer. Said it's down in the thirties. There's ice crust on the ground too." Sadie handed her a warm mug. "Not much wood to be found, but the grazing's all right."

The campers woke around them. Men

murmured to the stock while the women coaxed children from cozy beds. Delly waved to Junior, who stood by the Johnsons' wagon. Couldn't that boy ever stay by his own fire? He looked, and acted, for all the world like a boy on a grand adventure. Maybe he was. Unless he followed in his uncle's footsteps, he wouldn't travel across the continent again.

Sadie handed her a bowl of corn mush with pieces of bacon and a drizzle of honey. "Eat. We don't have much time."

Remorse filled her. She'd slept that long? How could she, and leave Sadie to care for the children? "Honey?"

"I did some mending for a woman who brought along a couple of hives to restart her colony when we get west. She had some jars set aside." Sadie bumped Delly with her hip. "I don't sleep much, so I've been working for others while you lazy people sleep in."

"Hmmm." Delly glanced at the fire. Buffalo chips, or Meadow Muffins as some called them, surprised her with their lack of smoke or scent. If only she didn't have to think of where they came from. Her stomach flipped. Or touch them. Thankfully, the younger girls weren't as squeamish at picking up the things.

Zeke strolled by and tipped his hat. "Morning, Mrs. Williams. Sadie."

"Good morning, Mr. Williams." The dreaded flush crept up Delly's neck, and she buried her face in her mug. Only a blind and deaf person would miss the intimacy of them sharing a last name, especially when he said hers with a husky growl.

Silly fool. If he saw her blush, he'd know he affected her more than she wanted to let on.

Moments later, the signal whistle blew, and they scrambled to get everything packed back into the wagon bed. Sadie tossed Delly a pair of gloves, and she shoved her sore hands into them.

They'd begun traveling on the north side of the Platte, eating dust and watching the wind blow.
Dust pelted her skin as they traveled, and Delly pulled her face rag as close to her eyes as possible. She'd relented earlier and let the children ride in the wagon. Now, they squabbled over being confined to tight quarters, and complained about dust drifting inside. Feeling and thought ceased to exist as Delly kept the wagon moving forward. Even Sadie sat hunched and silent.

Mercifully, Zeke called a halt earlier than normal. Sadie climbed from the wagon seat and shaded her eyes with her hand as she glanced at the trail behind them. Worry lines furrowed her brow.

"Who are you looking for?" Delly joined her. Seemed every time they stopped, Sadie's attention was glued to the trail behind them. "Are you afraid a bounty hunter's going to come? Zeke won't let them take you."

"No, no one." Sadie blinked rapidly then turned to begin unhitching the oxen.

Delly shrugged. Her friend would tell what sorrowed her when the time was right.

"The wind today is the worst yet!" She blinked against the stinging dust as the wind whipped her skirt and tangled it around her legs. "How am I supposed to get a fire started?"

"I guess we'll be eating a cold dinner," Sadie replied. "Won't be the last time."

Delly shoved her shoulder against the nearest animal which balked against the stinging particles of dirt. "Move, you miserable beast!"

Drenching, bone-chilling rain soon joined the wind. Delly gladly turned the animals over to her son, and she and Sadie escaped to the dry inside of the wagon. Dorcas handed them each a couple of hard biscuits and a slice of jerky. "Thanks." Delly perched on top of the stack of flour sacks.

Zeke stuck his head over the wagon bed. "You ladies, all right?"

Delly jerked and dropped her food into her lap. "You scared me."

"Sorry. Have to yell above the wind."

"We're fine." She tucked a few stray strands of hair behind her ear. "You should get to shelter. It's raining something fierce."

"I will once I've checked on everyone. Wanted to make sure you were settled first." He clapped his hand over his hat and the let the flap close.

"Best get those stars out of your eyes, Miss Delly." Sadie lowered the flame on the lantern as the wind buffeted against the wagon's bonnet. "Ain't hard to see you've got feelings for our wagon master."

Dorcas lifted her head from her pillow. "What's that mean?"

Sadie laughed. "Miss Delly knows."

"Stop. I do not have 'feelings' for Mr. Williams." Delly smiled and wrapped a quilt around her. "What about you? Got a beau somewhere? How old are you?"

"I'm sixteen, and I do have a fellow meeting me out west." Sadie ducked her head. "Out where we'll be free. It'd be mighty nice if he catches up with us. He'd be real handy on this trip. He's been trained as a farrier and is a right good blacksmith too."

"So, that's who you keep looking for." How romantic. A lover traipsing all the way across country to follow his sweetheart. What would that be like?

Ezra had courted with flowers once in a while, but both of them knew they married out of necessity more than love. He needed a ma for his kids, and Delly needed a man to provide a living for her. Well, not anymore. She'd remain the young'uns's ma, but she'd be self-sufficient now with the land.

Having lost track of her siblings years ago, she couldn't help wondering what they'd think of their little sister's good fortune. She also couldn't keep her mind off what Zeke's plans might be once they reached their destination. Would he be looking for a bride then? Would Delly change her mind about another marriage? She spread out on the mattress. Not likely. It would take a rare man indeed to change her feelings on the matter.

"Yep." Sadie smiled and ducked her head. "He's a right fine man."

Delly couldn't help but think that Sadie meant Zeke along with her beau.

The previous night's rain had settled the dust.

Sadie took the reins while Delly mended dresses quickly showing signs of wear. When the sun came out, the children ran barefoot along the trail, their laughter mingling with Sarah Johnson's as they picked wildflowers.

The heavier wagons bogged down in the mushy trail, slowing progress. Delly climbed from the wagon seat to stretch her legs and sank ankle deep in the mire. Her steps squished, until she removed her mud-encased shoes and sunk her toes into the mud. Her body ached. The slushy mess soothed her toes enough she was almost tempted to bury herself up to the neck.

As the day wore on, clouds rolled back in, cooling them with a breeze. Delly pulled off her bonnet and raised her hair off her neck. The motion barely refreshed her. The air thickened.

"Looks like a storm tonight." Zeke stopped beside her and slid from his horse.

Delly regretted leaving her shoes behind. He'd think her a country bumpkin. She tilted her head, letting her hair fall. "Moved in fast. This country has the strangest weather. Cold in the mornings, hot during the day, and stormy at night. Humidity to rival Missouri."

His gaze flicked to her hair. "I'm taking Junior off guard-duty tonight. You might need him at the wagon."

"It's going to be bad?" A grip of fear clenched her heart.

"It might. Storms can be unpredictable. It's best to be safe." He tipped his hat and swung onto his horse.

Delly didn't know what was colder, the rising wind, or Zeke's manner. They'd walked such a short distance together she wondered why he bothered getting off his horse. She'd seen the admiring look in his eyes before he'd turned as frigid as a block of ice. Sometimes the man seemed as moody as a woman. Did he have regrets about letting them come? They hadn't caused any extra trouble.

Why should she care? Wasn't this what she wanted? For them to keep their distance from each other?

Before they'd completed their end of the day circling of the wagons and accomplished supper preparations, the wind howled with the ferocity of snarling dogs. Delly grabbed a rain slicker in an attempt to protect her skin from icy drops of rain then helped put away the cook stove and pots. The wind ripped the slicker from her hands and tangled it around a wagon wheel. "Children, get in the wagon!"

Sadie yelped and leaped out of the way of a tumbleweed. Thunder boomed with the sharpness of a rifle and hail fell from the sky.

Delly ducked and shrieked as lightening slashed the sky. Her feet slipped on balls of ice. The more she scurried for shelter, the less ground she covered. Wind slashed at the wagon's bonnet, ripping at the canvas. The front wheels lifted a few inches off the ground.

The wagon wasn't safe. She'd sent her children into danger. Her stomach clinched. "Get out of the wagon!" The wind tossed her warning aside.

The canvas covering lifted like clothes on a clothesline. The wagon rolled, spewing some of its contents into the mud.

Giving up trying to regain her footing, Delly crawled. Her hands and knees sank into the mud. Her babies. They were all she had. "Junior, help me!" Baby Sarah's wails rose above the wind. Delly choked back sobs. She wouldn't survive without them. Please, God, don't take the children. Not a one.

Junior grabbed Delly beneath the arms and helped her struggle to her feet. Sadie reached the overturned wagon first. She tossed more things into the mud in her fury to find the children. A sob caught in Delly's throat as, one-by-one, Sadie pulled the little ones to safety.

Delly wrapped them in a hug. Besides a few scratches, they appeared frightened but unharmed. *Lord, what was I thinking bringing children on this journey? We should have taken our chances in Missouri.* She looked around for Zeke. Why wasn't he caring for his family?

~

Zeke galloped to Delly's wagon. Cyclone's hooves slung mud, caking his legs and splattering his duster. His heart beat in rhythm with his horse's pounding hooves until he thought it would burst free. "Everyone okay?" His heart skipped a beat when he saw Delly kneeling on the ground, surrounded by the young'uns.

He'd been across outside the circle checking on the livestock when he saw the wagon flip and thought the sight would knock him to his knees.

Instead, he'd bolted for his horse.

The wind had died, along with the rain, and the women stood ankle deep in mud, surveying the scattered contents. The canvas sported a couple of rips, but otherwise appeared untouched. Junior stood, hands on hips, clearly at a loss as to what to do next. Zeke bit his lip in an effort not to smile at the typical greenhorn picture the family made. "Get that wagon unloaded, and we'll soon get it set to rights."

His laughter escaped. "I never dreamed I'd see a wagon driven by women overturn because it was too light. It's usually the other way around."

"It's not funny. And it's your wagon!"

"Kept empty for your family. I expected Ezra to arrive with more belongings." And counted his blessings that the family hadn't. It was never a good thing to discard treasures along the trail.

"They were all sold to pay his debts." Delly handed the baby to Dorcas and turned to face him, blue eyes blazing in a mud-splattered face. "The children were in the wagon when it turned over. Someone could have been killed. Maybe you should've weighed it down more." She covered her face with her hands and began to cry. Her thin shoulders shook.

Remorse punched him in the stomach. He pulled her close. "I'm sorry. I really am." He chuckled, doing his best to keep the sound from bursting forth.

"You're still laughing." Her voice muffled against his chest.

"Y'all make a funny picture. Covered in mud,

standing in the stuff to your ankles while Junior stands back and watches." He rubbed her back. She'd lost weight. He followed her spine with his fingers, and vowed to go hunting for fresh meat at the first opportunity. "Everyone's fine. Let's get you situated. There are other wagons that need repairs."

He raised her face and placed a kiss on her forehead. No one could've said who was more startled by the gesture, him or Delly, who blushed a becoming shade of pink under the mud splatters. He shocked himself with his forwardness. Her cheeks reddened further as he continued to stare, and Zeke braced himself to be slapped. When it didn't come, he cupped her face and wiped away the mud beside her trembling mouth.

An almost overwhelming desire to kiss her overtook him, and he pulled back before acting on the thought. He called to some men to help right the wagon, and stepped back to a safe distance.

By tying ropes to the oxen and pushing from the opposite side, the men were able to set it correct. The soft ground had prevented the wagon bed from breaking, and other than a stained and dirty bonnet and a couple of repairable rips, the wagon looked travel worthy.

"Thank you." Delly sloshed toward him, bunching her skirts in one hand.

Zeke yanked his gaze away from her ankles. "You're welcome. I'd best be going to check on the others. Hopefully, we didn't lose too many supplies."

She glanced around. "Mainly tin dishes and

bedding. Nothing that can't be washed."

They stared at each other for several seconds until Zeke pulled away before he drowned in her gaze. His stomach churned at the emotions whipping through him as strong as the wind only minutes before. "Good night."

"Good night." Her whisper followed him as he turned.

Mr. Oglesby yelled for assistance, and Zeke increased his pace. He scowled, coming to his senses. There wasn't time for love. Not on the trail west. He knew that from personal experience.

Could this really be his last trip? Was he finally ready to settle down? Could he leave behind the adventures of traveling for the day-to-day life of a rancher? Leave behind near misses like they'd just had? He thought so.

He dreamed at night of waking the next morning to the sight of a bride's face. He'd try to set romance aside while traveling, but once they reached Oregon, before they had a chance to part ways, he'd think real hard on asking his tiny strong-willed sister-in-law to be his wife.

~

They didn't fare any better the next night. Another storm dumped rain in torrents, quickly leaving the ground a lake of brown. Delly wouldn't allow Sadie or the children to seek shelter in the wagon. Instead, they donned slickers and huddled beneath it.

"This is silly," Junior stated. "Hiding with the women. I'm going to check on the livestock. That lightening is getting closer. It might scare the cattle.

Hear the thunder?" He crawled and disappeared from their sight.

Moments later, shouts of stampede rang through the camp. Delly shivered, not able to determine whether she did so from the cold or fear for her son's safety. Gunshots split the night and the pounding of the livestock's hooves faded away.

She sighed with relief when Zeke's tall form approached their wagon. She jumped out to greet him. "Have you seen Junior? He went out to check the animals. What if he got trampled in the stampede?"

"He's fine. A smart boy. He climbed a tree as soon as the animals bolted. He's out helping round up the ones that got away. Let him be a man, Delly. He's old enough. Besides, I'm keeping an eye on him." His gaze moved over her shoulder and his eyes widened. "Did you take shelter *under* the wagon this time?"

"Yes." She glanced to where Sadie sat in several inches of water, her arms wrapped around the young'uns. "I wasn't taking any more chances of the wagon tipping with someone inside. And the wind was too strong for the tent." She stiffened and planted her fists on her hips, daring him to laugh.

"I guess I can see the sense in that. It's a smart move." The corner of his mouth twitched. He laughed silently at first, then the sound burst from him like a geyser she'd seen once. He held up a hand in apology and shook his head. He bent over, hands on his knees, and continued to laugh until tears streamed down his face.

"Go ahead and laugh, you big buffoon!" Delly

punched him in the shoulder and whipped around. How could she find herself growing attached to a man who laughed at danger? Found humor in children placed in harm's way? She sighed. She'd deal with him after she changed into dry clothes. She marched to the wagon and climbed inside, calling for Sadie and the children to do the same.

She yanked her soaked garments over her head and let them fall in a huddle to wagon's bed. Her brother-in-law was a cad!

9

With everything a sodden mess from last night's storm, Delly was more than glad for a day to enable them to dry out their belongings and bake bread. After washing laundry in a shallow creek a short ways from the wagon, she hung a shirt over a bush to dry in the day's sunshine.

They couldn't have stopped in a prettier place. Wildflowers, brighter in color because of the recent rain, covered the prairie. She lifted her head to watch an eagle soar and dip above her head. What would it feel like to fly with no worries? She'd most likely never know. Life was burdened with trouble and turmoil. Her mind whirred with Zeke's ridiculous proposal.

Maybe she should've taken him up on the offer. Then, she wouldn't have the sole burden of caring for children under such primitive conditions. Daily, she thanked God for Sadie.

The aroma of baking bread surrounded her. She breathed deeply. Peaceful days full of tranquility and beauty were so few on the trail, she cherished them when they came. *Thank you, God, for today.* She removed her bonnet and lifted her face to the sun and the kiss of a breeze.

"Morning, Mud Dog." Zeke tilted his head as he meandered by.

"Stop calling me that." She snapped a towel over a bush.

"Can't." He chuckled and continued on his way.

Every time he passed, he'd shake his head, smile, and make a joke about her huddling in the mud, or call her Mud Dog, until Delly wanted to bash him. Then she'd remember the feel of his lips on her skin, and get confused all over again. A kiss on the forehead could've meant anything. Maybe a form of endearment he'd give a younger sister. Is that how he saw her? An empty-headed girl landing in one scrape after another?

She sighed and moved to the wagon. She lifted a strip of canvas cloth, slapped on some caulk, then plastered it over one of the tears in the wagon cover. "You're the ugliest thing I've ever seen."

"Hey, Delly. Talking to yourself?" Alice stopped, a basket of clothes propped on her hip.

"Repairs are endless. Look at this thing."

Alice laughed. "Mind if I join you?" She plopped on a fallen log before Delly could answer. "Abby and Seth are driving me out of my mind. Said they're bored. How anyone could complain of boredom with all the work needing to be done is beyond me. Thought maybe they could play with your young'uns, and I could chat with you and Sadie. Plus, this baby is sitting heavier than my others did. It feels good to get off my feet, if only for a minute."

Delly smiled over her shoulder. "Sure. I've got one more rip to cover then I'll join you by the fire." She thanked God for these dear friends. Without them, she'd have given up a long time ago. She made the last patch and grabbed her mending from the wagon.

"Indians!" Junior dashed up, hat in hand, face red from running. "Uncle Zeke said they're Pawnee." He squatted next to the fire and focused his gaze on Delly. "This is Sioux territory, but they're Pawnee passing through. I've been wondering if we'd see any Indians other than the ones that operate the ferry."

Alice dropped the sock she was darning in the mud.

Sadie leaped to her feet and clasped her hands to her bosom. "They won't be coming over here, will they?"

"Nah. Uncle Zeke said they was peaceful. As long as we leave them alone, they'll pass us by. He said Indians hardly ever attack white folk anymore." He pointed. "But I shore do wish they'd stop. I've a hankering to meet one."

They could move quickly away for all Delly cared. She shaded her eyes and peered across the prairie.

More than fifteen mounted braves rode by at a slow trot. With bare chests and heads covered with feather headdresses, they made a formidable sight. Fringed buckskin covered their legs. They raised lances thick with fringe. Despite their impressive demeanor and lack of violence, Delly breathed a sigh of relief when they rode out of sight and her heart rate returned to normal.

"I hope that's all the interaction we have with savages," Alice said, rising to her feet. "I've enough to worry about. Especially now that I'm getting close to my time." She placed a hand on her growing stomach. "I'd best get to my own fire. Don't want an Injun snatching one of my children. Besides, those little ones of mine are always hungry, not to mention Ben, and I'm the only one knows how to start a fire, seems like."

Delly watched her go. "Should we be worried, Sadie?"

"About what?"

"The Indians. Alice. She does seem to be having a hard time getting around and she's got at least three months before that baby's due."

"Don't know. The trail could be a mite hard for a woman so close to her time." Sadie used her skirt to protect her hands from the hot coffee pot. "But, we'll think positive and pray hard. God's got it in control."

Delly hoped so. She glanced to where Alice leaned against her wagon.

On a small hill in the distance, Zeke sat on his horse, rifle crooked in his elbow. The tension from the Indian sighting drained away. She had nothing to worry about with Zeke on guard.

~

The next day they stopped beside a creek to stock up on fresh water. Plenty of dry wood laid around the banks, and Delly piled some in the back of the wagon. After depositing her last armload, she climbed down, turned, and smashed her face into a darkly tanned, naked chest gleaming with sweat.

Her gaze rose to the painted face of an Indian. Her cheeks burned. Seeing the shirtless men from a distance was definitely different than close up. She couldn't remember ever having seen her father without a shirt. Ezra and Junior, yes, but her son was still more boy than man, regardless of what he perceived himself to be.

A musky odor rose from the Indian and stung her eyes. It took all her willpower not to bury her nose in the crook of her elbow.

The children! Delly's heart plummeted to her stomach. She'd read of Indians kidnapping white children. She whipped her head to locate them. They played beside the Johnsons' wagon, drawing pictures in the dirt. There was no sign of Zeke or his men. Women washed laundry and baked bread. Where was Sadie? Delly closed her eyes, breathed a prayer of safety for them all, and turned back to the brave. She'd have to handle this herself.

He watched her without expression; his eyes as dark and deep as a cave. Despite her resolve to be brave, Delly shivered and swallowed against the lump in her throat. She slid her hands into her skirt pocket where she'd stashed a small knife after seeing the Indians the day before. The smooth blade gave her strength, and she wrapped her fist around the handle.

The brave yanked Delly's sunbonnet from her head and tossed it to the ground. He yanked the pins from her hair letting it tumble to her waist. She whipped the knife from her pocket, and stepped back until she pressed against the wagon.

"Don't come any closer! I'll cut you." She brandished the small knife in front of her.

The Indian's eyes hardened for a second then he laughed, throwing his head back in abandonment. With a grin still on his face, he grabbed a handful of her hair and dragged her closer until their bodies touched. He said words she didn't understand, but with the way his eyes had roamed her body earlier, the meaning was clear. Her face burned with mortification. Would he ravage her here or drag her into the bushes?

Delly pulled free with enough force to tug at the roots of her hair and bring tears to her eyes. Would he scalp her without a weapon? Did he know how to do that? She lunged toward him, knife raised. He grabbed her wrist in an iron fist, spun her around, and bent her arm back. Pain shot through her shoulder.

Tears sprang to her eyes. She stomped her foot as hard as possible on top of his. He grunted but didn't loosen his grip.

"Let go of me, you savage!" She kicked backward until he wrapped his arm around her waist and lifted her off the ground, pinning her arms to her side and leaving her legs flailing.

"I see you've met Red Feather." Zeke said something in the Indian's language and clapped him on the shoulder. Red Feather released her and crossed his arms. "He's harmless enough. Says he's protecting himself from you. You can put the knife away. He won't hurt you."

"Easy for you to say. He already did. Almost pulled my hair out of my head." She held a hand to her aching scalp and stepped behind Zeke, taking comfort in the breadth of his shoulders. "What does he want? Aren't you going to do anything about him attacking me?"

Zeke spoke a few more words then turned back to Delly. "He wants some of your hair. Said it shines like the brightest star and cascades in a rippling waterfall." Zeke grinned. "I have to agree with him."

"My hair?" She clapped her hands to her head as if doing so would hold it in place.

"And he'd like to make you his squaw. Said he likes women with a spirit of fire."

Delly opened her mouth, then snapped it closed. Did every red skin out here want to take her as his wife? Her gaze traveled from the beaded moccasins to the smooth chest and up to the face of a grinning Red Feather. Now, she'd heard everything. Delicious Williams, Indian squaw. "You'll have to tell him thank you, but no."

Zeke said something else before turning back to her. "Just some of your hair then. He's willing to trade for it."

"But..." She glanced around at the growing amount of spectators. Seemed half the wagon train watched with horror. Except for Sophia Miller. That woman's cool smile wouldn't melt butter. She'd most likely rejoice if Delly were carted away to some Indian camp, leaving Zeke alone.

What would happen to everyone if Delly refused? Would the Indian's good nature disappear to be replaced with violence? She refused to allow herself to be captured, or one of her children stolen.

"The rest of his party is waiting to see if we're willing to trade. Are we?" Zeke glanced around the group, then fingered Delly's hair. "Might be able to get yourself some nice things that'll hold up better out here."

Delly lowered her hands, and stared into his eyes. Her mother had told her that a woman's hair was her glory. How much would it be worth to an Indian? The thought of parting with it made her chest tighten. The Bible said vanity was a sin. That a woman's beauty should come from within. So be it.

She sniffed and nodded. Hair would grow back, but she did like the sultry look in Zeke's eyes. "All right. I'll trade for three pairs of moccasins."

"He'll consider your hair worth more than that." Zeke leaned closer. "He also said if you go with him as his woman, you can keep all your hair, and he'll give me his pony. Sounds like a fair trade to me." His eyes twinkled.

Gracious! "No, thank you." She narrowed her eyes. "Why don't you say something when these Indians make remarks like that? It isn't proper. Didn't you tell him I said no?"

He put his lips near her ear. His breath tickled her neck, and a flock of sparrows took flight in her stomach. "Yes. I also told him you're mine. He likes you. So, do I, spirited woman with star-fire hair." Zeke straightened and placed his hand on the small of her back.

The day suddenly grew warmer. What

happened to the man who couldn't string two words together in her presence?

Delly bit her lower. Her heart danced. Did he have any idea what his casual statements of affection did to her? Could he feel her tremble beneath his touch? She forced an answer through a constricted throat. "Dorcas has some ribbons she wants to trade. What else does he have? The whole family could benefit from a pair of moccasins." If he thought her worth so much, then she'd trade for all she could get.

Zeke translated and Red Feather's bronze face brightened. He chattered something and sprinted to where the other Indians waited. Within minutes, he returned with five braves and two squaws. They carried blankets, trinkets, and wild honey.

Delly retrieved her knife from where the Indian had tossed it and hacked off her hair at the shoulders. She handed Red Feather a length as long as his pony's tail. He waved it above his head and whooped.

Tears filled Delly's eyes despite the smile she forced. She touched her head. Without the waist-length weight, curls abounded, springing around her shoulders in abandonment. Her sorrow turned to laughter. She felt freer and a lot cooler.

"You didn't have to give him so much of it." Zeke twirled a finger around a curl.

"Do you like it?" Please say yes.

He laughed. "Makes you look sassy. Not that you needed any help, Star Fire." He tweaked her nose and sauntered away, whistling.

Star Fire? At least it was better than Mud Dog.

Did Zeke look upon her as his woman or had he only said so to get Red Feather to back off? Delly fanned herself with her apron. She hated to think he only said those things to keep the Indian from getting further ideas. She shook her head, causing her curls to bounce. Zeke did the right thing, and Delly was silly to dwell on something that couldn't be.

~

At first glance of Delly being manhandled, Zeke's heart had stopped, and he'd reached for his rifle. Then he'd recognized his old friend and relaxed. Although white women were still rare in the west, more came every day. Red Feather had chosen well. Delly hadn't over-reacted and gone into hysterics. Instead, her strong backbone made her willing to defend herself with nothing but a little pig sticker. Downside was, her spunk is what drove Red Feather into making his outrageous suggestion to make her his squaw.

Most Indians weren't used to a white woman standing up to them. Most swooned or screamed so shrilly, the Indians were tempted to shoot in order to shut them up.

He chuckled thinking how quick Delly'd been to bargain. At least a foot of the most beautiful hair he'd ever seen for a few pairs of moccasins. He shook his head. A high price to pay to his way of thinking.

The other day, he'd overheard her comment to Sadie about how frightened the journey made her. How she feared for those she cared about every day. What she didn't see was how much stronger she grew with each mile they traveled. That kind of strength was needed in Oregon.

What would it be like to be married to such a spit fire? He doubted anyone could say it would be boring. Although petite, Delly was just the woman he wanted to help him grow his ranch big enough for others to take notice. They'd have a passel of kids to leave their legacy to. And people would travel miles to purchase a horse from The Rocking W Ranch.

Mrs. Ezekiel Williams. He liked the sound of that. Too bad neither of them planned marriage in the immediate future.

10

Delly stared at her feet. Knee-high moccasins hugged her legs with the softness of doe skin. She ran fingers through her now shoulder length hair. By far, she'd made the better trade. She felt ten pounds lighter and cooler.

Intricate bead work decorated the sides and across the top of each foot. She wiggled her ankles. "These are amazing, Sadie. I can't imagine putting on another pair of confining shoes."

"My momma would faint right over if she could see me." Sadie giggled, admiring her own set. "Then she'd probably want to try them on herself."

Delly didn't know enough of her mother to make that assumption. And, Lord knows, her father wouldn't have cared much one way or the other. Not considering how he'd dumped his six offspring at the nearest orphanage before Delly turned three. Obviously, his concern about anything to do with Delly definitely wouldn't extend to her choice of footwear. Her gaze fell on her own brood, drawing pictures in the loose soil around camp. Abandoning even one of them would be like cutting off her right arm.

"What's in Oregon for you, Delly?" Sadie lifted the tin coffee pot from the fire and topped off their drinks.

"Independence." She breathed in the hearty brew. "Kind of like you, I figure."

Sadie snorted. "I doubt you white folk have a clue what freedom means to us."

"Your father loved you. I can't say the same." Delly sipped the hot liquid.

"Still you was free." Sadie plopped back on her stool.

"Yeah." Maybe in the broad spectrum of freedom, but not one day in all of Delly's eighteen years could she say she relied on no one but herself. She'd lived her own brand of slavery and wouldn't do so again. Ever. From her mama's breast, to her father's uncaring arms, to the cold orphanage, and finally … marriage to a man who squandered their money, according to the debtors who'd come knocking on the door. The deed resting between the pages of her Bible became more important with each step they took west.

Zeke strolled by and tipped his hat.

Delly lowered her gaze. Thankfully, he hadn't asked her to hand over the precious document. How would she dissuade him if he asked for it? She had to keep it in her possession. She had to! If for nothing else than the feeling of security it gave her.

"What day is it?" Delly pushed off the stool and began placing the last of their breakfast dishes in the wagon.

"Well…I think it's Sunday."

"I thought so. The days run into each other to where I don't know morning from night sometimes. Most times I fall into bed too exhausted to do much of anything but sleep." She wiped her hands on her apron. "I'm going to speak to Zeke about having a Bible reading when we stop at noon." She sighed. Resting for the entire day held a lot of appeal, but she'd take what she could get. "I've been lax on building the children's faith." Not to mention her own wavering one.

She strode toward the other side of the wagon circle, nodding at women bent over fires or tending to children, and searched for Zeke. He stood with a group of men from the committee. They seemed to be in a heated argument.

Zeke towered over the others, arms crossed. Crimson stained his cheeks, and his lips were set in a firm line. Delly stayed on the outskirts. Apprehension rose with the shouted voices, and she clenched her hands in the folds of her skirt. Maybe she should come back later.

The men paused and glanced her way. Only Zeke's face softened to see her. He strode to her side. "Is everything all right?"

She shook her head. "I can talk to you later. This looks like a bad time."

"It's fine. What's on your mind?"

"I wondered if it would be possible to have a Bible reading when we stop. There's not a preacher signed up with us, is there?" A nice sermon would be what they all needed. Something to lift their spirits and keep them going. She cast a worried glance at the waiting men who continued to glare.

"Afraid not." Zeke grasped her elbow and drew her closer to the group. "It's funny that you should walk up just now. We're discussing that very thing."

She cast a worried look at the men.

"Gentlemen, this little lady would also like a day of rest on Sunday."

"Sure she does," Mr. Oglesby retorted. "All the women want a day to sit around and gossip. If they can get out of doing a hard day's work, they'll jump at any excuse. Look at my Sophia. Always reclining in the wagon instead of working." He crossed his arms. "The committee voted to keep moving. We'll get there sooner. Can't get stuck in the mountains with snow. We can't give into the fanciful notions of a bunch of women, either. All they need is a half a day on Sunday."

Nothing but sit around and gossip? Delly frowned. Mr. Oglesby obviously had no idea how much work a woman did every day. Especially trekking across the wilderness. Her heart went out to his daughter, despite her persnickety ways. Maybe Sophia didn't drive a wagon, but Delly saw her at every meal hunched over the fire attempting to cook for her family. More often than not, the odor of burnt biscuits surrounded her. Delly gave her credit. She did more than when they first set out.

Delly took a deep breath to control her temper. "It would benefit the children also, Mr. Oglesby. The Lord has said that man needs a day of rest."

The man's face reddened. "Don't argue the Good Book with me. Rest when you get to

Oregon." He turned to stalk away, then stopped and looked over his shoulder. "The world is run by men and should stay that way. *That's* what the good Lord intended."

Delly's hands trembled as she bunched them in her pockets. She wanted to march over there and smack the smug look off his face.

"If our guide didn't spend so much time sniffing around your skirts," Mr. Oglesby continued. "We wouldn't have this problem."

Zeke bolted forward too fast for Delly to discern his intentions until he had Mr. Oglesby by the collar of his shirt and spun him around. The forceful movement caused the older man to lose his footing and land hard in the dirt. Zeke hauled him to his feet. "I will not tolerate your insulting Mrs. Williams." His eyes flashed. "She's done nothing immoral to warrant those kinds of words."

The group of onlookers stepped back, clearly in agreement Oglesby earned the knock to the ground.

With one hand, Zeke gripped the older man's shirt. "You mind your manners, or I'll mind them for you. I was hired to get this group through, and that's what I'll do. Resting on Sundays, travel permitting, is good for the stock. Surely you care about your beasts, if not your family. If we can afford a day of rest, we'll take one. And we're taking the whole day today." He released the man and gave him a shove. "Get back to your wagon."

Mr. Oglesby brushed the dust from his pants. "You'll regret this, Williams. Mark my words. Nothing good comes from stopping. We can be overcome by Indians, disease, the other wagon trains can pass us and get the best grazing. There's a million reasons to keep going." His eyes narrowed. "Don't force us to hire another wagon master when we reach Fort Laramie." He squared his shoulders and left at a trot.

The other men glanced from Zeke to Oglesby and back to their own wagons, yet not one followed the irate man. Instead, they shuffled back to their families.

Delly smiled, her heart swelling with gratitude over Zeke's defending her. "You're welcome to join us. You too, Mr. Oglesby," she called then nodded to the others watching her. "Any of you. We'll be reading from the book of Genesis in thirty minutes." With a swish of her skirts, she turned and marched back to her wagon.

~

Zeke shook his head as Delly stalked away. The girl had grit, that's for sure.

"My wife's pretty keen on stopping." Mr. Robbins said. "I'm not willing to argue with her over this. I see the wisdom in it." Others raised their voices in agreement.

Zeke grinned. "Thank you. Now, I'm going to listen to a pretty girl read from the Good Book." He slapped his hat on his head and followed Delly.

She'd pulled up a three-legged stool by the time he joined them. Several others sat around her in a semi-circle. Delly's gaze fell on them one by one. "We'll start at the beginning," she said. "Since this is the beginning of a new life for us."

Sadie scooted over on the quilt she sat on, and motioned for Zeke to join her. "Are you a religious man, Mr. Williams?"

"No, ma'am. I reckon I'm not. But I do enjoy a relationship with my Savior. Will that do?"

She nodded. "I reckon that'll do just fine."

Close to half the travelers joined them as Delly read. Several of the women mended as they listened. Children sat enthralled or dozing. When she'd finished and closed in prayer, someone pulled out a harmonica and played a soft hymn. Voices rose as they recognized the song. Spirit refreshed, Zeke vowed that as long as it was in his power, they'd take this day of rest. Especially if it let him spend some time in his sister-in-law's presence.

Delly approached him after the others had left for their own fires. She laid a hand on his arm, sending trickles of heat through his skin. "Thank you for standing up to Mr. Oglesby. It meant a lot to me. I think this time of prayer and scripture helped, don't you?"

"It helped me." He took her hand in his, noticing the new calluses. "Are you using the salve in the medicine box?"

"Can you imagine what they'd be like if I didn't?" A dimple winked close to her mouth.

Zeke couldn't believe how much this little bit of a girl could rattle him. She took his breath away with one glance from her eyes. What a fool he was to think he could look at her as only a friend. But that's all they could be. He dropped her hand as if burned. She bit her lower lip and turned her face away.

"Uh, Delly, do you want to ride my horse?"

"What?" She clasped a hand to her throat.

"He's a beast."

"With me. Do you want to take a ride with me?" Good grief. Was he back to talking in circles around her? "We'll ride double. I'll have you back in plenty of time to help with the noon meal." He held his breath waiting for her answer.

She stared at him for a moment, then smiled and nodded. Zeke put two fingers in his mouth and whistled. Cyclone trotted to his side. Delly held her ground, despite the widening of her eyes, and the increased rapidity of her breathing. Zeke hoisted himself into the saddle and offered a hand down to help her. She perched sideways in front of him and called to Sadie that she'd be back soon.

"We'll head toward the river." Zeke turned the horse's head. The grass grew tall and green, waving in the breeze. Rising and falling like the waves he'd seen in the ocean. Wildflowers broke up the expanse with splashes of color. Across the river, the mountain range painted a line of purple across the horizon.

"It's beautiful." Delly turned her face to his, and set his blood racing. "Is Oregon as wonderful?"

"Better. Waterfalls flowing over rocks taller than a church steeple, falling with enough power to send spray into the air. Trees so tall they brush heaven's floor, flowers so colorful they hurt your eyes, and dirt so rich you can grow anything. Rains as much as it doesn't. My land is only a few days ride from the ocean. I'll take you there sometime. There's nothing like it."

"I can picture it. A piece of Eden right here. I can't wait to get settled in a place to call my own."

Zeke spurred the horse into a gallop and tightened his hold around Delly's waist, relishing in the feel of her back against his chest. He was tempted to ask her about handing the deed into his safe keeping but didn't want to spoil the moment.

Her bonnet fell between them, and her curly locks brushed his face. He breathed in the scent of her: flour, soap, and something uniquely Delicious. He could stay that way forever. On Cyclone, with this girl in his arms, racing across the prairie.

"This is glorious!" She held her arms out. "Like flying."

"Yah!" Zeke laughed and kicked the horse's sides. "Let's fly faster."

By the time they reached the river, they were short of breath, and Delly's face had flushed to the color of the sunset. With one arm, Zeke lowered her to the ground before sliding off himself.

She bent and plucked a handful of flowers. "We should have brought us a picnic." She gasped. "That was forward of me. Presuming you'd want to stay out here for lunch."

"No more so than letting me take you away on my horse." Oglesby would have a field day when he found out.

Delly's face reddened deeper and she turned, squinting against the sun, to stare across the expanse spread before them. In the distance, the river shimmered like a ribbon. Zeke took her arm and pulled her to face him. "I'm joshing. There's no need for formalities here." He took a flower from her hand and tucked it into her curls. He grinned. "Things are different out west. They move faster.

Not as much time for courtship. I didn't mean to hurt your feelings, but you can be as forward with me as you want. We're family, remember?"

She smacked his chest and stepped back. "You didn't hurt my feelings. I don't know how to be coy or to play feminine games. My mouth has loose hinges. Whatever I think, I say. And who said anything about courtship?"

He laughed. "Forward speaking is one of your endearing charms." He took her hand and tucked it in the crook of his elbow. "Let's walk."

They stopped beneath a tree. Delly spread her skirts and sat. Her fingers deftly formed the flowers she'd picked into a chain.

Zeke leaned against the tree's trunk. "What do you want, Delly? When we reach our destination."

She lifted her head and glanced toward the west. "My own place. To be my own boss, no longer fetching at another person's whim. To care for my children and teach them to be self-reliant."

Figured she'd want something other than a husband to care for her. He tangled his finger in one of her curls, and smiled as her fingers stilled their work on the flower chain. "We've got the sweetest place in Oregon. I hope to build my share into a fine ranch." Before he did something that might get him in trouble, he released her hair and straightened.

"Cyclone will father many beautiful horses. I've three mares with wonderful lines being cared for by my uncle Rupert, and along with fifty head of cattle, I've got a right good start to my ranch."

"I'd like to see it." Her whispered words drifted on the breeze. "I've got a gourd filled with vegetable and apple seeds, two mangy dogs, a passel of kids, a goat, and an ornery mule." Laughter burst from her. "It isn't much, but it's a start."

"You'll be settled before you know it." Zeke's heart plummeted. "Some man will snatch you up and take care of you. With your face, you'll have your every whim satisfied."

Her face paled and she jumped to her feet. "How many times do I have to tell you, I didn't come out west to catch a man!"

"I didn't mean to imply that." He rose and captured her hand. "But women are scarce out here. The men will be lining up."

"Then I'll run them off with a shotgun!" She whirled and marched away.

Independent little minx. He grinned and caught up with her to reclaim her hand. "I'm glad to hear that, Delicious Williams." Glad indeed.

His stomach started grumbling before they headed back, and he let Cyclone have his head until they reached the train. He stayed on the horse's back, safe from temptation. He'd make do with some hard tack from his saddlebag.

He wanted to grab Delly to him and claim one powerful kiss after another. But that would tarnish her reputation, and he wouldn't risk it. Not to mention the punch in the jaw he'd receive for his effort. Who would've thought that a day spent doing nothing but strolling with a woman on his arm could make him so happy?

Delly smiled. "Thank you for a pleasant morning."

"My pleasure." He tipped his hat and rode toward the front of the train. Yep, he was in danger of being smitten. His stomach dropped to his knees with the knowledge. He saw everything he'd sworn against falling to the wayside like discarded belongings.

Giving his heart to a woman on this trail could only lead to heartbreak.

11

Three days later, they camped on the banks of the Platte River. Dorcas and the three younger children, along with the dogs, ran circles around the wagon, screaming and barking. When they knocked over a rack of fresh laundry, Delly had enough. "Take those dogs somewhere else. Now I've got to rewash everything!"

"Sorry." Dorcas took to amusing her siblings by skipping stones and was soon joined by Seth and Abby Johnson.

Delly gathered the muddy clothes and strolled upriver away from them.

"Good morning, miss." A man's deep voice broke the peace.

She glanced up into the face of a dandy. The man twirled a finger in his mustache. He tipped his hat and glanced around them. "Where's that unfriendly wagon master?"

"Have we met?" She set her laundry on the river bank. Her skin prickled at the nearness of the stranger.

"Not officially. I attempted to join your train and was declined. Ira Bodine's the name."

Delly's mouth dried. This was the man Ezra warned her about. "Sorry to hear that, Mr. Bodine." She turned back to her wash, wishing for her knife.

"You don't appear very friendly either." He sat and leaned against a fallen log. "Not friendly at all. And here I am hoping to enjoy the company of a lovely woman."

"You are mistaken. I'm a widowed woman with no interest in a man's attentions." Delly scrubbed a shirt on the washboard and glanced up in time to see the children race toward the wagons.

"My mistake. Maybe I can remedy that." He pulled a cigar from his pocket and lit it with a match he struck on a rock. "I sometimes ride short distances with wagon trains I meet up with. Since finding you here, I might have to spend a bit more time with yours."

She tossed the clothing into a basket and straightened. "Don't waste your time on me. I'm not interested." She turned to leave. He grabbed her arm and the fresh laundry landed in the mud beside the water.

She glared at him. "I'm not *interested* in your attention," she repeated. Didn't the man understand? "And you've muddied my clothes. You're wasting your time and mine." She stared into his sharp angled face. Dark brown eyes were shaded by the brim of a black hat.

"It's my time to use as I see fit." His smile didn't reach his eyes. "I could take you away from all this, Mrs. Williams. Yes, I know who you are."

He waved his arm toward the wagons. "I'm a man of rather comfortable circumstances. A beautiful woman like you shouldn't be slaving over a washboard." He reached a hand to her curls. "A pity you cut your hair, but it'll grow back. As thick and gorgeous as before."

He gripped her hands and scowled. "Hands like a scullery maid. Expensive creams would repair most of the damage." He stepped back as his gaze traveled over her. "And a beautiful gown would show off your assets. Yes, I think we could have a mutually satisfactory relationship."

She glanced at the wagons too far away to hear if she screamed. Why hadn't she stuck her knife in her pocket? Delly stiffened her back and jerked free. "I'm perfectly content where I am." She bent to retrieve her fallen wash.

Bodine grabbed her arm again and yanked her to him. She yelped against the pain in her wrists. "We'll see about that." He pulled her to him, his mouth reaching for hers and grinding her lips against her teeth.

She placed both hands against the purple brocade vest he wore and shoved. "Get off me!" The man stumbled back.

"Step away from her, Bodine, or I'll put a bullet through you." Zeke stepped from around a tree, a revolver in his hand. Delly dashed to his side. With a swift move of his arm, Zeke thrust her behind him.

Bodine held up his hands. "I see how it is. Guess you've already won the prize. Thanks for the kiss, Mrs. Williams." He winked at her and sauntered to his tethered horse. "I'm sure we'll meet again. You let me know when you're tired of hanging with cowboys and want the pleasure of a real gentleman's company."

Zeke tensed beside her. Delly laid a hand on his arm. "He's not worth it." She stepped away and retrieved the clothes. Luckily, only one shirt landed in the dirt this time. With Zeke standing silent guard, she washed it before tossing it in the basket.

Back at the wagon, Zeke spun her to face him. "Don't go off alone anymore. We're in Indian Territory. With them, snakes, and lowlifes like Bodine, it's not safe. Not even for your necessary time. Understand? Take a group with you— always." He pulled a pistol from the waistband of his pants. "And this. I'll teach you to shoot it."

Her face heating at his casual reference to private things, she accepted the gun. "I know how."

She watched him march away. Indians! She stretched to locate her children. Junior led the animals to the river for water. The others played near the Johnson wagon. Delly sighed and hung clothes to dry for the second time that day.

When she had the laundry finally completed, she stretched, popping the kinks from her back. She realized she hadn't seen Sadie since before she'd headed to the river. Keeping the wagons in sight, she headed for a grove of trees set away from where they'd camped.

She found Sadie in the embrace of the largest man Delly had ever seen. His ebony skin glistened beneath overalls. Toes protruded through holes in tattered boots.

"Delly!" Sadie stepped away, a sheepish smile on her face. Her cheeks flushed scarlet. "This is Luke. My intended."

Luke lowered his eyes. "Ma'am."

"She's all right." Sadie placed a hand on his arm. "She's good people."

Delly rubbed the back of her neck then extended her hand. "I'm pleased to meet you." Luke stared impassively at her hand.

Sadie gripped it instead. "He's escaped that wagon train we passed a day ago. He's a trained blacksmith. We can't send him back. I'll tell anyone that asks he met up with me. It'll be the truth."

"Was he following you? You said he'd catch up in Oregon." Delly planted fists on her hips. "You lied to me." Couldn't anyone in this life tell the truth?

"I'm sorry." Tears trickled down Sadie's face. "He's been checking every train until he found me. Please don't send him back."

What more could this day hold? Delly took a deep breath. "Can I get into trouble over this?"

"It's Indian Territory. Free land." Sadie released her and folded her hands. "Please."

"All right. I'll have to tell Zeke, though. What if the rest of the train makes a fuss? He'll have to do what they vote. I guarantee Mr. Oglesby won't want to shelter a runaway."

"He don't have to know Luke's a runaway. I'm freed, they'll think he is too." Sadie rejoined Luke. "All the others need to know is that Luke is with me. They'll want to keep him once they find out he's a blacksmith."

"Who's he going to ride with?" Delly wouldn't lie to Zeke, not even for her love struck friend. She caught a glimpse of Sadie's determined expression. "Oh no. He can't ride with us. It wouldn't be proper."

"Not any more proper than you riding off alone with Mr. Williams? He can stay with Junior by the animals. He'll just take his meals with us. You chaperone me, and I'll do the same with you. Nothing wrong with that."

"Fine." Delly stood in front of Luke and waited until he lifted his head. "But you'll have to sleep out by the stock. No offense."

He smiled. His teeth flashed bright as stars against a moonless sky. "That's right fine with me, ma'am."

"Call me Delly. I'm not your mistress, nor do I want to be. Never cottoned to slavery." Good Lord, what would she do now? Harboring a runaway. What would Zeke say?

A large rain drop plopped on her head, followed by a close second. "My laundry!" She hitched up her skirts and sprinted for the clothes.

The rain continued into the evening and, as there was no wind, Delly consented to let the children sit in the back of the wagon. They perched wherever they could in the tight space. She gathered together some quilt pieces from her trunk while Sadie worked on the never ending pile of mending. The children practiced their letters.

Since she hadn't spoken to Zeke all day, the opportunity to inform him about Luke hadn't presented itself. The knowledge ate at her. She was fairly certain he'd feel as she did about the situation, but if he didn't, and he sent Luke away, Sadie's heart would break.

"I don't know why I have to do this way out here," Dorcas whined. "There's no school for thousands of miles."

Delly threaded a needle. "You don't want to grow up stupid, do you?"

"No, but why can't I wait until we get to our new place and then study? I don't need all this to be a cowboy. And that's what I'm going to do when I grow up."

"Really? Cowboys are dirty all the time. Especially on cattle drives. You hate being dirty."

"I don't care. So, do I still have to practice?"

"Yes."

"Why?" Her shoulders slumped.

"Because it's raining and there's nothing else for you to do. It's either that, or help Sadie mend."

Dorcas pouted. "I hate rain."

"What are y'all doing?" Junior poked his head through the canvas opening.

Delly smiled and motioned for him to come in. She handed him their Bible. "Here. Read."

"What?" He glanced at her in astonishment.

"Read. We can't let your schooling stop completely until we reach Oregon, now can we?" She patted his shoulder, handed him a towel, and then moved over so he could squeeze in.

"Where's Luke?" Sadie asked.

"I left him to watch the animals," Junior muttered. "I should've stayed with him." He set the Bible on his legs. "If you want me to read, why can't I read the guidebook? That's what we need out here."

"The Bible will help you anywhere."

"I know, but can't I please read the guidebook?"

She smiled and pulled it from a pocket sewn into the canvas. "Read about this river we're following. Then you can read a passage from the Bible."

He scanned the pages. "Well…the Platte River runs all the way into Wyoming Territory. In some places you can't hardly see across it 'cause it's so wide. There's lots of little streams and waterways that run into it."

"You aren't reading." Delly stitched one quilt piece onto another. "Stop skipping around."

He scanned some more pages. "Fort Laramie's less than two weeks travel from where we are now."

"I sure hope we stop for a few days." Her needle poked through the fabric, in and out, leaving behind a sense of accomplishment as a vision of her completed quilt filled her mind.

"What for?" Junior glanced up. "The more we travel, the quicker we get to Oregon."

"I want to take a hot bath."

"A bath! Women want the silliest things." He lowered his head back over the pages. "I'm going to climb Chimney Rock and carve my name in it. We'll get there before Laramie. Who cares about a bath?"

"I do," Dorcas spoke up. "It's hard staying clean on the trail."

"Well then, you're as silly as Ma. You're just

going to get dirty the next day."

"And you're beginning to get a little sassy for your britches, aren't you? Your uncle doesn't go around dirty all the time," Delly pointed out, remembering the scent of the pine soap he used. "Besides, Dorcas wants to be a cowboy when she grows up. I guess she'll be the cleanest one there ever was."

"I'm sorry for sassing, Ma. But I'm becoming a man out here. I don't need to be treated like a child."

"Not too old for me to swat." Delly sent him a stern look. "If you want to be treated like a man, then act like one."

"Aw shucks. You ain't never hit me. And Dorcas can't be a cowboy. She's a girl!"   He crawled toward the canvas opening. "I never would've come to visit if I'd known I was going to have to read and get a lecture on cleanliness. Or hear some fool story about a little girl wanting to be a cowboy. I'm going to look for Uncle Zeke."

Delly laughed and reached for the Bible. Maybe Junior's hunt for his uncle would lead them both back here.

12

The clouds disappeared by morning, revealing blue skies and little wind. Landmarks Court House Rock and Chimney Rock towered over the plains of Nebraska Territory. Flat, with scattered brush, and a horizon that stretched forever.

Delly lifted her skirt and grimaced at the sight of her feet. In order to save her shoes, and her pretty new moccasins, she'd taken to going barefoot most of the time now. Her feet were as ugly and calloused as a cow's hooves in spite of the salve Zeke had given her. She'd need a chisel to get rid of the roughness.

Good thing she wasn't looking for a new husband. She swore she got uglier and more weather-worn with every day, despite the admiring glances Zeke and the Oglesby boys shot her way.

"Hey, Ma!" Dorcas ran alongside her. "Look over there." She pointed to the east. A massive herd of animals grazed. "What are they?"

"I don't know."

Junior trotted past on Old Blue, his rifle slung

across his lap. "It's buffalo. I'm gonna shoot one. Get the fire ready. We'll feast tonight." He grinned and hurried to catch up with the older men who'd galloped past.

The train rolled forward while guns blasted in the distance. Delly's skin crawled as the herd moved en mass, a black cloud that ate up the ground between them. "Dorcas, get the children in the wagon. Hurry, now." Her mouth turned as dry as the desert.

With trembling legs, she climbed on the wagon seat beside Sadie. It seemed she was always telling her children to seek the safety of their home on wheels.

A subtle vibration shook the seat beneath her, steadily increasing in intensity. She glanced behind them and clamped a hand over her mouth to stifle a scream. God, help them. They were going to die.

The horizon rose and fell like a mighty moving wave as thundering animals barreled straight toward them. Dust hung heavy in the air, blocking out the sun and thrusting them into the dimness of dusk. "Make it quick, Dorcas!"

After she helped the younger ones climb to safety, the little girl hurled herself inside. The noise deafened, and threatened to drown out thought as well as spoken words. Delly grabbed the reins and hollered for the oxen to move. They balked, fighting against their restraints. The dark cloud grew larger and rolled toward them with the speed of a freight train. The ground rumbled. Tears poured down Delly's cheeks, while Sadie chanted over and over for God to save them.

Delly whipped the reins harder. "Ya! Ya!" The

animals refused to budge, straining against their harness. They shrieked and rolled back their eyes.

Sadie's mouth opened in a silent scream. She clutched Delly's arm. Her fingernails pierced the skin. Delly whipped her gaze back toward the approaching herd. They'd be trampled. Dead on the prairie. Left for the animals. A sob caught in her throat.

She leaped to the ground and dashed to grab the harness. "Come on, you beasts!" She tugged, urging them forward. She glanced to where the other wagons moved forward, widening the gap. How could they leave them to fend for themselves? Delly yanked harder. "For once in your miserable lives, do what I say."

Luke darted to the wagon and jumped up beside Sadie. "Hold 'em still! You don't want them to bolt with the herd."

"I'm trying to make them move forward!" Delly's arms pulled. Her muscles ached with the strain. "They don't want to go anywhere." They were as frightened as she was. Given the chance, she might've cried and run in circles too.

The other wagons were far enough ahead to be safe from the approaching wave of death. They were alone. The others should've waited! Where was Zeke? He was supposed to protect them. There were times when Delly thought twice about managing on her own. This was such a time.

Didn't anyone take bother to glance back? She cried in earnest now. Rocks danced at her feet. The children screamed from inside the wagon. Luke darted inside, emerged with a pot and tin ladle, then jumped from the wagon.

"Luke, get back inside!" Sadie shrieked. "Oh, Lordy."

"It's a stampede." He planted his feet, legs apart, and stood his ground. "Don't seem like we're going anywhere anytime soon. Can't stand still and let death take us. You climb back up, Miss Delly. I'll handle this."

"What are you doing?" Sadie's screams pierced Delly's ears. "Are you crazy? You're going to head them off with dishes?"

Luke raised the pot above his head.

He intended to divert the stampeding herd. Delly scrambled back onto the seat and crawled through the back of the wagon, squeezing past children and tossing things aside, while frantically searching for the pistol Zeke had given her after her run-in with Bodine. Why hadn't she listened and kept it closer at hand? Her own stupidity would get them killed.

Weapon in hand, she climbed out and stood with her back against the wagon's bonnet, and braced herself. Her heart pounded with each thundering hoof. The dust thickened air made it difficult to breathe, even through the rag she wore over her nose and mouth. She closed her eyes and prayed before raising the gun above her head.

Her eyes shot open, and she squeezed the pistol's trigger. Luke banged on the pot with the force of a marching band.

Zeke galloped up, rifle blazing. "Get that wagon out of here!"

"They won't move." Delly's shoulders sagged.

The herd stampeded closer. Feet away from the wagon and firing guns, they split, thundering past the wagon in two seemingly unending lines.

Delly coughed against the dust. Her heart pounded with each thundering hoof. It seemed an eternity before the animals were past. Their path marked by trampled grass and brush. Dust hovered in the air, falling like dried rain upon their shoulders.

Her legs refused to hold her, and she sagged against the canvas and let the sobs overtake her.

~

Zeke replaced the rifle into its sling. "Fools. Every one of them. Riding off like they were on a picnic. Firing their weapons as if they had no sense." He hated this part of the job. Watching out for grown men who had no more sense than a child.

Delly plopped to the ground. Tears left tracks on her face.

Lifting her to her feet, Zeke pulled her close. Why did it seem this woman was in the middle of danger every time it came upon them? He was the one who most likely wouldn't survive the trip. Not with Delly around.

"Junior rode out with them." Despair outlined her body. Her eyes stood out among the layer of dirt on her skin.

"I'll find him." Zeke cupped her face then released her. After launching into his saddle, he spurred Cyclone toward the group of returning men. His heart had almost failed him at the sight of Delly standing on the wagon seat firing a hand gun in the air. He shook his head. The woman needed to develop a healthy fear. She should've grabbed the children and ran at first sound of the stamped. A wagon wasn't worth her life.

He squinted against the afternoon glare of the sun. One man lay slung across a horse's back. *Not the boy, Lord!* He sent his horse into a gallop. What would he tell Delly? How would he survive the death of yet another family member?

He reined Cyclone to a halt and willed his racing heart to return to normal. It wasn't Junior. The body was too large. "What happened?"

"It's Oglesby," Melvin explained. "Buffalo hunters shot to head the herd in our direction when they saw us coming. Guess they figured it'd scare us away from what they thought was theirs." The man shook his head. "Ogleby's horse spooked and reared. He fell, and the beasts trampled him. There's not much left."

Zeke lifted the blanket covering the body and grimaced. There was nothing left to distinguish this man from any other, besides his clothes. The buffalo's hooves had caved in his skull and all but obliterated his features. He sighed and let the blanket fall back. No way to clean him up before his family saw. The blood had dried quickly in the heat, blackening the blue shirt the man wore. Flecks of brain matter clung to the lifted blanket and peppered the man's hair. Zeke's heart went out to his family, and he swallowed against the bile rising into his throat.

He scanned the group. "Where's my nephew?"

"I'm here." Junior trotted up on the mule.

"Your ma's looking for you. Get back to the

wagon." Zeke pulled his hat firmer on his head, regretting his stern tone of voice when Junior's smile turned to a frown. What had the boy been thinking, taking off after the others? It could've been him lying mangled beneath the Indian blanket. How would he have told Delly her stepson was dead? He made a vow to keep a better eye on the boy until he grew to have more sense. Keep a better eye on all of them. Somehow, despite needing to check on all the others, he'd make Delly and the children more of a priority. Maybe put Melvin and Hiram to work seeing to the other emigrant's needs.

Junior nodded, before kicking the mule into action.

Zeke glanced over his shoulder at the line of waiting wagons then reached for the reins to Oglebys's horse. "I'll take him to his family. We'll be stopping here to bury him and allow the family time to grieve."

Mrs. Miller wailed before Zeke reached her. The sound resonated off his ear drums and wrung at his heart. She grabbed her two-year-old son close to her. "I told him not to go. I told him."

"And got smacked for your trouble," a man, a brother Zeke thought, stated. He stepped forward and relieved Zeke of his father's body. He lifted his chin. "Thank you, Sir."

Zeke nodded and waited for one of them to ask what happened. They didn't. Instead three pairs of shimmering eyes stared at him. He cleared his throat and removed his hat. "We'll stop here today to give you time to bury him." He sighed. "I'm sorry, Mrs. Miller. Sophia. You let me know if I can help with anything. I'll get someone to dig the grave, drive your wagon…"

"We'll be all right. Thanks. We take care of our own." Her brother turned, put his free arm around his sister, and they shuffled away leading a gray horse that carried a heavy burden.

Zeke allowed his gaze to follow them before he turned toward Delly's fire. She glanced up from where she added beans to the pot.

"Are you all right?" She wiped her hands on her apron and stood before him. "Junior told me what happened. Should I see to Sophia?"

He dismounted. "I'm fine. Mrs. Miller has her brother and son. Seems that's all they want." He dropped onto a stool. "I hate when we lose someone. Especially when it's to foolhardiness."

"It wasn't your fault." Delly handed him a cup of coffee which he accepted gratefully. "Even though her father may have been heavy handed on occasion, it's all she knows. There was nothing you could do to stop it. The men took off as soon as the buffalo were spotted. Whooping and hollering. Did they get any?" She sat cross legged beside him.

"What?" He stared into the dark brew.

"Buffalo."

"A couple. Before the hunters stampeded the herd." He glanced around trying to locate Junior and spotted him heading off with Ben. "Looks like Junior went to get your share. There'll be meat to go with the beans tonight." He smiled at the sight of the gun tucked in the waistband of her skirt. "Glad you put the gun to good use."

"Yes, thank you." She nodded to where Sadie

stood with a big man, he hadn't met. "Luke would've tried running them off with a spoon and a pot." Her giggle sounded like music to him. Zeke pushed to his feet. "He started beating on pots and pans to beat the band. Yelled louder than any Indian I've ever heard."

Zeke brushed a stray strand of hair off her face. "Please, don't put yourself and the children in harm's way again. You scared ten years off me."

She nodded. For a second, he thought she'd lean into his hand. Instead she stiffened.

"I guess I'd better meet this foolhardy hero."

Delly matched steps with him, laying a hand on his arm. "Sadie's taken up with him. I think they were trying to meet up when he ran across our train. He must've been delayed." She turned her face away.

"What are you hiding?"

She sighed. "I think he's a runaway. Sadie says he's a good blacksmith." She added as if to take away the severity of the problem. "We could use him, couldn't we?"

Zeke rubbed the bridge of his nose between his forefinger and thumb. The challenges never seemed to end. "I don't cotton with slavery myself. I won't turn him in, but I won't stop his owners from taking him back, if they find him before we reach Oregon."

"Zeke." Her eyes pleaded.

"Don't scold." He grinned down at her stern face. "You're doing real good on the trail. I'm proud of you. But there are things in life that even a tough spine can't get rid of. Or fix."

The look she gave him said she wasn't partial to his explanation. "Some nights I'm so tired, I can't get comfortable. And Junior's doing the work of a man. Dorcas doesn't complain either, except for the dirt, and Sadie's a god send. She'll come in handy when Alice's baby comes in August. Luke could be a gift…"

"Don't talk to me about babies." Zeke stopped. God, preserve them. "A baby is not a good idea on a trip like this. Sadie's a midwife?"

Delly nodded. "Said she's done some birthing."

He ran his hand along the bristly growth on his chin. "I need to meet this Luke." He again asked the Lord what he'd gotten himself into.

When they reached the man, Sadie stepped in front of him, folded her arms, and set her chin. She reminded him of a little bulldog ready to protect her young. "Mr. Williams. This is Luke. My intended."

Zeke smiled at her feistiness and extended his hand. "Heard you're a blacksmith."

"Yes, sir." Luke hesitated before stepping around Sadie and accepting the handshake. "A good one."

"Well, you aren't lacking in bravery, if not in smarts. Trying to divert a stampeding herd with a pot and spoon. I've never seen that before." He shook his head. "It'll be nice having another man to help look over these women. They have a talent for finding trouble."

Delly huffed and crossed her arms.

"I'll protect them with my life, if need be."

Zeke studied the man in front him, noting the firm handshake. Luke didn't meet his gaze but for a second. He figured that was because of the man's background. Intelligence shown from his eyes, softening when he glanced at Sadie.

Then Zeke asked the question he'd dreaded on the walk over. "Are you a runaway?"

Luke swallowed, his Adam's apple bobbing. "Depends on what you call a runaway."

Zeke laughed. "Fair enough. Welcome. Do you know how to drive a team?"

"Ain't much pertaining to animals that I don't know."

"Sadie you can move aside now," Zeke said. "I'm not going to run him off." He couldn't predict what the others would do, though. He prayed it wouldn't cause trouble. "Thank you, Mr. Williams." Tears shimmered in Sadie's eyes. "We were feared you would."

"I can't say what the future holds, but for now, it'll be nice having another strong man along. Especially one willing to risk his life for others." He tipped his hat at Delly, nodded at the others, and strolled to his horse. When had he acquired the talent for picking up strays?

13

"Ma, come here." Junior pointed to the oxen. Every time he tried putting on their harnesses, they balked and moved away. "They won't let me hitch 'em. I need you to hold them still."

She set the camp stove she'd used for breakfast into the back of the wagon. "That's unusual. They've been docile so far, if not a mite stubborn and skittish." She ran her hands over them. Their flesh twitched at her touch. "They're covered with sores." She showed him the raw marks around their necks. "Haven't you been taking off the harnesses every night? Especially when it rains?"

He bowed his head and shuffled his feet in the dirt. "Mostly."

"Mostly?" She placed her fists on her hips.

He raised his eyes without moving his head. "Some nights I don't. It's our turn to ride toward the end of the line and the poker games have usually started by the time I get the wagon unhitched." He lifted his head and jutted out his chin. "I didn't think it would matter once in a while. All the guys play. I've been winning…mostly."

Her son is gambling? Like his father? Delly

clutched her throat. Her stomach churned. How could she not have noticed?

Delly bit her tongue to squelch the sharp words wanting to burst forth. "These oxen could determine whether we make it to Oregon or not. They must be cared for properly." She took a deep breath. "You know the dangers of playing cards. But, you're not a child anymore. You've grown up a lot on the trail, and you're going to do what you want, regardless of my wishes " She patted the nearest ox. "Just make sure you unharness the oxen first—every night. Switch the sorest ones with the extras. I'll get the salve for you to put on them."

"Thanks, Ma." He dashed off to her bidding. She smiled at the small sign of childhood still left in him. She sighed. She'd need to talk to Zeke. See whether he could speak with Junior about following in his father's footsteps.

"I'll take charge of the oxen, Miss Delly."

"Good morning, Luke." She shook her head. "It's kind of you to offer, but my son needs to learn responsibility."

Luke grinned. "Maybe I could keep an eye on him? Make sure he does it right."

She laughed. "You mean do it for him and let him run off and play."

"Regardless of what he thinks, he's still a boy. A boy doing the work of a man and trying to live up to it. Let him take night watch. I'll care for the animals."

She pulled the salve from her apron pocket. "It's a deal. Here. The smell of this turns my stomach. I'll gladly turn it over."

Shouts of "move 'em out" drifted down the line, and Luke set to work as soon as Junior arrived with the replacement animals. Delly donned her face rag and climbed onto the wagon seat, leaving Sadie to walk with Luke.

The sun rose and the day slipped into their normal monotony. The oxen, used to the routine, followed the wagon ahead and left Delly alone with her thoughts. She focused on her physical tiredness. Every muscle ached, barely relieved by nights spent in the cramped tent or back of the wagon.

She tried to be grateful for the opportunity, saying her blessings each night, but most of the time her eyes closed before she could squeeze a prayer from her lips.

A dust cloud rose in the distance, pulling her from her thoughts. She raised her glance to the sky. Late afternoon. Had she spent the entire time dwelling on her thoughts?

"Can you see what it is?" Sadie stepped close to the wagon. "Is it more buffalo?"

Delly stood and craned to see. "I can't tell, but I hope not." The wagon ahead of her stopped and she pulled back on the reins.

Zeke rode up. "There's a drove of cattle ahead. We'll be stopping for the remainder of the day. I don't relish eating their dust. I'll speak to them about letting us pass first in the morning. Where's Luke?"

"He went back with the animals." Sadie frowned. "Something wrong?"

"Just a wheel that needs tending to. Might be some money in it for him. I've been spreading the word that we've got a blacksmith with us now."

"You doing okay, Delly? You look a mite peaked." He studied her face, his eyes grave beneath the brim of his hat.

Her traitorous heart leaped at the concern in his voice. Being self-sufficient was exhausting. What would it be like to have a man like Zeke take care of her? She shook her head and stiffened. "Just tired."

"Why don't you let Sadie drive more? You don't need to do everything yourself."

"Don't treat me like I'm a child." She lifted her chin. "There's enough of them in the back of the wagon." She averted her face, embarrassment rushing through her. "I apologize. There's no need for shrewishness."

"Take care, Delly." His look softened as he continued to study her, before tipping his hat and steering Cyclone to another wagon.

Delly smiled at the warm look he'd given her. If she didn't know better, she might think he cared more for her than as another traveler. Then she chided herself for romantic notions. He treated them all the same. With care and understanding. Sometimes, she acted like a silly girl, instead of a woman with children.

Zeke had made it clear on more than one occasion that a wife wasn't in his plans. Other than his spur of the moment proposal, he'd not said another word to tell her different. She shook her head and climbed from the wagon. She was a fool, dwelling on something she neither wanted or needed.

She had a fire burning by the time Alice

shuffled toward her, burdened with a Dutch oven. Abby followed, her young arms loaded with the ingredients for bread.

"This is the perfect opportunity to get some baking done." Alice set the pot in the embers of the fire. "Got to take the chance when you can. Mind if I share your fire so we can visit a spell?"

"Sounds good." Delly brushed off the skirt of her calico dress. "I'll do the same."

Dorcas and Abby took the little ones off to play while the women baked. A child's cry pulled Alice away with the promise to return as soon as she'd handled the latest crises.

Once the bread was set to rise, Delly plopped on the three-legged stool and pulled out a novel. Maybe a cheap dime western could take her mind off the trail's troubles. If only Zeke didn't fit the hero like the book was written about him.

"What 'cha read in that book of yours?" Alice returned and set the oven next to the fire.

"A love story about an outlaw turned good by a feisty woman."

Alice nodded. "I don't read good myself. Never had the time. Can sign my name and my young'uns. That's about it. Tried reading the Bible a couple of times but got flustered over all the big words."

Delly slid her book back in her apron pocket. "I could help you"

She waved Delly's offer aside. "I'm too old for that now. Got other things to occupy my time. You will too, once you're settled down having babies." Alice glanced sideways at Sadie who joined them with a basket of mending.

Delly could tell from the way Alice kept shooting glances at the other that she had something on her mind. She bit her lip to keep from giggling when Alice blurted out her question. "That boy follow you all the way from Missouri?"

Sadie startled, spilling some flour. "Pretty much."

"Guess what I don't know, can't hurt me, right?" Alice shrugged. "Guess some might say that was romantic."

"You don't?" Delly stirred the fire's embers then pulled her shawl from the wagon. The air chilled with the setting sun.

"Don't have a lot of time for that type of nonsense." Alice lifted the lid from her oven, revealing a mound of golden bread. The smell rose, teasing Delly's taste buds. "Although the way our wagon master looks at Delly might put me in a romantic frame of mind."

"Don't be silly." Delly removed her own pan from the fire and admired the completion of her loaf. "A little romance is nice. Every girl wants some in her life. You aren't any different, it's just not for me outside the pages of a book." She flashed Alice a grin. "I've seen the way you and Ben look at each other. Even after children."

Delly wrapped the bread in a saved sheet of greased paper. "Has anyone seen Junior? He's usually clamoring for something to eat by now. The boy never can wait for supper."

"I saw him head to the front of the train." Using her skirt, Sadie lifted a pan of beans from another fire. "Right after dark."

"Keep an eye on the children, please." Delly wiped her hands on a hanging towel, grabbed the pistol from the wagon, and set off for the front of the line. Maybe she should find Zeke. No, the man was busy. Delly wasn't his only concern. Whatever trouble Junior got himself into, she could handle. If not, she'd fire her gun and Zeke or one of his hands would come running. Big, strapping, wagon master, or not, Delly was perfectly capable of minding her own children.

To the right of their circle, a large fire roared, and she switched directions to follow the sound of raucous laughter. Her stomach soured as curse words filled the air. Maybe she should've waited and taken Luke with her.

Junior sat with five strange men, obviously the drovers Zeke mentioned, tossing money and cards like they were candy. Her heart sank. The strange men around him were dirty, smelly, and spewed curse words faster than Delly's feet could carry her to her son's side. She stuffed the pistol into the pocket of her dress.

"Junior. It's time to go." She clapped a hand on his shoulder and pulled him to his feet. Once he stood, she turned with a flick of her skirt and marched several feet away. She turned and waited, one foot tapping.

"Ma, you don't belong here." Junior tossed a glance toward the men around the fire. "I shouldn't have left yet. I've been winning, and they'll be angry."

"I don't care. These men look dangerous, and you're gambling with them. Gambling!" Her hands trembled and she clasped them in front of her. "Where's your money?"

He handed it to her. "Two hundred dollars. Won fair and square. But they're going to be mad that…"

"I don't care." She stuffed the money into the bodice of her dress and clutched his arm. "Let's go."

The money seemed to burn her skin through the thin fabric of her shift. Everything in her wanted to toss the greenbacks into the fire. Reasoning told her the money would come in handy when they set up their homestead, ill-gotten or not.

Junior yanked free. "I can't go yet. The men need an opportunity to win back some of their money. You're making me go against the code, Ma."

"I said, let's go." She grabbed him again.

"I said no." He yanked away and crossed his arms. "Give me some of the money, at least."

The belligerent look on his face pained Delly. Where had her loving son gone? The responsible big brother to the others? She'd lost him somewhere after they'd set out on this trip. The boy replaced with a headstrong young man. She again questioned the wisdom of leaving what had been familiar.

"Fine." She handed him a fistful of dollars. "But don't come crying to me when you lose it all." She'd be the one heartbroken when he succumbed to the fate of his father.

"Hold on there, little missy." A man stepped out from behind the nearest tree. He wore his hat pulled low over his face. The pants and shirt he wore were covered in dirt and stained with perspiration. He stank like cattle and liquor. Delly swallowed back nausea and lifted a hand to her nose.

Junior tugged on her sleeve, and she shook him off.

"How about you hand over the rest of that money," he growled

She stepped back. "You're mistaken. I don't have it."

"You aren't being truthful with me." He grinned with tobacco stained teeth. Before she could take another step he lunged forward and grabbed her arm. "I saw you stuff it down the front of that purty dress. Now hand it over, or I'll go fishing for it. Might be we could make a deal beneficial to both of us."

Bile rose in Delly's throat. She slipped her free hand in the pocket of her dress, taking comfort from the presence of the pistol. She contemplated screaming for help, but realized with the location of the wagons, no one would be likely to hear. Most of the train would've bedded down for the night. Why hadn't she told anyone where she was headed?

The man grabbed a fist full of her dress and yanked, ripping it down the front, exposing the white beneath. The wad of money fell to the ground.

"Now you owe me something for my trouble." He pulled her close, trying to wrangle a kiss. Her heart beat so fast, she'd swear the man could feel it thump. She turned her head and bit his hand. He punched her, knocking her to the ground.

Delly raised a hand to her split lip and tasted blood.

"Let go of her!" Junior launched himself on the man's back. "Nobody hits my ma."

Delly took advantage of the man's distraction to get to her feet and whip out the gun. "You step back and let me and my son be."

The man laughed. "You going to shoot me?"

"If I have to." *Please, God, make him back down.*

He flung Junior off his back and took another step toward Delly. "This is going to be fun."

Zeke thought his heart would stop when Delly crumpled to the ground. His steps faltered in amazement when she whipped out his pistol. The situation escalated from there. Junior picked himself off the ground then rushed to his ma's side, raising his fists to a fighting position.

"We'll both take you on, mister."

The man laughed and pulled his own weapon. "Think you can take me on, do you? Think that purty gal there can pull her trigger faster than me? Want to turn around and take it at ten paces, or start shooting from the hip where we stand? Either way, I'm going to spill blood."

Zeke stepped from his hiding place, revolver in hand. "I wager I can take you." He motioned for Junior to take Delly back to the wagons then, not taking his eyes off the other man, bent and retrieved the money. "Here. Now go. Next time, I might not be so generous."

The man smirked, counted off some bills and

handed the rest to Zeke. "Just want what's mine." He spun and headed back to the fire.

Zeke put his revolver away and headed to the wagons. His anger grew with each step of his booted feet. That woman would be the death of him. Rather than going after Junior on her own, she should've fetched him. He admired her dedication and love for his brother's children, but some things were better left for a man to do.

Delly stood backlit by the campfire. Wide-eyed the others watched from behind her. Zeke slowed his steps and counted to ten. The only one who didn't look terrified at his stormy approach was the dark-haired spitfire in front of him. What did the others think he would do? Hit her?

She'd tucked her torn dress up into her slip and glared at him. Her fine chin tilted in defiance.

"What were you thinking?" Zeke grasped her arm and pulled her out of sight of the others. "Do you know what that man was capable of? Most of those cowhands hadn't seen a woman in months, much less a pretty clean one."

She jerked free. "I've had enough manhandling for one night, thank you." Delly marched back to the fire, where the others had mysteriously disappeared, and poured herself a cup of coffee. She glared at him over the rim of the tin cup.

She had the gall to be mad at him? He whipped off his hat. "Are you so naïve that you don't know what that man intended when he grabbed you?"

"I know exactly what he intended." She lowered her drink. "That's why I pulled the gun on him. I would've shot him if I had to."

"You would've…you knew…" He found himself at a loss for words. How could she sit there and calmly drink? Then he noticed her hands trembling, despite the brave front she tried to portray. "Come here."

Delly's cup fell to the ground, and she launched herself into his arms. He held her tightly. "When I saw you fall, I saw red. I wanted to kill the man." Zeke tilted her face to his. Blood had dried at the corner of her split lip. He licked his thumb and wiped it away. "Are you okay?"

"I'm fine." She leaned her forehead to rest on his chest.

Lord, what had he done to deserve the growing attachment he felt for this woman? Or her apparent increasing attachment to him, whether she wanted to admit it or not? He glanced up to see the children peering from the wagon's bonnet.

"The west is a dangerous place." He lifted her face again. "You've got to be more careful. Laramie is only a hundred miles from here. There's new trouble for you to get into on the other side of the fort. Don't drive me to distraction on the way." He kissed her forehead and stepped back before digging into his pockets. "Here's most of the money. The man just took what he'd lost. Put it somewhere besides the inside of your blouse. Maybe wherever you stuck our deed. " He handed it to her and turned to Junior. "Come on out."

His nephew crawled reluctantly from his shelter. "Yes, sir."

Zeke shook his head. "Do you realize the trouble that could've happened?"

The boy met his eyes. "I could've taken him."

"I know you would've tried." Zeke clapped him on the shoulder. "But as man of this family, you've got to look ahead. See what trouble might come up and see what you can do to prevent it. Playing cards with rough men is not safe. There's enough danger on the trail, without going and looking for it. If you ever put one of your family members in danger again, I'll pull you over my knee. I don't care how big you think you are. Got it?"

"Yes, sir."

"And what do you think you're doing gambling in the first place? Don't you remember what happened to your pa? Tarnation, boy!" Zeke kicked a rock at his feet. "What would you getting shot do to your ma?"

"I'm sorry, Uncle Zeke, but I'm good at cards, and we need the money." Junior's chin quivered.

"You don't need the money. I have plenty." He exhaled and his shoulders drooped. He wasn't cut out to be a family man. Knowing that, only a fool would entertain notions of settling down with a woman and a quiver full of young 'uns.

14

Zeke halted the train in the shadow of Chimney Rock on June fourth. Delly glanced at the nearby Platte River, the lush grass and firewood lying close at hand, and grinned. The day's rain had slowed to a drizzle and the clouds dissipated. Things looked brighter than they had in days. A rainbow of fox glove, lark spur, and rose moss covered the ground.

Junior announced right off his intentions to carve his name in the towering landmark and dashed off before Delly could assign him any chores.

"Delly," Alice called. "If you're heading to the river, could you take Abby and Seth? Abby can get a start on my laundry. I'll catch up to you in a few minutes."

"Sure. Take your time." Delly hefted her basket of laundry, ordered Dorcas, Abby, and Seth to follow her, and set off through the tall grass, leaving Sadie to mind dinner and the babies.

Mindful of Zeke's warning to always keep the wagons in sight, Delly hesitated at the top of a small rise. She glanced behind her. She wouldn't be able to see the wagons, but she could hear them. Mules brayed, oxen bellowed, dogs barked, and children laughed. She headed toward the water. "Don't wander off, children. Stay where you can hear my voice."

In the distance, Junior and others brave enough to scale the face of the rock, were dark specks against its surface. Delly smiled, tucked her skirt between her legs and up into her waistband, then dragged her laundry into the river with her. Scattered along the banks, other women washed and chattered like the crickets singing in the brush. Delly relished the privacy the small rise put between her and them. Constantly surrounded by people tended to give her a headache.

"Only I hope there won't be too much of it when we reach Oregon. A neighbor or two not far away would be nice." She giggled and glanced around to see whether anyone had heard her talking to herself. She spotted Alice's basket of clothes, left untended by her daughter. If Alice didn't arrive soon, Delly would start the wash for her. The children needed the play time.

Using a large boulder for balance, she scrubbed one of Zeke's shirts against the washboard, watching in satisfaction as the dirt and sweat disappeared. Like her sins. Head mistress at the orphanage often remarked as Delly grew how doing laundry was a daily application of what the Lord did for them. Washing them clean. Making each day a new beginning.

Washing Zeke's clothing brought him close to mind. If only Ezra had taken after his stronger, younger brother. Life might've been so different if Delly had married Zeke instead. Maybe a marriage of love rather than what one partner could do for the other. Would the tender kisses and warm glances continue after marriage with a man like Zeke or would the flowery words disappear like with Ezra?

Having been orphaned at such a young age, Delly had no idea what that type of marriage was like. She got an inkling from the way Alice and Ben related to each other, but still couldn't fathom how a man and woman reacted beneath the same roof. Did they carry on conversations? Touch each other's hand as they passed by? Would Zeke be like that when he found that one lucky woman?

Could Delly be that lucky woman? Probably not. Not with the way she seemed to be a thorn in Zeke's side. He deserved someone sweeter and more ladylike.

Would Sophia Miller be that woman? Sophia still made a point of passing their fire each night and making moon eyes at Zeke. He'd smile and nod a welcome. Did they spend time together when no one was watching? Delly slapped a pair of pants against a rock.

Ugh. She needed to focus on her work and not what ifs. She changed directions faster than a twister.

Delly glanced around her for sight of the children. Besides the far off murmurs of the other women, silence greeted her ears. "Dorcas? Abby?" She tossed the wet shirt into the basket and sloshed her way to shore.

She rounded a large sage brush, gasped, and

stumbled backward to the river. She lost her footing and fell, staring at the six Sioux braves staring down at her. Other than buckskin breech cloths and war paint, they wore little else. Two of them held their hands over the girls' mouths. Delly prayed Seth had gotten away.

The one she determined was the leader held a finger to his lips and made a cutting hand motion across his neck. Delly nodded. She understood the universal language of death. Her blood chilled. She wouldn't have been able to talk if she'd wanted to. Nothing but cotton seemed to fill her mouth. The lead Indian waved for her to join them.

The Indians grinned at the sight of her sloshing through the water, skirt around her waist, bloomers hampering her movement. Delly untucked her skirt.

One of them grabbed her arm, and she yanked free. "Get your hands off me," she hissed.

The Indian backhanded her, knocking her to the ground, then hauled her back to her feet. He growled some words then pointed to the back of one of the Indian ponies.

She wiped her mouth. Did they have a chance of escape or would fighting endanger the other women scattered along the river bank? Abby's and Dorcas's eyes were twice their size in their tear-streaked faces. Delly would have to wait for another opportunity to escape. She nodded, and mounted. Within seconds, the braves tied her and the girls behind them on the back of Indian ponies and galloped away from the wagon train.

An attack of trembling shook Delly hard enough to make her teeth chatter. Her face hurt where the Indian hit her. She pulled against her bindings. Stuck like a rabbit in a snare, and the hunter was approaching.

~

"Mr. Williams." Sadie stepped beside him as he groomed his horse. "Have you seen Miss Delly?"

"No. Not since we pitched camp." Zeke faced her. He'd found signs of Indians during his ride earlier, but they'd headed away from the camp. His heart hitched. "Did you check the river?"

"She was doing laundry." Sadie twisted her apron. "The clothes are there, but her and the children aren't. Delly left me in charge of the little ones, so I stood on that rise and there ain't a sign of none of them. She'd never leave the clothes lying in the dirt like that."

"No, she wouldn't." He dropped the brush back in his bag. Seth Johnson sprinted across the prairie toward them.

"Injuns took them." He fell to his knees in the dirt. "I hid…in…the bushes."

Luke appeared at Zeke's right. "I found horse tracks. Unshod ones. Down by the river."

The news stabbed Zeke's heart. He shouldn't have been gone so long on his scouting trip. *Please, God.* He had to take control. "Sadie take Seth to his parents. Luke, do…"

"Uncle Zeke, Indians!" Junior joined them, dirt streaking his face. He leaned over to catch his breath. "I was climbing down from the rock. I saw them take ma, Dorcas and Abby."

Zeke forced his legs not to give out. Chimney Rock was a mile away, and with Junior running on foot, the Indians could have as much as two miles or more head start. Dark was coming fast. "Luke, do you ride?"

"Some."

Zeke tossed him a rifle. "Grab the first horse you see. Junior, sound the alarm, and find Hiram. Tell as many of the men to follow us as you can round up, and tell Melvin he's in charge until I get back. We ain't waiting." He tossed his saddle onto his horse and tightened the girth. "Luke, try to stay up." He mounted and kicked his horse into a gallop, glancing over his shoulder to make sure Luke was behind him.

Luke followed, riding without a saddle, and his long legs flapping on each side of the animal. His elbows stuck out like a bird ready to take flight. If not for the direness of the situation, Zeke would've laughed. They started at the riverbed and followed the tracks east. Behind them, Junior clanged out the warning.

The bell donged, ringing across the prairie as steady and powerful as the erratic beat of Zeke's breathing and the pounding of Cyclone's hooves. Each stretch of the horse's long legs took Zeke that much closer to Delly. That much closer to her rescue.

Several times the tracks vanished in the muddy waters of the Platte River or the small creeks branching out from it. Zeke glanced back and spotted the dust from the other men who trailed them. Thunder rumbled in the distance, and he groaned. The last thing they needed was rain to wash away any evidence of where the Indians had gone. "Come on. The others will have to catch up."

Within the hour, the heavens opened and wiped out the remaining tracks. *God, we need your help. I can't do this alone, no matter how much I think I can.*

The wind increased. Icy drops of rain slithered off his hat and down his back, leaving him as cold as the fear threatening to choke him. "No!" Zeke reined in his horse and stared into the darkening sky. This couldn't be happening.

He turned to Luke. "Can you ride in this?" Rain poured steadily from the brim of Zeke's hat, obscuring his vision.

"Yep. Hopefully them Indians will have to stop because of the girls. Hostages could slow a person down."

~

The speed of their flight kept Delly plastered against the back of the Indian in front of her. She held her breath against the musky odor of his perspiration. The rain came as a blessing, washing the smell away.

Abby wailed above the sound of the storm. Delly turned her head to check on the two girls. The brave she held onto jerked her hands tighter around his waist. The rain plastered her hair to her face. Held close behind the man in front of her, hands tied, she endured. Closing her eyes, she prayed.

She held herself together by sheer willpower. She had to for the sake of the girls. What did the Indians want them for? Slavery, or worse—wives? Would they be adopted into the tribe? She couldn't allow that to happen. She'd die before letting the girls be taken as slaves.

"Let me go." She tugged against his restraint.

"No."

"You speak English?"

"Some."

"Where are you taking us?"

"Pale face pay money and whiskey for woman."

A white man? Delly's heart accelerated. Who? And what about the girls? She peered behind them, searching for a sign of rescue. The rain hid any sign of pursuit. Delly blinked back tears.

Night fell before they stopped in a ravine. A few mesquite bushes, prickly pear, and thorn trees dotted the landscape, highlighted by the lightening. High, sloped walls rose on two sides of them. With the force of the downpour, Delly feared a flash flood. Surely the Indians were too smart to camp in place where they'd be at risk.

The Indian untied her hands from his around him and retied them together. He slid from the horse, leaving her to manage on her own. The skin on the inside of her thighs felt as if someone had taken sandpaper to them. She fell from the horse; her legs refusing to bear her weight. The braves pointed and laughed, then shoved Dorcas and Abby down beside her.

One of them clutched a rope and tied the children's hands behind their backs. Another started work on a fire beneath a slight overhang.

"Please. The girls are cold. Leave their hands free." Delly implored her captor. "They won't leave without me." Although she'd beg them to.

He shook his head and stalked away.

The girls and she scooted beneath the meager shelter of a mesquite bush. The prickly leaves poked through the drenched fabric of Delly's dress.

The Indians hooted and passed around a brown bottle. *Oh, Lord, is that whiskey?*

"I'm scared." Dorcas pressed against her.

Abby snuggled closer and sniffled. "What are they going to do with us?"

"I don't know." Delly shivered. Whether from cold or fear, she wasn't sure. Probably both. With her hands tied, she couldn't hold the trembling children. Instead she had to content herself with their presence. No way would she increase their fear by telling them they would be sold.

The Indians started on their second bottle before the leader approached. He pulled Delly from her shelter and to his feet before running his fingers through her hair. His gaze traveled down her body, making her self-conscious of her wet clothes. She willed herself not to shrink back. Instead she stared defiantly back at him.

He laughed and patted her cheek sharply before returning to the fire. Delly released her pent breath. She had to get them away. They couldn't wait on Zeke and the others to rescue them. It might be too late.

She glanced at the girls. A bruise darkened Abby's jaw. The ribbons had disappeared from Dorcas's hair and a scratch marred one cheek. Both girls' faces were streaked with tears. How long since the Indians took them? Surely, Sadie had raised the alarm by now. Tears stung the back of

Delly's throat. What had happened to dear Seth?

Dorcas and Abby maneuvered until their heads lay in Delly's lap. She leaned her head against the bush and watched as the Indians drank themselves into a stupor. She'd tried rubbing the rope tying her hands against the trunk, but hadn't done anything but scrape her hands.

A rock poked her buttock, the bark of the tree dug into her spine, and her chaffed legs stung. Tears welled in her eyes. She blinked them back. Crying would not help them. She laid her head back and closed her eyes. *Lord, the guidebook didn't say a thing about what to do if captured by Indians. Do I keep my mouth shut and cooperate, or show some spunk and demand they release us?*

She swallowed against the acid churning her stomach with the details of the plan she sketched. But something needed to be done, and now, to insure the children's safety. "Hey, you!"

The braves glanced her way. The leader lumbered to his feet and shuffled toward her.

"I have a trade for you." Delly willed her lips to stop trembling.

He stared impassively.

"Take me and let the girls go. I'll be your squaw. Anything you want." After all, other Indians seemed to find her desirable as a wife, why not this one?

Delly took a deep breath and returned his stare. She could do this. Whatever it took. She'd worry about getting herself away later.

The Indian trailed a finger down her neck and toward the collar of her dress. Delly forced out a shuddering breath and fought not to flinch or pull away. Ice water rushed through her veins. The man grabbed the neckline of her dress.

He laughed and shoved her aside. "Need money more. Got wife."

Delly curled into a ball and cried. She finally let sleep claim her.

The next morning the sound of galloping hooves jerked her awake. Zeke! She straightened. Her heart stopped at the sight of a fancy man riding a tall roan. The pale face the Indians mentioned? The man turned. Ira Bodine. Her blood drained as Ezra's words of warning returned.

Bodine grinned, slid from his horse, and tossed the reins to one of the Indians.

"What a welcome surprise, Mrs. Williams." He removed his hat and bowed. "I expected you, but here are also two beautiful little girls."

"What is the meaning of this?" Delly fought to still her trembles. The last thing she wanted was for the man to see her fear. "I demand that you release us at once."

"A little high and mighty, aren't you?" His smile faded as his eyes hardened. "We'll see how long that lasts."

"What do you plan to do with us?"

"Sell you, of course. Unless the wagon master is willing to trade the deed for you. But then again, my plans are grander than even that. Once the deed is in hand, the wagon master will be killed and I'll keep you." He nodded toward the Indians.

"They'll keep the two girls. Raise them as their own, or use them as slaves. It makes no difference to me." He switched his gaze back to her. "But you, I have plans for. There are a lot of gentlemen in the west who will pay good money for a white woman with your looks. One that is unmarked and without disease. Unless, of course, I can persuade you to stick with me? I own several gaming houses. Men would come for miles around to lay gold dust at your feet. Do you sing?"

She shook her head. "I'll never go with you willingly." She needed to warn Zeke somehow. He'd ride into a trap.

He shrugged. "Then I'll have to sell you. Pity, really. You'd be better treated with me. It's strictly business, Mrs. Williams. Nothing personal. You can change your fate simply by saying yes, and handing over the deed." He slapped his hat back on his head. "I'd better get this bunch moving. We'll meet again in a safer location in a few days." He marched to the nearest brave and woke him with a hard kick.

Too late, Delly realized the Indians drank themselves into a stupor. She and the girls could've escaped in the night. But to where? And on foot?

"Ma, I don't want to live with the Indians." Dorcas whispered. The two girls started to cry.

"Shut them up." Bodine swung onto his horse. "These braves will have hangovers and might not be partial to the whimpers of little girls."

The Indian who'd ridden with Delly sat up and scowled in her direction. He groaned and cupped his hands around his head.

"Shh." Delly kept her gaze on him and scooted farther beneath the tree branches. "Nobody's going to live with the Indians." Not as long as she drew

breath. She'd think of something.
Zeke, where are you?

15

Delly's muscles screamed in protest as the Indian yanked her to her feet. Pinpricks stabbed her feet as circulation resumed. She kicked the man's shin and received the back of his hand to her lip in payment. The taste of copper filled her mouth. Her already swollen mouth throbbed.

With all the anger she could summon, she glared at him. He could get her back on that horse, but she'd fight him every step of the way. Hopefully, her attempt at stalling the Indians would give Zeke the time he needed to find them.

Blood dripped down her chin. The brave motioned her forward. Delly shook her head. With a grunt, he stomped away. With her hands tied behind her back, Delly couldn't wipe her lip. She spit and raised her eyes to where the Indian towered over her again. In his hand he held a rope with a loop at one end.

Her blood froze as he slipped it over her head like she was an unwanted dog. With another fierce tug that almost took her to her knees, the brave mounted his horse. Delly gasped. He intended for her to walk.

Dorcas screamed and slid from the animal she'd been perched on. She pummeled the Indian's leg. "You can't make her walk." The brave raised his fist.

"Get back on the horse, Dorcas." Delly lifted her chin. Her plan may have backfired, but she'd never let on the Indian had won, and she wouldn't have her daughter in danger because of her stubbornness.

"But, Ma." Dorcas's cornflower-blue eyes shimmered with tears.

"Now." She couldn't bear it if he struck Dorcas. She'd endure whatever she needed to in order to prevent that from happening.

The child nodded and allowed herself to be put back on the horse. Delly closed her eyes, prayed for strength, then stared into the face of her captor. He grinned and kicked his horse into motion.

As the morning wore on, Delly's spirit sagged. Obviously the previous night's rain led Zeke down the wrong path. Each step took her and the girls farther away from him. Unless, by his coming, he'd put the rest of the train in danger. Could that be the reason for his delay? Would he allow the loss of three to save the others?

She couldn't see him doing that, but how well did she really know him? He thought nothing of jumping into a river to save a child, but to enrage a handful of Indians? Maybe Delly was expendable.

By noon, sweat poured down her brow, her steps dragged. She could no longer jog to keep up. Perspiration burned the raw skin on her throat. She wished she'd decided on a more docile approach to captivity. Several times her legs gave out, only to have her hauled back up with a tough yank that left her neck sore. Perspiration burned like fire ants over her raw skin. She licked lips dried from the sun and squinted against the glare. What she wouldn't give for a sip of water.

It appeared they'd done nothing but follow what looked like a river bottom, full of rocks and bushes struggling to survive. Storm clouds gathered over head, filling the distant sky with rumbles. Delly glanced at her captor's back. Surely, they knew the dangers of traveling a ravine during rain.

The Indian up-ended a whiskey bottle, drained it, then tossed it to the ground where it shattered against a boulder. Delly's skin prickled as lightening flashed and the first drops of rain began to fall.

Her skirt tangled around her legs. "Please, stop." She fell to her knees, then prostrate. The Indian dragged her a few feet before he stopped, yelled something to his comrades, then dragged Delly to a bush where he discarded her like a pile of wet laundry.

She lay still and gave her tears free rein as despair threatened to wash over her with as much violence as the rain's downpour. Zeke wasn't coming.

Within minutes, the girls were shoved toward her. They curled up against her, providing a semblance of warmth against the rising chill. The ground beneath them quickly turned into puddles of mud. Delly struggled to a sitting position. The last thing she wanted was to drown in the mud.

Pain and fear quickly turned to alarm as the water continued to rise. The Indians whooped, drank, and splashed their drunken selves through the ankle deep water.

"Girls." Delly used a tree to push to her feet. To their right sat a waist high boulder with a flat top. "We've got to climb on that rock. You'll have to help me. I can't do it with my hands tied."

With the agility of monkeys they scampered up and both grabbed an arm to tug Delly beside them. Their perch offered no protection from the rain, but at least they were out of the water.

~

Zeke spotted the ravine moments before they galloped to the edge. They'd lost half a day trying to track in the rain and ended up going off course. He reined in his horse and held up his hand for Luke to slow. They dismounted and belly crawled until they could peer over the ledge.

"There they are." Luke pointed.

Delly and the girls huddled on top of a large rock while the rain continued to pour from the sky. A tattered rope hung from Delly's neck. Biting back his anger, Zeke scanned the area, noting the six drunk braves and empty whiskey bottles. This would be easier than he'd thought. He motioned for Luke to draw back.

"We aren't going to wait for the others. They can't be far behind, even if they did get lost like we did. But there's no telling how long this group will stay here." Zeke stared into Luke's wide eyes. Fear and determination shone back. "I'll sneak around to the other side. When I start firing, that's your signal to do the same."

"I'm here." Hiram squatted next to them. " I out rode the others, and didn't lose the tracks quite as easily as the two of you."

"Thank you, God." Zeke clapped him on the shoulder, grateful for the other man's tracking skills. "Shoot as fast as you can. Don't worry about aiming. We want them to think there're more of us. We may be able to get out of this without anyone getting killed. Got it?" The last thing he wanted was the retaliation of these Indians' friends, unleashing their fury on the wagon train.

"I'm not a very good shot, Mr. Williams." Luke's shoulders hunched.

"Just pull the trigger."

Luke nodded and tightened his grip around the rifle. Zeke crouched and hurried to around the rim to the other side of the ravine, bringing him closer to Delly and the girls. His foot slipped on loose gravel and he paused, waiting for a cry of alarm. He slid more, sending a small avalanche down the hill. *Please, don't let them see or hear me descending. Don't cry out, Delly. I'm coming.*

Would the Indians kill the girls if they thought they were surrounded? Zeke prayed not. He made his way more carefully until he estimated he hid opposite from Luke and Hiram, then ducked behind a boulder. He peered above the rock.

One of the braves approached Delly and stroked her hair. She tilted her chin and said something. Zeke grinned, imagining the barrage of venom-spiked words she most likely spewed. The fact she and the girls still lived, gave him hope. If his plan failed, he prayed there'd be another chance to free them.

He raised his arm and aimed. His first shot shattered one of the bottles. The Indians yelped and scrambled for their horses. Luke and Hiram fired from the other side. The Indians returned fire half-heartedly and leaped onto their mounts. Zeke fired again and the Indians galloped away, leaving their captives behind.

Zeke smiled. The braves didn't want them for themselves. If so, they would have fought harder to keep their prizes. Who did they work for? He slid his way down the hill.

"Zeke!" Delly straightened. "Thank God."

He fell to his knees beside her and cupped her face in his hands. "Are you all right?" He noted the rope burn around her neck and her swollen face. He second guessed his motivation of a peaceful rescue, instead his fingers wanting to curl around the butt of his pistol and put a bullet through the men.

"I'll be fine, but Abby's face is bruised from where one of them slapped her."

Zeke pulled a knife from his belt and sawed at her ropes. "There's no end to the trouble you get into, is there? Didn't I ask you to wait until we reached Laramie?"

"Very funny. Just cut me free."

The blade sliced through the fibers and he laughed when she lunged at him, throwing her arms around his neck. They fell back into the dirt. He returned her hold and kissed her, finally laying claim to the lips he'd desired for weeks. She tasted of dirt, tears, and something so sweet his heart thumped with a furious erratic beat. "You definitely keep life interesting." She'd most likely regret her impulsive action the next day, but Zeke didn't care. She fit in his arms, whether he wanted her to or not. He'd examine his feelings later.

Delly leaned an elbow on his chest and stared into his eyes. "Did you come alone?"

"No. Luke and Hiram are with me. The others are less than an hour behind us." He wanted to kiss her again. But the other two faces staring imploringly into his stopped him. "Let's get you three home."

He whistled for his horse and the others. Within minutes they rode to join them. Zeke mounted, then pulled Delly onto the saddle behind him. Luke and Hiram each lifted a girl up behind them.

Delly nuzzled against his back. "You smell better than my last companion."

"Thanks." He patted her hands which were wrapped around him. "That doesn't say much for the other guy." The odor of his perspiration rose in a cloud. Didn't say much for her sense of smell, either.

"Bodine was behind this. He was going to sell the girls to the Indians. He said he had another buyer for me. He wanted to lure you here with a trade, then kill you. Me for the deed." Her voice shook. "Thanks for coming after us."

Bodine! Zeke's hands trembled where he held the reins. Everything in him wanted to head out after the man and leave the wagon train in Hiram's capable hands. But, he couldn't leave Delly behind. Not after what she'd gone through. He forced his voice to remain calm.

"Wouldn't have it any other way. I can't imagine reaching Oregon without you. It would be a mighty boring trip if you weren't here." He flicked the reins and sent his horse into a slow gallop. His heart stopped when he thought of what might've happened had they not got there in time. He'd have to do something to keep his family safe, even if it meant checking on the other emigrants less often.

They met the other men as they headed back. Abby's father slid from his horse and ran toward them. He pulled her from in front of Luke and wrapped her in a big hug. Tears streamed down the man's face. "Thank you, men."

Zeke nodded and continued toward camp. By the time they reached the wagons, Delly's head bobbed with sleep, and he tightened his grip around her to prevent her falling. By morning, she'd most likely regret their kiss, but for this moment, he'd savor the feeling of her arms wrapped around him.

Sadie sobbed and covered her face when they approached the fire. Junior wiped his eyes and thrust out his chin in an obvious attempt to look tough and unflustered. At the sight of the sleeping Dorcas, Sadie struggled to her feet then rushed the child into the wagon to feed her and change her into clean clothes.

Junior handed him a cup of hot coffee. "I'm sorry I didn't look out for them better. I know I promised you I would."

"They're fine, son. You can't watch over them every minute." He clapped the boy on the shoulder. "These things can happen. If you'd have been there, they would have taken you too." Or worse, killed him. They wouldn't have had much use for a half-grown boy.

Zeke extended his hand to Luke. "Good job out there. I'd be proud to ride with you anytime."

Luke's teeth flashed, and he returned the hand shake. "Didn't know I could ride like that." He patted his backside. "I'm going to feel it tomorrow. Never rode anything but a farm horse or a mule before, and then nothing more than a trot."

"Well, again, I'm glad to have you along." Zeke slid from his horse and patted Delly awake. "You should go in the wagon and get some sleep."

She nodded. "I don't think I really knew what this trip would entail. It's one trial after another."

"Trials make us stronger." Sadie joined them and handed Delly a cup of coffee. "Mr. Williams is right. You need to get your rest. Dorcas fell back asleep right away, poor thing. Luke and I will take care of things out here." She smiled up at him. "And my man deserves a fine dinner."

"I'm pretty hungry too," Zeke spoke up. "Think you could fix me something before the two of you get all mushy?"

"It's already cooked, Mr. Williams. I'll fetch you a plate."

After a meal of beans and rice, he leaned against the wagon wheel and stared into the fire. Now that Delly and the girls were out of danger, anger and fear overtook him. His hands shook. He knew what he'd be capable of if he ever saw Bodine again and the thought took his breath away.

It wouldn't be the first time he'd shot a man,

but that was in the past. Now he did everything he could to prevent another's death. But that was before he found himself head over heels about a slip of a girl. He'd have to do something about her, and fast. Before she got one of them killed.

~

Delly shook out her dirty dress, then hung it over the backboard. Zeke must think her wanton and addle-minded. Turning down his proposal one minute, and throwing herself at him the next. With a groan, she tugged her nightgown over her head.

Widowed less than a month, had it only been that short a time? and her mind turned to a handsome man with shoulders that stretched a mile. How could she face him come morning?

She'd tell him how grateful she was for his rescue, and skirt around the issue of her behavior. Hopefully, he'd chalk it up to a woman's hysterics. She'd made it clear she had no intentions of marriage. He'd said the same. So, there shouldn't be a problem, right?

She grabbed her Bible and turned up the wick on the lamp. There had to be something in God's Word to tell her what to do in a situation like this. Her fingers paused in flipping the pages. His will. Delly had not once stopped to ask God His will. Not when she promised Ezra to head west, and not in the situation with Zeke.

The deed poked from under the leather front cover. What if Delly were never meant to come?

16

When they arrived at Fort Laramie, the sun sat high in the sky and beat with summer's ferocity on Delly's head. She removed her face rag and wiped her perspiring brow. "Finally, a few days of rest and fresh food."

The rectangular shaped fort wasn't large enough to hold all their wagons so Zeke called for them to form their customary wagon circle outside the walls. Heat waves shimmered around the fort, causing it to appear like a desert mirage. A few trees managed to hold onto life, and someone, in an attempt to make the place more welcoming, had planted wildflowers by the gate.

Zeke leaned against the wagon, his tilted face shadowed by his hat. "I'm going to meet with the captain. Would you like to go with me?"

"I'd love to." Delly held out a hand for him to help her down, while averting her face. Maybe he could act like nothing transpired between them, but she couldn't. Even after almost a week of avoiding him, her face heated. She didn't believe he was used to kissing women willy-nilly, but nothing more had been said.

Zeke laughed and grabbed her by the waist to swing her to the ground. Obviously he did remember and felt the urge to poke fun at her red face.

The captain greeted them with a smile and a handshake. Zeke wasted no time in filling the man in on Delly's abduction. She blushed under his sharp scrutiny and tried to make light of her situation.

"You're lucky to be alive, Mrs. Williams." He removed his hat and ran a finger down his handlebar moustache. "We've had some unpleasant encounters with the Sioux recently. Stupid, really. An incident over a cow that got out of hand. But it did result in deaths on both sides. They haven't been particularly friendly lately. Took over the Platte ferry and killed the two men who ran it. We have to keep the cannon manned around the clock now."

Delly shuddered. "They didn't seem to be on the war path. They captured us for a man named Ira Bodine. The Indians seemed more interested in whiskey than us."

The captain scowled. "That man brings trouble every time he rides through here. We'll keep an eye out for him. He's nothing more than a fancy hired hand. We'll throw him in the stockade if we have to." He replaced his hat. "Enjoy your stay and be careful. Our red-skinned neighbors are resenting the flood of white people moving across this land." He tipped his hat and marched away.

"I'll leave you to your shopping, "Zeke said, his eyes sparkling. "I've business to attend to."

"I'll meet you back at the wagons." What did the man have up his sleeve now? With a skip in her step, Delly headed for the trading post, bypassing Sophia Miller who seemed to have an unwarranted interest in their conversation with the captain.

Inside, Delly fingered a bolt of pink flowered calico and another of blue checks. Curtains for their new home, and clothes for the girls. She calculated the money she had stashed then grabbed the fabric, plus a bolt of plain muslin. She moved on to essentials. Soon, her arms laden with parcels, she stepped outside onto a wood plank porch.

Sophia stormed up, dragging her young son behind her. "You'll do just about anything to capture Mr. Williams's attention, won't you?"

"Excuse me?" Delly shifted her parcels.

Luke jogged to her side and took her packages. "I'll take these back to the wagon for you."

"Thank you. They were getting heavy." She transferred her attention to Sophia. "I'm not sure what you're talking about, but you sound mistaken to me."

"Getting yourself kidnapped." The woman smirked. "We haven't run across unfriendly hostiles the whole trip. Why'd they choose you? What do you have up that mountain trash sleeve of yours, anyway?"

Delly wished she had a weapon stashed up her sleeve. Anything to wipe the hateful words from the other woman's mouth. But that wouldn't be Christian. Two wrongs did not make a right. "I have no claims on Mr. Williams." With a swish of her skirts, she stepped off the mercantile stoop and headed toward the wagons.

"Hey." Zeke jogged to her side and grinned, twisting his hat. "I've found that bath you've been longing for."

"What?" Delly squealed. "Really? How did you know about that?" Her smile quickly faded. Had their kiss, given at a moment of weakness after he rescued her from the Indians, given Zeke ideas? A bath sounded lovely, but not at the expense of Delly letting go of her ideals and goals.

"Junior told me. No strings attached." He crooked his arm.

She bit the inside of her lip before slipping her hand into the crook of his elbow. It was mighty hard to turn down the offer of a hot bath. Maybe the warm water would settle her stomach. She glanced back to see Sophia glaring at them. A shiver ran down Delly's spine.

Zeke led her to a small room behind the Captain's quarters. Inside, sat a metal tub full of steaming water. Zeke ushered her inside and stepped out. "I'll send Sadie to help you. You deserve a time of pampering. There's a pretty smelling soap for you to use too."

Tears stung her eyes. "Thank you." And when she'd finished, she'd treat Sadie to the same.

"Miss Delly?" Sadie poked her head inside. "You ready for me to wash your hair?"

"Heavens, Sadie, I'm not even in the water yet. Come in and close the door."

Sadie did as she was asked.

Delly dropped her dress in a puddle on the floor. "You do mine and I'll do yours. And please, drop the Miss. Aren't we close enough friends by now?"

"Old habits are hard to break." Sadie stuck a hand in the tub. "Nice and warm."

Delly shed the rest of her clothes and stepped into the water, sinking down until nothing showed but her head and knees, she closed her eyes while Sadie poured water over her head.

"I got me some news to share." Sadie said.

Delly opened her eyes. "Good news?"

Sadie rubbed a bar of rose smelling soap between her hands then spread it through Delly's hair. "I'm thinking so. Luke done asked me to marry him."

"That's wonderful." Delly's turned to face her and gripped her friend's hands. "When?"

"There's a lay preacher staying at the fort. So, tonight." A grin spread across Sadie's face. "I'm marrying my love, Miss Delly."

"Hurry up and rinse me, Sadie. We've got a wedding to get you ready for." Delly ducked under the water. Her friend was getting married. Although marriage wasn't for Delly, she couldn't be happier for Sadie. She'd seen how she and Luke looked at each other. Witnessed how he'd give his life for his woman. The two proved that love did exist in the world.

The ceremony took place in the center of the wagon circle. Sadie Cwas radiant in a pale yellow dress, her hair hanging free around her shoulders. Luke towered over her petite frame, wearing patched, but clean overalls. A simple, humble picture that loosed the tears from Delly's eyes. She sniffed and put her arms around the shoulders of her children.

"You all right?" Zeke stood beside her.

"They make a pretty picture."

"They do. If it's okay with you, I'm giving them the tent. Junior usually bunks down with me under the supply wagon anyway."

She glanced at his strong profile. "That's mighty nice of you."

He chuckled. "I can be nice."

He could. That's what made it so difficult for Delly to keep her mind, and heart, focused on the land in Oregon and being self-sufficient. Zeke's many admirable qualities made keeping her distance more difficult with each passing day.

She tried to tell herself that his risking life and limb to save her and the girls was just what a wagon master did for anyone, but she was starting to think that maybe Zeke had growing feelings for her. The idea scared her to death.

After Luke bent to his kiss his bride, Delly turned. "I've got food on the fire for tonight's celebration. I'd best tend to it. See you later, Zeke."

Bending over the hot coals, Delly stirred the pot of beans. Her stomach heaved. What was wrong with her lately? More fatigue than she deemed necessary, even with the daily grind of traveling, and food rarely looked appealing.

She straightened and clutched her stomach. It couldn't be. God wouldn't do that to her, would he? She mentally counted the last time she'd had her … monthly. It'd been a while. Subconsciously, she'd written it off due to fatigue and not enough nourishment. How could she keep her condition a secret? She glanced at the children playing in the shade of the wagon. One more mouth to feed.

17

They were two days out of Fort Laramie when they passed the first of the recent graves. The wagons passed close enough for Delly's mind to register more details than she would've liked. She couldn't pull her gaze away from the grisly sight. Some had been dug up by animals and bones lay scattered around the mounds. A comb lay next to one, a woman's hair stuck in the teeth. As they rolled along, they came by discarded wagons and mattresses. One of the beds held the remains of someone who'd died and been left behind.

Delly shuddered. Icy tentacles of fear wrapped her heart in its clutches. She tightened her hold on the reins and glance at Zeke who rode by their wagon. "What killed these people?"

"Cholera, I think. Keep moving." He spurred his horse and galloped past.

"Lord, help us," Sadie clutched her throat. "We've traveled into the Devil's land."

Delly tightened her face rag around her face. She'd heard the dreadful stories of people dying like flies. Alive one moment, dead the next. *Lord protect us. Keep us safe.*

A woman, thin to the point of starvation, wailed beside a grave, obviously left behind by an earlier train. She clutched a man's hat and rocked on her knees.

"Stop." Delly turned and bent into the wagon.

"What are you doing?" Sadie's voice rose shrilly.

"I'm giving her some food and water." Delly jumped to the ground. "Then I'm going to convince her to come with us. She doesn't look sick, just starved."

"Get back in the wagon." Zeke put his horse between her and the woman. "You can't help her now."

She moved sideways, trying to get around the prancing animal. "I can try. We can't ignore her plight." How could anyone with an ounce of compassion drive away and leave her?

He dismounted and grabbed her arm. "Please. I beg you not to go to her. She could be ill. There's got to be a reason she was left behind. You'll put the entire train in jeopardy. If you aren't concerned for your own safety, think of your children, of Alice and Sadie."

Delly's eyes burned with unshed tears. The naked fear on Zeke's face gave her pause. She glanced from him to the woman then nodded and set the food on the ground. With a shuddering sigh, she climbed back into the wagon, glancing behind them as they moved ahead until the woman vanished from sight.

"We should've helped her more." Delly couldn't remember a time she'd ever walked away from someone in need.

"You fed her." Sadie patted her shoulder. "That's all you can do now. You've got children to look after. And another one on the way, if I'm not mistaken."

"How did you know?" Delly took a deep breath.

"Ain't hard to figure out with the way you've been acting. Tired all the time. More so than the rest of us, and I caught you looking peaked a few mornings."

Her secret wasn't secret anymore. How would Zeke react with one more responsibility? Delly was quickly realizing that her wanting self-sufficiency might be a fool's dream, and that Zeke wasn't the type of man to stand aside and not help his kinfolk. She sighed and focused on the landscape stretching before her.

The trail they traveled that day seemed like a road of death. Discarded wagons and belongings. Hurriedly dug graves. And hanging over it all was the ever-present cloud of exhaustion and fear. The sun slipped past the horizon before the train stopped. Almost as if Zeke thought he could help them outrun the threat of death.

Every muscle in Delly's body protested as she climbed from the wagon seat. She hadn't been able to get the picture of the dying woman out of her mind. Tears started fresh and cut a path down her cheek.

"Delly. Sadie." Alice dashed up to them as fast

as her expanding waistline would allow. Tears cut tracks through the dirt on her face. "It's Seth. He's vomiting and complaining of stomach cramps. They started last night but I thought it was something he ate. I don't know what else to do for him. He won't take any food or water. Help me."

"We'll come right away." Delly reached into the back of the wagon for the medicine box.

"Yes," Sadie's hoarse whisper drew Delly's attention.

Luke stared at his wife. The whites of his eyes shined with unshed tears. "He ain't the only one taken sick. People are talking about ill family members."

Cries of cholera drifted through the circled wagons, widening the terror. People hunched over the reins of their teams, faces pale beneath their hats and bonnets. Several families panicked, wanting to put as much distance between themselves and the ill as possible, and headed into the prairie on their own.

Delly leaped out of the way as one wagon lumbered past her. Their lives had gone from dull to dreadful in the space of a day.

She glanced over her shoulder as she and Sadie climbed into the Johnsons' wagon. Zeke and Luke stood with slumped shoulders, dread on their faces. Her children peered out from the safety of the wagon's bonnet.

Delly held up a hand to stop Alice from joining her. "No. Go back to our wagon. You've got to think of the baby."

"And you don't?" Sadie hissed.

"Hush." Delly glared. If she didn't help, questions would be asked. Questions she had no answers for. She twisted her lips. Pregnant from one night with her husband. While she'd cherish her baby, she couldn't help but wish it had chosen a better time.

Alice buried her face in her hands. "But Seth *is* one of my babies. I need to do something."

"You got help. Sadie and I will do all we can." She ducked inside the wagon's bonnet. "See to your daughter."

Seth lay on his side, his legs curled close to his small body. The stench of sickness hung heavy over him.

Sadie met Delly's eyes and shook her head. "I seen this before. He's awful dehydrated and can't keep nothing down. I'm afraid he ain't going to make it."

Delly opened her box and carefully spooned some bismuth into the boy's mouth. His lips hung slack, and the precious medicine dribbled from the sides. "We have to try." They'd had one case of cholera in the orphanage and the head mistress had used bismuth. Delly prayed it would work.

"Delly?" Zeke called from outside.

She stuck her head and shoulders outside. The fresh air was like a breath of heaven. "Yes?"

"Do you think it's cholera? The Oglesby boy just took ill. We've moved him from the corral to a tent." Zeke twisted his hat in his hands. "We need to quarantine the ill."

"I'm not sure. I think so, and Seth is too weak to be moved."

"I read in one of the eastern newspapers that dehydration is a major concern. You've got to try and get fluids into Seth. Do you hear?"

She nodded. "I'll try."

Sadie joined her. "Won't matter now. The poor thing just went to be with Jesus. We'll try the water on the others. We were too late for Seth. I'd best tell his ma and pa."

By nightfall, Delly had prepared Seth's body and fed her own family before she collapsed in a heap by the fire. The emotions she'd held in all day caught up to her and she succumbed to her sobs. Alice's own cries of grief drifted to her ears on the evening breeze.

Zeke joined her, dropping to his knees in a cloud of dust. "We lost two more. A mother and her child." He sat cross-legged. Delly leaned into him.

"It's so fast." She sniffed. "Seth died within hours. Alice said he felt poorly at bed time last night, but she thought it was from drinking bad water." She sniffed. "Do you think it's because I stopped to help that woman?"

"No. Cholera seems to hit with no reason. If what you told me is true, Seth was sick before we stopped."

"I'm not a doctor. I don't know what to do."

"I want you and Sadie to wash your hands. Every chance you get. Use soap, especially when you touch someone and move on to someone else. Promise me. I know I can't keep you from helping, but I won't lose you. God knows there'll be enough deaths."

"You've seen it before?"

His shoulders slumped. "I was married before. On my first trip west, my wife and son took ill with cholera and died."

"I'm sorry." She listened to his heart beat against his cheek and thanked God for this man who cared about the people under his command. He'd do all he could to help them. The knowledge gave her strength. She too, would do all she could.

"I read in a newspaper that some doctors believe the disease is carried from one person to the next." His voice rumbled beneath her head. "They think fluids and cleanliness work best against the illness. And boil all drinking water if you aren't already. I told everyone to do that from day one, but I'm afraid some slacked off, not wanting the extra work.

Delly thanked the Lord that she and Sadie had followed Zeke's orders. Although it meant extra work, all water for human consumption was boiled before being poured in the barrels.

"I want you and Sadie to take shifts. I don't know what I'd do if you got sick too. Luke is already beside himself with worry. He lost his parents to cholera years ago."

She sighed. "How many more are sick?"

"About twenty." His arms tightened around her. "There will likely be more dead by morning. You don't have to do this, you know."

"I want to." Caring for the people of the train helped keep her terror at bay. At times it rose like a snarling beast and threatened to engulf her. Drown her in black fear that smelled of death. Even taking turns with Sadie watching the children and caring for the sick left her steps dragging and her limbs heavy.

Digging deep, she found the strength to rise and shuffled away to give Sadie a rest from watching her brother. She was relieved that Sophia and her son were bunking with another family and she wouldn't have to deal with the woman's hysterics.

John Oglesby slept fitfully, tossing and moaning. Despite his discomfort, Delly dozed, waking hours later to a weak, but smiling young man. She felt his forehead.

"Much cooler, John." She grinned at him. "Do you think you can take some water?"

"Yes, ma'am. I'd treasure a drink."

She gave him a dose of bismuth then sips of water until he fell back, exhausted from the effort. "You rest now. It's the best thing for…"

"Delly!" Sadie called from outside. "Come quick."

"Who is it?" Delly's heart seized in a fist of dread. She climbed from the wagon and gripped Sadie's arms. "Who?"

"It's Dorcas. She's had the dysentery and vomiting."

Delly lifted her skirts and sprinted to her daughter's side. Dorcas lay in the tent, thrashing in delirium. Zeke sat beside her, trying to spoon broth between her lips. He glanced up with red-rimmed eyes. "I can't get her to take any. It just runs out of her mouth."

"Dorcas, you listen to me." Delly dropped to her side. Her chest ached from the weight of possibly living without the joyful little girl who dreamed of being a cowboy. "You take this broth or we'll force it down you." She grabbed the bowl from Zeke. "Hold her down."

He placed a hand on each of the little girl's shoulders. Delly managed to dribble a bit into her mouth then reached into her pocket for the medicine. At this rate, the bottle would be empty before she could save many more. But her daughter she would save, or die trying. She grabbed a clean rag and dipped it into some water, dribbling it between Dorcas's lips. *God, please, don't take her. Not my feisty little girl.*

~

Zeke gazed at the dark circles under Delly's eyes then at the dirt and perspiration stained dress that covered her body. He lifted a hand to brush the limp hair from her face.

She slapped his hand away. "Don't fret over me."

"Delly."

"Don't." She buried her face in her hands. "I never should have come on this trip. It's been one trial after another. Addle-brained, that's what I am, and full of pride, thinking I could do this. Me, an orphan nobody wanted. Just go."

He crawled from the wagon and leaned against the side. What could he do to ease her pain? Three times he'd made this trip as wagon master. Other than Becky's death, they hadn't encountered the evil devastation of cholera either time. Why now? What had he done differently? He'd warned the others to boil their water before drinking it. He wondered if Alice had simply been too tired one time, or someone else too lazy.

He didn't know how long he waited before going back inside to check on Delly. She lay on the pallet of quilts next to her daughter; her face as pale as the muslin beneath her cheek. He gathered her to him. "Please, God. Don't take another one."

"What?" She muttered against him. "I was sleeping. Her fever broke, and I'm so tired."

His voice shook. "I thought you'd taken the illness too."

She shook her head. "I've been following the instructions you gave me and drink plenty of water." She shoved her hair out of her face. "How many?"

"Two new cases and ten more dead." Relief at Delly's wellness left him ragged. He sagged against a nearby trunk. "Alice felt poorly, but Sadie cared for her and she's improving. I think she was more grieving and worried than truly sick."

"Ten." Delly leaned against him. "So many."

He wrapped his arms around her, relishing in her softness. He never thought he'd fall for a woman with a will of steel. He couldn't imagine life without her now, and he didn't know what to do about the revelation. How could he risk love again when life out west was so uncertain?

"I've tried to get the bodies buried. Some people don't want to let go. One of the wagons that left on their own came back last night. By morning they were all dead." He kissed the top of her head then stood. "We're lucky, I guess. Some wagon trains lose more. Sometimes as much as half." He peered into the early morning sun. "We'll stay here until we're sure no one else is getting sick. We don't want to take the illness with us. I'll get us something to eat. Do you want more broth for Dorcas?"

~

At the end of a week, the survivors stood over the graves of twenty-two of their friends and family. Most of them had lost at least one family member, others more. The dreaded cholera swept through leaving sorrow and death in its wake.

Delly glanced at her raw and cracked hands. She'd constantly washed them with lye soap as ordered. She clenched her fists, relishing the pain in her chafed knuckles. Pretty hands wouldn't bring back Seth, or help Alice in her grief. Yet the pain in the tight skin reminded her she still lived, as did the baby she carried.

Alice hadn't attended the mass funeral. Ben wouldn't allow it. He was afraid she'd lose their unborn child.

Guilt weighed Delly down. Her family had been spared death. What made them different than the others? Had she prayed harder? Found more favor in God's eyes? Why did He take one person and leave another?

Zeke stepped forward and recited the Lord's Prayer. His voice quavered yet he continued. Once the simple service reached its end, and dirt was piled on the graves, the weary travelers headed to their wagons, prepared to drive over the graves to obscure them from wild animals and Indians bent on scavenging.

One woman, Mrs. Holtmeyer, lay prostrate

across her husband's grave despite the orders to pull out. Zeke begged her to come with them. He tried bargaining with her, then resorted to ordering her to climb into her wagon.

She shook her head and sobbed louder. He pulled her to her feet and tossed her kicking and screaming over his shoulder. He sat her in the back of her wagon and tied the bonnet closed. With no family to help her, Luke volunteered to drive her team. The woman cursed and screamed her husband's name several times before becoming silent.

Delly shuddered, each draw of breath a pain deep in her chest. She wanted nothing more than to curl up in the back of the wagon. The harsh reality of life on the trail left her wanting to crawl into a hole and hide. To stick her children somewhere life's evil couldn't reach them. Tears ran down her face and soaked the rag tied around her face. Promise or no promise, she should never have come west.

18

The wagon train traveled through the Black Hills, according to the guidebook, and bounced over rocks and holes. They'd gone several days drinking only the water from their barrels, and Delly looked forward to fresh water from the springs. Pine and Cedar trees dotted the landscape. In the distance, the snow-covered peaks of Mt. Laramie towered above green valleys and lime-covered ledges.

She climbed gratefully from the wagon seat, her muscles protesting the movement. Zeke cut the rope he'd used around Widow Haltmeyer's ankles to prevent her from running into the desert and helped her out of the wagon. The woman sat silently on a boulder and glared as Delly and Sadie prepared supper.

Her silent stares raised goose-bumps on Delly's arms, and she avoided making eye contact. Each evening they'd offered her food, only to have her reject it. This was the first time since they'd left the graves that Zeke had let the woman sit untied longer than needed to take care of her bodily functions. Delly squared her shoulders and smiled at her, hoping she'd take nourishment that night.

"Would you like some coffee? A biscuit?"

The woman continued to stare straight ahead. Was she regretting the decision she'd made with her husband to come west? The one about starting a new life? What had they left behind? Maybe a life of leisure or a prosperous farm, yet they'd left, lured by the promise of a land filled with milk and honey.

Delly turned back to the fire and stirred the beans. She'd headed to Oregon, her heart full of a dream. Why did moments of despair and second-guessing her decision still plague her? Her heart ached for Mrs. Holtmeyer, but there was no going back. For either of them.

The woman bolted, disappearing into the stand of trees behind the wagons. Delly hitched her skirts and dashed after her. The widow paused at an overhang, glanced over her shoulder, took a step, then disappeared. Delly screamed and rushed forward.

Below her feet ran a ravine so deep, darkness covered where the woman had fallen. Delly dropped to her hands and knees and strained to hear. Nothing.

"Delly!"

"Over here" She sat cross-legged and wrapped her arms around her middle. Hurt ran so deep through her, she thought someone had torn her in half.

"Where is she?" Zeke asked.

"She's gone over the edge."

He squatted and peered over then scooted back beside Delly. "Sometimes the grief is too much. I thought I could keep her with us by tying her up.

Keep her safe until she came to her senses. But I couldn't keep her tied all the time. It wasn't right." He choked off his words.

Delly laid a hand on his arm. His muscles tensed beneath her touch. "Sometimes the sorrow is so painful you can't find an escape outside of death. She bided her time. There wasn't anything you could do." Or Delly for that matter, but it didn't ease the agony in her heart.

"She told me once she had no family other than her husband." He sighed. "I guess I'll give their wagon to Luke and Sadie. She didn't have much, but it's more than they've got now."

Crickets serenaded them from the bushes. Locusts buzzed from the trees. If not for the horror lying within feet from them, Delly might have found herself enjoying the ambiance.

~

They emerged two days later from the Black Hills into the most desolate country Delly had ever seen. According to the guidebook, she overlooked what some called the Devil's Crater. A fitting name as far as she was concerned. Not a tree or patch of grass as far as the eye could see. The narrow Platte River was barely visible in the distance.

"This must be what hell looks like." She snapped the reins to encourage the oxen to move forward and kept her eyes on the billowing bonnet of the wagon in front of her. Luke and Sadie's wagon now took the spot behind her.

Dust kicked up beneath Sadie's skirts as she walked beside Delly's wagon. Her friend's eyes twinkled beneath the layer of dirt on her face. From a poverty-stricken freed slave to a married woman with material possessions, Sadie's dreams were coming true. Delly prayed Oregon would be everything they all dreamed of.

A few more months and she'd be free of the dirt and dust of the trail. She'd have a home of her own. It couldn't happen soon enough.

The sun continued to beat on their heads late into the afternoon. Her head pounded. By the time they stopped on the banks of the winding Platte River, her shoulders sagged. The oxen strained against their harnesses, crazy for a drink. The animals fought Junior and Luke as they struggled to unharness them.

As the day turned to evening, a dust storm blew in. Everything that wasn't under shelter or tied down blew away. The children took refuge inside the wagon, despite Delly's fear of it overturning in the high winds, and huddled beneath a pile of quilts.

Delly struggled to light a fire so she could cook. The wind scattered her kindling, blew out her tiny spark of flame, and pulled her hair from its bun. Finally, a flash and a flame. The wind increased and a spark jumped from the ring of rocks and settled on her skirts. She shrieked and jumped back. The strong winds whipped her skirts and fanned the flames. "Help!"

She beat at her legs with her hands. Sadie grabbed the nearest pot, filled it with dirt, and tossed it in her direction. The wind caught it and blew the cloud of dust away before even a speck landed on Delly.

Zeke dropped the reins to his horse and dashed

to her side, wrestling her to the ground, where he beat the flames until they were out. He yanked her to her feet. "What were you thinking? You don't make a fire in this kind of weather. Woman, you're going to give me grey hairs. One day, Delly. Give me one day that I'm not having to save your bacon!"

Delly stared at the hole in her skirt. Anger replaced fear. Planting her palms on Zeke's chest, she shoved. "I was trying to put together a meal to feed you, you ungrateful lout!"

"Delly…"

She stuck her nose in the air and flounced away. "I'm not speaking to you."

"You're being unreasonable."

She whirled to face him. "*I'm* being unreasonable? Day-after-day, I struggle to take care of this family, drive the wagon, ford raging rivers, eat dust, and feed you." She stalked over and jabbed his chest with her finger. "I'm so mad I could spit." She lifted her skirt and dashed away.

How dare he? Tears stung her eyes. If they weren't so far toward their destination, she'd turn around and head back to the city this instant. She climbed into the wagon and plopped on the pile of blankets that served as their bed. She forced a smile to reassure the children that everything was all right.

After the wind died down, she sighed and stared out the bonnet opening. Sadie strolled by arm-in-arm with Luke. Her dear friend seemed to thrive on the rigors of life on the trail. Some of that attitude would do Delly well. Knowing it and mustering it up was a whole different story.

Here she was, with all of her needs met. So what if she had to work for every morsel? Tears leaked down her cheeks, dampening her hair. An ungrateful fool. That's what she was. Being so focused on owning land of her own, she'd not once asked what God's will was. Instead, she'd headed off like a ninny and now paid the price.

~

Seeing Delly on fire had gripped Zeke's heart in a fist of ice. He'd watched, confused, as she stalked back to the wagon and climbed inside. He turned to Sadie and Luke as they approached. "She scared me. When her skirt caught fire …"

"It'll be all right. The trail's getting to her is all. She'll see your way in a little bit." Sadie kicked dirt over the smoldering embers and watched Luke's long stride toward the corral. "It's as much my fault as hers. Lighting the fire, I mean. Maybe I need to do more. Relieve some of her burden, instead of disappearing with my husband. I'll go see what kind of cold supper I can put together."

Zeke was an idiot. He shouldn't have yelled at Delly, but the sight of her skirts on fire had cast all reason to the brisk blowing wind.

A scream shattered the night. He sprinted toward the far side of the wagon circle.

The acrid smell of smoke filled the air. Shooting flames illuminated the night. Men grabbed nearby water buckets and dashed past him. He sprinted to join them.

Another family had been foolhardy enough to try lighting a fire, and the strong winds had blown the embers to land on the canvas covering of the wagon. Days without rain had left everything dry as tender. Men milled around the fire and tried to approach the wagon. Frightened screams from inside rent the air. The stinging odor of burning cloth hung in the air.

Luke doused himself with some of the precious water and, covering his face with his arm, leaped into the wagon bed.

Zeke turned to Hiram beside him. "Who's in there?" His heart clinched. They'd had more disasters half-way on this trip then the past trips combined. Thankfully, he'd be leaving this life behind.

"The Turner's little girl. Mrs. Turner lit a fire and tried to use the wagon as a block against the wind. You can see what happened. The child was inside sleeping." Hiram removed his hat and wiped his forehead with a red bandanna. "Didn't take it long to catch fire in this wind. It's a shame, if you ask me. That fool colored boy has been fighting to get inside that wagon since he heard a child was inside. Probably climbed to his death." The man shook his head. "We've doused it with water, to no avail. The wagon's a goner."

"I would've gone in too." Zeke trotted to the wagon where flames licked the skirt of the bonnet. He glanced around to make sure the flames weren't spreading and held an arm up against the heat of the blaze. The heat seared his skin through the thin flannel sleeve of his shirt. "Luke!"

"I'm here." Luke emerged, carrying a child wrapped in a quilt. He stalked past Zeke to where the child's father restrained her mother. "Good thing she slept near the front. Fire wasn't so bad there." He handed the girl to her crying mother. "She's coughing a bit from the smoke, but she's alive and well. I'm afraid you're going to lose what's in that wagon though."

Mrs. Turner smiled through her tears. "Bless you. Without you, my daughter would've died. You showed a lot of nerve." She cast a glance at her husband who twisted the brim of his hat. "Unlike others." She sniffed and marched away, hunched over her sobbing child.

Zeke clapped Luke on the back. "Well done! You all right? Not burned?"

"A little singed, and my eyes are watering from the smoke, but I'll be all right. Don't tell Sadie. She'll have my hide and start fussing." He grinned and glanced around the circle. "She'll find out soon enough, I reckon."

Zeke laughed. "We had our own fire episode. Delly started a fire and set her skirts a blaze. Scared ten years off my life. I don't think your wife will gripe too much. She'll be proud of you. You're a hero."

Luke ducked his head. "I didn't do any more than what the Good Lord would want. What are the Turners going to do now?"

"They'll have to hook up with someone. I'll see what others can spare. The Turners still have their mules so they won't have to walk all the way to Oregon."

He made the rounds that evening, asking folks to lay their donations in the center of the circle. The generosity of those under his guidance brought tears to his eyes. People who had little still gave until the needs of the Turners were met with blankets, clothes, and utensils. An elderly couple let them share the space of their wagon in exchange for the Turner's mules taking a turn pulling.

Removing his hat, Zeke watched the pile at his feet grow, thought of Delly's safety and Luke's unthinking heroism and sent a prayer of thanks heavenward. He was truly a blessed man.

19

August already, and they arrived at the Sweetwater River a couple of hours before nightfall and discovered it would cost three dollars to cross. Delly eyed the rickety bridge which missed some planks in the middle. She sighed. With the outrageous fee charged, she expected it to be in better shape. There seemed to be no other way to cross. With only her wagon, and the Johnsons' behind her left to drive over, the bridge didn't look like it would hold up. The other wagons seemed to have sapped the sagging structure of its strength.

Zeke yelled and encouraged his horse into the swift flowing river. Luke followed close beside him on another horse, Junior right behind on Old Blue. Why did that fool boy insist on swimming the stock? He ought to leave the dangerous work for the men.

Halfway across, Junior slipped from the mule's back. Delly's heart skipped a beat and she screamed. Luke grabbed her son by the collar, pulling him onto his own animal. Junior kicked and thrashed to free himself from the reins. Delly released the breath she hadn't known she held and transferred her attention to the floundering mule.

The animal struggled to regain its footing, disappeared beneath the water, and resurfaced a few feet away. The whites of its eyes showed in fear as it was lost down the river. Another loss. The old animal was as much family as the docile old goat, Mabel. Daely blinked back tears. The children would be devastated.

Luke managed to keep a hold of Junior until the two of them reached the opposite shore. Junior collapsed on the bank and covered his face with his hands.

With a deep breath, Delly drove onto the bridge.

It swayed and creaked, as if buffeted by strong winds. The bridge lurched violently to one side, almost tossing Delly from her seat.

"Delly!"

She glanced to where Zeke stood, hands cupped around his mouth. "Hurry! One of the posts is giving way."

She cast a look over her shoulder. The Johnson wagon approached close enough for their oxen's nose to touch the back of her wagon. Beneath them the bridge sagged. The children screamed from behind her. Delly braced her feet.

"Giddup!" She whipped the reins. The oxen fought against the moving boards beneath their hooves and refused to budge. Delly jumped to the pitching bridge.

Her skirt caught on a nail, and she tumbled over the side of the wagon, landing hard to her knees on the deck. Maintaining a hold on the wagon, she struggled to her feet, then fell again as the bridge gave another violent jerk.

Using the wagon to pull to her feet she made her way to the harness. "Come on!" The bridge shuddered again. "We're going to die, you stupid beasts!" The Indian toll keeper ran onto the bridge and tried to usher the Johnson wagon backwards.

Zeke dashed to Delly's side and shoved her behind him. "Go, I'll get the team."

"I can help."

"No. Go now."

She grabbed the reins and set her jaw.

A muscle ticked in Zeke's jaw. "Why do you have to be so stubborn?"

"Why do you?"

With both of them tugging, they made their way across. The bridge collapsed beneath the back wheels of the Johnson's wagon as it lurched to the bank. The rickety structure washed down river, shattering against the rocks.

Delly collapsed, shivering, to the ground and laid her head on her knees. "I've never been so frightened in my life. These skirts are a nuisance. Not only did we have a falling bridge to worry about, but I almost landed in the river head first when I got caught on a nail."

"We'll have to think of something." Zeke squeezed her shoulder. "Go get a fire started so Junior can dry off. I'm going to check on the Johnsons. At the very least, we'll have to change a wheel." He took a few steps before turning back. "When I give a direct order, I expect it to be followed."

"I wasn't going to leave the children." Delly planted her fists on her hips. "No matter what bossy man told me to."

"I'm perfectly capable of knowing what's best for my nieces and nephews." His back stiffened.

"And as their mother, I know best." She lifted her chin. "They were left in my care. Mine. I will make the decisions regarding them."

He stepped closer. "I'm the wagon master. My orders are for everyone here. Mind that you remember that." He stormed away.

After a sleepless night spent dwelling on a stubborn man, Delly stared into her open trunk. No more skirts and petticoats for her. Yesterday's scare had taken years off her life. She pulled out a pair of Junior's britches. With a grin, she yanked off her petticoat, donned the male pants and slipped into a flannel shirt. The freedom! Why hadn't she thought of this before? She tied the pants tight with a piece of rope and belted the shirt around her waist.

The scent of frying bacon drifted through the wagon's bonnet. Delly took a deep breath and jumped to the ground.

Zeke paused in sipping his coffee. "What are you wearing?"

She straightened her shoulders. "A pair of Junior's pants." She rolled up the legs to the top of her moccasins. "You told me to think of something. I did."

"Take them off. You aren't running around dressed like that." Zeke scowled. "People can see your…well…your shape. It's not seemly."

She planted her fists on her hips. "Yesterday, I

almost killed myself falling from the wagon. All on account of feminine silliness. This is more practical and a lot more comfortable. I may never wear a dress again." She glared at him. "It's either these, or my bloomers. And they have a hole in the leg."

"You will not run around in your undergarments." His face darkened.

"I'll do what's necessary, and first chance I get, I'll modify the girls's dresses into split skirts for them."

"Over my dead body!" His eyes flashed beneath his hat. "I demand you change back into a dress."

She marched to the fire and poured a mug of coffee. Blowing into the fragrant brew to cool it, she avoided his eyes. Demanded, did he? She'd see about that. Let's see how he handled a woman with a mind of her own.

Sadie disappeared into the wagon. Several minutes later she reappeared dressed in an outfit more ridiculous than Delly's. Junior's clothes hung on her like a scarecrow's garment. When Dorcas reached between her legs and pulled her skirt through to tuck into her waistband, showing the ruffled edges of her bloomers and pale legs, Zeke's eyes widened and his mouth dropped.

"What?" Dorcas straightened. "This will do until I can ask Alice for a pair of Seth's old pants. If Ma can wear 'em, I can too."

Delly choked on her coffee, spewing it into the dirt, and glanced at Zeke. All seriousness had fled. His lips twitched then he exploded in laughter.

Once he'd caught his breath, he shook his head.

"My pa once told me there was no understanding women. I've seen it all now. Wait until Luke gets a hold of his bride."

Still shaking his head, he stalked away, muttering. When Junior paused to take in the hysterics of those around the fire, Zeke held up a hand. "Don't ask. Just keep walking."

It wasn't that funny. And what was to understand? Safety before convention Delly believed. Relieved the minor disagreement with Zeke was over, she set her coffee on the ground and reached for breakfast. The men would soon see the sense in the women's new clothes and that would be the end of it.

The call to move out rang through the camp, spurring them to action. Movement in pants allowed a quicker cleanup, and Delly climbed onto the wagon seat with a lighter heart.

They traveled up the Sweetwater Valley and the weather turned noticeably cooler. One of the mountains to the side of them wore a bonnet of snow. No wood or grass could be found beside the river, but the water ran clear and slow. When they stopped for the night, the men swam the stock across to feed where the grass was more plentiful.

With the fall of dusk, Delly's good mood vanished. She slapped her neck. "I don't know what's worse. The dust or these mosquitoes."

Sadie strolled past with an armload of dirty laundry. "I'll take the dust. It doesn't try to eat you."

Delly joined her on the river bank and grabbed one of Zeke's shirts. "I'll be drained of blood by the time we move on."

"Mind if I join you?" Alice squatted next to them with her own basket of laundry.

Delly smiled. "I'd like nothing more." She eyed the woman's protruding stomach. "How are you feeling?"

"Little Ben is pretty active." Alice stood and arched her back. "I was a little worried over the excitement of crossing that bridge back there, but everything seems to be fine. I'm glad to have you on this trail, Sadie, when my time comes."

Sadie nodded. "Is your cow still giving milk?"

"Some. I drink a little every day, like you said. It's hard though, when my children need it more."

Sadie scrubbed the last pair of pants. "It's that baby inside of you that needs the milk. You keep drinking it. Same thing I tell Delly, here." She tossed the washed pants into a basket. "And mind that you do as I say. You're looking peaked." She lifted the basket and strolled back to the wagon.

Alice turned and watched her leave. "She's a bossy little thing, ain't she? You in a family way?"

Delly nodded. "She can be, but I've found she's usually right. I don't know what I'd do without her. She's been so much help. Please, don't tell anyone of my condition. I'd like to hide it until we get to Oregon if I can. My hands are already so full, not to mention how Mr. Williams will blow his lid when he finds out."

Alice nodded and plunged a shirt into the water. "I know it ain't none of my business, but my Ben says he sees your oldest gambling a lot. It ain't fittin for a boy his age."

"I was afraid he was still doing that." She paused in helping Alice. "But I don't know what to do. He's making money, and seems like he's going to do what he wants. I'll have to leave him to God to convict of the wrongness of gambling."

"Well, people are also talking about you and Sadie wearing men's britches. Little Dorcas too." She rose and picked up her laundry. "Said it ain't lady like. Or civilized."

"Let me carry that for you." Delly took the basket. "Let people talk. This is more comfortable and a lot safer."

Alice fell into step beside her. "Ben would throw a fit if I were to do the same."

"I'll wear a skirt on Sundays, when we stop for our day of rest." She set the basket next to the Johnson wagon. "I'm not worried about what others might think. This trail is hard and has enough trials of its own without me worrying over every little thing." She gave her friend a quick hug.

"But now Abby wants a pair." Alice frowned. "I caught her with one of Seth's yesterday. I thought Ben would have a fit of apoplexy."

Delly laughed. "Let her wear them. It's only for a couple more months. There's plenty of time for them to be girls when we settle."

20

Zeke shattered the ice on the water bucket so Delly could make coffee, avoiding her gaze. His heavy handed attitude from the day before embarrassed him, but the woman needed to learn to follow orders. He couldn't watch her every second of every day. There were others he was responsible for.

Movement to the west caught his attention. A small band of Indians rode by, wrapped in skins against the frigid morning. He nodded a greeting. They glanced expressionless toward the white people who emerged from their beds, and continued past. The ten braves were accompanied by two squaws who pulled a litter piled high with furs.

Delly stepped close to his side. "Are they dangerous?"

He shrugged. "Seem peaceable enough, but I didn't see or hear them until they were on top of us." Might have something to do with the train his thoughts took, but he'd take an arrow to the leg before admitting to Delly how often she entered his mind.

He glanced around for Hiram. The scout should've noticed the group approaching.

"Maybe they want to trade."

"Doesn't appear so. They almost rode by like we weren't here." He frowned. "I think we should pull out. They didn't seem aggressive, but not friendly either."

"You do think they'll be trouble, don't you?"

"Anyone can be if they're hungry enough." He patted her shoulder then lifted his saddle to the back of the horse. "Get a quick breakfast together. I'm going to ride around the circle and let the others know."

They made eighteen miles that day and camped a short distance from Pacific Springs. As Zeke informed everyone to water the stock and refill water barrels, he turned to head back to his wagon. Several braves watched from the bushes. Zeke quickened his step and rounded the wagon to the sight of Delly slipping the rifle from under the wagon seat.

"Put it down." He took the rifle from her. "Don't show signs of aggression."

"But..."

Three of the braves came forward. One held his hand out. "Hungry." He pointed toward the barrels of food seen through the wagon's bonnet. He said something else and waved a squaw forward. Her arms were loaded with furs. "Trade."

The woman laid the furs at Zeke's feet and scuttled back. The Indians muttered among themselves when Luke appeared.

"I don't think they've ever seen a black man before." Zeke held up a hand to stop Luke. "Delly, pack them some food."

"I'll stay back here. Sadie, come by me." Luke drew his wife into the crook of his arm.

At the sight of Sadie, the Indians began speaking rapidly to each other. The one Zeke dubbed the leader marched to Luke, touched him on the forehead, then turned to say something to his comrades. The rest moved forward and stopped in front of Luke and Sadie, touching their skin and grabbing at their hair.

"Ouch!" Sadie slapped the squaw's hand who tried taking some of her hair. The bun she wore came loose and ebony curls fell around her shoulders. "Luke, do something. They're going to scalp me bald."

He pushed Sadie behind him at the same time Zeke stepped forward. "Stop." He leaned the rifle against the wagon and stepped between the Indians and the others before motioning toward the box she'd packed. "Take the food and go."

The group stared at the gun, back to Luke and Sadie, then lifted the box and melted back into the brush. Zeke rolled his shoulders to release the tension and turned to Hiram who sprinted to his side. "A group of us stayed right out of sight in case you needed us."

"I appreciate that, but it's over now." Zeke replaced the rifle beneath the wagon seat. "They're just hungry."

"Hungry, my foot." Sadie crossed her arms. "They almost pulled my hair out."

"At least they didn't ask you to cut off your hair." Delly scowled.

Zeke laughed. "They were just curious. They didn't mean you any harm." He hoped, glancing toward the trees. "I thought about sending men to hunt, but I think I'll wait until tomorrow." Harmless or not, the Indian's behavior left him uneasy. Hunger did strange things to people, and those Indians appeared hungry and downtrodden.

~

The next morning, Delly stepped to the breakfast fire where Zeke nursed a cup of coffee. "Junior said some of the stock is missing. Our goat and kid too. The children couldn't bear to lose them after Old Blue." She glanced around the circle. "Do you think those Indians took them?"

He tossed his coffee grounds into the dirt. "That's my guess. Luke, me, and some of the others are going out to look for them." He untied his horse from the back of the wagon. "I've asked Junior to stay behind with you. If the Indians took the stock, they won't have gotten very far." He mounted Cyclone.

Delly turned to Sadie. "Now's a good time to catch up our mending. Junior, why don't you check over the harnesses. Dorcas, get your primer and read to us." She glanced in the direction the men had gone. "If we stay busy, the time will pass faster, and Lord knows, there's no end to work to be done."

"I'd rather look for the goats," Junior stated. "And I ain't seen the dogs all morning." His chin quivered. "The only thing I got to claim as mine is those dogs."

He tried so hard to be a pain, but once in a while the little boy came through, and Delly couldn't resist that. "I bet the Indians lured them off so they could steal from us." She marched to where the rifle sat propped against the wagon. Those mutts meant a lot to her son. She wouldn't let them be taken along with everything else.

Besides, this would give her and Junior a chance to talk about his gambling without anyone around. They'd only be gone a short time. "Come on. We're going to find them."

"Are you sure?" Sadie frowned. "Mr. Williams said to stay put."

"We'll be fine. I've got this rifle, and Junior has his. We'll be back before the men return." Delly hitched up her pants, propped the rifle over her shoulder, then led the way into the woods bordering the trail. Zeke would have a fit at her disobeying orders again, but she hadn't missed the sheen of tears in Junior's eyes as he spoke about the dogs.

Pine trees stretched above them, blocking out the morning sun. "Will you be able to find our way back, son? How do you know they came this way?"

He pointed to some dung and whistled for his pets. Not receiving an answering bark, he headed forward. "I know the way back. Do you think they could have circled back to water?"

Delly trudged along behind him. "I don't see why. We give them water every night."

Damp leaves muffled their steps. After an hour, she sat on a fallen log, laid her rifle at her feet, and glanced around her. Her stomach rumbled. Not expecting to be gone so long, she hadn't thought to bring food or drink. If Zeke made it back before them, he was going to be furious.

An occasional bird warbled from the trees. Delly took a deep breath of cold air, letting the crispness bite the lining of her lungs. Junior slumped on a stump across from her, resting his elbows on his knees.

"It's no use. The dogs are gone. Same as Mabel and the kid." His chin quivered. "The little ones are going to be sad."

"So will we." She started to rise, and froze. Cold perspiration stuck her shirt to her back. Her palms sweated and acid rose in her throat. She should've listened to Zeke and stayed in camp. "Junior, don't move. Stay perfectly still."

"What?"

"There's a bear behind you." Delly moved in slow motion and stooped to retrieve her rifle.

"A bear!" He leaped to his feet and whirled.

The animal rose on its hind legs and roared. His huge paws raked at the air. Junior darted to Delly's side.

"I told you to stay still." Her arms trembled as she raised the rifle. *God, help us.*

The bear fell back on all four legs. It huffed and slapped against the ground. Delly's breath stuck in her throat.

"Back up real slow. Don't startle it or make it mad."

"I'm scared, Ma." He raised his rifle.

"So am I." Her heart pounded and drowned out the forest sounds. Together, they backed away, pausing with each step. Delly struggled to force herself to take small, quiet breaths.

Junior stepped on a dry twig. The sound snapped through the woods as loud as a gunshot. They froze.

The bear roared, and charged.

Delly shoved the boy out of the way and squeezed the trigger. The gun's recoil knocked her to the ground and she dropped the weapon. She whimpered and scrambled through the leaves until she clutched it in her fist. She crawled frantically toward the thick underbrush. *God, help us*! She glanced over her shoulder. The bear swung its massive head toward her. She leaped to her feet, and ran.

The animal thudded the ground behind her, quickly gaining ground. A fallen tree blocked Delly's path. She tried scaling it and fell when her foot caught on a branch. The bear swiped at her, raking her shoulder. Fire burned through her.

She dropped the rifle and curled into a ball. Escape eluded her. All reason left her. Survival became of the utmost importance. She tried melding with the ground. The musty odor of forest floor and leaves clogged her nose. Her shoulder throbbed, and she wrapped her arms around her head. *Don't cry. Don't scream. Don't breathe*. Tears forged a course down her cheeks.

Breath, hot and rancid cascaded over her, rancid and sour. Bile rose in her throat. The bear continued to batter her like a rotten log, rolling her back and forth, like a cat with a toy. Each breath became a burning agony. Delly chanted silently for

God to save her.

"Hey!" Junior fired his rifle.

The enraged bear turned, its back paw slicing across Delly's thigh. She lost control and screamed.

The bear roared and rose. Junior fired again. The animal fell to the ground with a moan. Delly closed her eyes. Pain washed over her with the intensity of the desert sun.

"Ma!" Junior knelt and shook her.

"Don't touch me."

"You're bleeding awful bad." His words caught. "I'm sorry I didn't listen. You told me not to move and I did anyway. Can you get up?"

"I don't think so." She kept her eyes closed, fighting not to vomit. Every move, no matter how small, shot fire through her body. She forced her words through her clenched teeth. "You'll have to go and get help."

"I won't leave you here."

"You have to. Cover me with your coat and go find your uncle." She felt him lay his coat over her and heard the leaves rustle as he put her rifle within her reach. Darkness pressed in. "Hurry."

21

"Uncle Zeke!"

Zeke whirled toward the voice. "Junior?"

The boy burst from the trees and bent over, struggling to breathe. "You've…got…to come. Now."

Zeke grabbed his shoulders and stared into his eyes. "Where's your ma? We've been looking for you for half an hour."

His nephew pointed. "Back there. She's…hurt bad. A bear got her."

Zeke's blood ran cold. Adrenaline prickled his skin. He yanked his rifle from its saddle holster. "Show me. Luke, I might need you. Hiram, watch the train."

"Yes, sir."

They set off at a sprint, heading farther up the mountain.

Tears trailed down Junior's face. "She told me not to move. But I did. It's my…fault. I never listen to her. She's bleeding an awful lot."

Zeke increased his pace. *Please, God, don't let me be too late.* He faltered at the sight of the fallen bear, then rushed to Delly's side. Blood soaked into the ground beneath her. He laid his ear to her chest. Unconscious, but alive. He wrapped Junior's coat more snugly around her and lifted her into his arms.

"Luke, you and Junior take care of the bear. There's good meat to be used." They nodded and he took off as quick as he could. Delly groaned, spurring him faster.

Sadie met them at camp, one hand clasped to her bosom. "What happened?"

"A bear." Zeke laid Delly in the back of the wagon. He climbed in after her and rummaged through their things until he found the chest that held their dwindling medical supplies. Dorcas's face appeared in the bonnet opening.

"Dorcas, boil water and send Sadie to help me. Keep the little ones out of here."

Using his Bowie knife, he sliced through Delly's pant leg. Where the fabric stuck to the wound, he pulled it free. Blood soaked the quilt beneath her. He choked back a sob at the sight of her ripped flesh. The scrape on her shoulder wasn't bad, but the weight of the bear had torn some of the flesh from her thigh, leaving a wide gash. With a speed born of fear, he ripped a petticoat into long bandages.

"Hurry with that water! And find me some whiskey."

Sadie set the pot next to him. "Here. We'd already started boiling for coffee. Tell me what to do."

Dorcas tossed him an amber colored bottle. "Got it from Tucker. I told him you wouldn't be mad, 'cause you need it. That's right, ain't it?" She glanced at Delly. "Will Ma be all right?"

"I don't know. Go outside. Luke and the others will want dinner."

"But…"

"Now. You don't need to be here for this." He hated being curt with the girl, but he didn't have time to coddle a child when Delly's life held in the balance. "Hold her down, Sadie. I'm going to pour this whiskey into her wounds. She'll most likely wake from the pain."

He gritted his teeth and poured. Delly's screams pierced his eardrums. He fought against a desire to release his fear in a primal yell of his own. "I'm sorry, sweetheart. I'm sorry." He soaked a strip of cloth with more of the whiskey and tied it tight around her leg. Her gaze locked with his. Her eyes wide and glassy. Zeke forced himself to smile, and knew he failed the meager attempt at putting on a good face. Instead, he concentrated on doctoring her shoulder.

By the time he finished, she'd fallen asleep. He sat back on his haunches and rubbed his hands across his face. "We have to watch for infection. I couldn't stitch her. I don't know how to stitch gouges. She'll have a nasty scar, and maybe a limp. She's in God's hands now."

Sadie knelt beside him and wrapped him in her thin arms. "That's the best place to be. The *best* place. You go rest. I'll watch her awhile."

"No." He shook his head. "I'm not leaving her."

"You need to talk to your nephew. That boy's out there crying his heart out 'cause he thinks this is his fault. It ain't. Neither one of them listen worth a hoot when someone says to stay put. Junior's figured that out. Go easy on him." She took a deep breath. "You go help him. I'll watch her real close. I promise."

"Okay, but come get me if she wakes." He pulled another quilt over Delly's motionless body and climbed from the wagon.

Junior stood beside the fire. Zeke squared his shoulders, then moved to stand in front of him. What could he say to ease the boy's mind? How would Junior handle the guilt if his stepmother died? "We've got her patched up. She's sleeping. Wasn't your fault, son."

"She told me not to move." Junior didn't bother wiping away his tears. "I got scared and ran. She pushed me out of the way and took up the rifle. You should've seen her. She stepped in front of me. Like she was my real ma." He threw his arms around Zeke's neck. "I should've been protecting her. Not the other way around."

He patted the boy's back. "That's the way she is." Putting his hands on Junior's arms, he held him away and stared into his eyes. "She'd do it again, in a heartbeat, because she loves you."

"But I'm still playing cards."

"Her love is unconditional, like God loves us. Do you understand what I'm saying?" He released Junior then pulled the other children into his arms, planting a kiss on the baby Sarah's chubby cheek. "Now, we pray. What were y'all doing in the woods anyway?"

"We went looking for the dogs and Mabel,"

Junior said, his words sounding muffled as he kept his face buried in Zeke's chest. "Did you get the other animals back?"

"All but one oxen. They'd already butchered it, and the dogs showed up soon after. We got the goats too." He wanted to tell the boy how foolish they'd been, heading off because of a couple of animals, but held his tongue. Wounding the boy's feelings further wouldn't accomplish anything.

"Mr. Williams," Sadie called. "She's awake."

He tussled Junior's hair then sprang into the wagon bed and kneeled beside Delly. As quiet as a wraith, Sadie slipped outside. Zeke brushed the damp tendrils from Delly's hair. She smiled weakly at him.

"You hurt me." She teased, her words barely above a whisper.

"I'm sorry. But you ought to be blaming the bear."

"I want a rug made from its fur."

He grinned. "Anything. You should sleep now."

"I can't sleep. It hurts too much." She closed her eyes. "Sorry to cause you more trouble. The grey hairs on your head ought to be too numerous to count with all me and the children put you through." Tears fell from her eyes, wetting her pillow.

Zeke shoved his head through the canvas opening. "We need laudanum."

"There ought to be some in the chest," Sadie told him.

"Alice has it," Delly said. "She wanted it for Seth."

"Check the Johnsons'." Zeke clenched his fists as Delly whimpered.

After what seemed an eternity, Junior appeared with a small blue bottle. Zeke clapped him on the shoulder then turned back to Delly. "Here, sweetheart. Take a swallow of this." He propped her against his arm and dribbled the liquid between her lips. She grimaced and laid back, closing her eyes.

The night loomed before him. Zeke leaned against a crate and stretched his legs in front of him, keeping an eye on Delly. His anxiety grew as her temperature rose, and she tossed beneath the covers. He'd lose her, just as he'd lost Becky. "Sadie!"

She entered the wagon, a shawl thrown over her cotton nightgown. "She's doing poorly?"

"She's hot as an iron. I need snow to wash her."

"I'll get it. " Luke yelled. "It's too cold for Sadie. Don't want her catching a chill."

Sadie smiled. "That man dumps snow over my head one minute, then says it's too cold the next."

"He's a good man."

"Yes, he is. So are you, Mr. Williams."

Together they packed snow around Delly, keeping a steady stream of buckets coming into the wagon. Zeke didn't care how many things got wet. All he cared about was the beautiful woman in front of him.

"You ought to let me care for her, Mr. Williams." Sadie removed a sodden towel. "It ain't proper, with y'all not being married and all."

"I won't leave her." He reached for another bucket. "I'll worry about convention later."

"But Miss Sophia is still grumbling…"

"Enough!" Sophia be hanged. If the woman couldn't get it through her mind after months that Zeke had no interest, then she'd reach Oregon a disappointed woman. She should've turned back after the death of her father.

They camped for two days. Despite the complaints of a couple of the wagoneers, Zeke refused to move until Delly's fever broke. Instead, he left Hiram in charge. A couple of impatient pioneers headed on without them.

Zeke rubbed a chin rough with whiskers. His eyes felt full of dirt from lack of sleep. With Sadie's help, he'd kept Delly cool with melted snow, while Luke and the other men hunted and searched for wild roots and berries. He couldn't remember having been this tired in his life. He closed his eyes.

"Zeke?"

"Delly!" His eye lids popped open. "Praise God!" He pulled her into his arms. "You're awake."

"How long have I been ill?"

"Too long." He ran his hands over her face and arms. "How are you feeling?"

"Sore, but I want to go outside and see my children."

"Are you sure?"

She nodded, and he swooped her into his arms. When he emerged from the wagon, Junior burst into tears, wiping his nose on his sleeve. "I'm so sorry, Ma."

"Put me down, Zeke."

"Delly…"

"Please." She looked imploringly at him. "I

need to stand. If only for a moment."

He nodded. She needed to show her son she'd be all right. He let her down, keeping an arm around her for support.

"I'm going to be fine, Junior. See." She tried taking a step and Zeke reached for her before she fell. "It'll take a few days, but I'll get there, and we'll have a fine rug to grace the floor of our new home."

Junior threw his arms around her and stooped, laying his head on her shoulder. "I thought I'd lost you."

"Miss Delly?" Luke stepped beside her holding a crutch carved from a small tree. "This will have you walking in no time."

"How thoughtful, Luke."

Zeke lifted her. "She won't be using it for a few days, though. She's going back in the wagon." He turned toward the rest of the train. "We're pulling out tomorrow, folks."

A cheer rose above the camp, echoing through the trees and sending woodland birds into flight.

22

They pulled out the next morning, Sadie driving, and Delly bundled in the back of the wagon with Dorcas and the little ones sitting beside her—chattering non-stop. Baby Sarah slept on a pile of quilts, a drop of drool beside her lip. The other children ran beside the wagon.

Full of curiosity over Delly's encounter with the bear, Dorcas bounced with questions. "Were you scared? 'Cause Junior said he was."

Delly fiddled with the fringe on the red shawl she wore. "I didn't really think about it until I lay on the ground with the bear on top of me. Then I was terrified. I thought for sure I'd be meeting Jesus that day."

The little girl sidled closer to her, smelling of dirt and mountain air. "More like the devil according to Junior. He said that bear roared and huffed, slapping the ground with his big old feet." She shivered. "I think I would've sat down and cried and let it eat me. Did you cry?"

"No." She tucked a quilt around the two of them.

"Did it smell bad? The bear breath. Like rotten meat? 'Cause I heard once that they stink real bad. Did you play dead?"

Delly closed her eyes and leaned her head back against the few crates they carried in the wagon. She recalled the rancid odor as the animal breathed on her. The terror as it stood over her and roared. She sighed. "Yes, it smelled very bad."

"You're lucky to be alive, Ma."

"Yes, I am."

"Junior hasn't gambled once since you've been sick."

"Then something good has come of all this." She opened her eyes and watched as pine trees moved past them. The squawk of a crow echoed above the creak of the wagon. Her leg pained her with each jolt of the wagon.

But the physical pain didn't hurt nearly as much as the emotional one. More and more she questioned the wisdom of her undertaking the journey with children in tow. Fearing every day that an accident would leave a person helpless or dead, was quickly becoming more than she could bear.

She'd always considered herself strong. Now, with a leg that would most likely never be the same, what kind of a pioneer would she make? She'd walk with a limp like a broken-winged bird.

Zeke's ministrations during her time of fever had kept him away from the other emigrants, adding to Delly's sense of guilt and failure. The man's heart was too big to comprehend. Now, with Delly crippled, there's be one more burden he felt he needed to take on. Delly couldn't let that happen.

There had to be another way.

She rubbed her stomach, barely feeling the just emerging bump. Somehow, she'd find a way to raise this baby, and the other children, without imposing on Zeke.

The wagon lurched going uphill, and Delly grappled to hold on as she slid toward the backboard. Another jolt slammed her against the wood. She yelped at the shooting pain through her shoulder.

Dorcas stood to help her and pitched head-first to the ground outside.

"Dorcas!" Delly peered out. The little girl lay on her back, eyes wide, mouth open, staring at the sky. "Sadie, stop the wagon."

"I can't. Mr. Williams said we had to keep the team moving forward or we'd slide down the hill. Once we start, we wouldn't be able to stop and we'd crash into the wagon behind us."

The Johnson's wagon rounded the bend, and Dorcas still didn't move. Heart in her throat, Delly pulled herself painfully to her feet and climbed out of the wagon. The jump to the road jarred her leg and she cried out, falling to her knees. She crawled over and ran her hands over Dorcas's arms and knees. Finding nothing broken, she shook her. Dorcas opened her eyes. "Come on, we've got to get off this road. Can you walk?"

"Yes, I just had the wind knocked out of me." She touched her head. "And I hit my head."

Ben Johnson yelled a warning for them to move. The oxen bellowed.

Dorcas leaped to her feet and scampered to the

rock face, pressing her body as close to the granite wall as possible. Delly crawled. Rocks dug into her knees. The ground vibrated beneath her hands, and she whimpered with each movement by the time she reached her stepdaughter.

The Johnson wagon moved past. Alice craned her neck toward them as they passed. "I'll tell the wagon master!"

"Thank you." More proof that traveling west had been a fool's errand. She couldn't even prevent her daughter from falling out of the wagon when she sat right next to her.

"You're bleeding." Dorcas pointed to her leg.

Blood soaked through her pant leg. Her thigh throbbed. Perspiration beaded on her brow. "I'll be fine. Run ahead and get your uncle." She noticed the bump on Dorcas's forehead. "Have Sadie put something on that first chance."

Dorcas nodded, hiked Seth's pants up, and darted away.

~

"Uncle Zeke!" He pulled roughly on his horse's reins, turning the animal. Dorcas sprinted toward him. "Ma's bleeding again. I fell out of the wagon, and she came after me. Banged up her leg again."

"Catch up to Sadie." He set his horse to a gallop and dismounted before coming to a complete halt. Delly slumped against the rock face with her eyes closed. Would he manage to get her to Oregon in one piece? If trouble could be found, she was in the middle of it.

"Delicious?" His gaze traveled from her head to her feet.

"I'm fine. I hurt my leg again getting out of the wagon. I just need to rest for a minute."

Luke and Sadie's wagon, driven by the oldest Oglesby boy rattled past them. The braying of mules and bellowing of oxen reached his ears. He pulled her to her feet. "I've got to get you on my horse. The stock is coming, and we're in the way."

Her eyes widened as the animals came into sight. "Hurry."

Gunshots from the drovers rang over the herds' heads, pushing the animals faster. Luke appeared around the bend, took one look at them, then darted in front of the herd, waving his arms and yelling. The animals continued, and he dove into the bushes to avoid being trampled.

Zeke swept Delly into his arms and dashed for his horse. "Come on, honey. Put your foot in the stirrup."

"I can't. I don't have enough strength in my leg." She glanced over his shoulder. "They're coming right for us. There's no time for you to seat me. We're going to be trampled."

Zeke slapped his horse on the rump, causing it to jerk and gallop ahead. He positioned Delly against the cliff wall and plastered himself against her back. She squirmed beneath him. "Be still."

Frustration against their helplessness rose. He pressed closer until he felt he'd crush her. Her breath whooshed against his wrist. The animals thundered closer. He closed his eyes, knowing the space between his back and the surging animals wasn't wide enough. Better him, than her. A whole man had a better chance of surviving than a wounded woman.

Dust filled the air and clogged his throat. An oxen's horn caught in the hem of his shirt and pulled Zeke with him. Previous years of wrangling cows gave him the skill he needed to wrap an arm around the beast's neck. He kicked against the ground until he regained his feet. Fire burned through his side. The animal dragged him, Zeke's boots leaving ruts in the dirt. Getting his feet under him, he ripped free of the horn, leaving behind a scrap of his shirt, and fought his way back to Delly.

The animals passed, and she turned to face him. "I thought we'd lost you." Her gaze flicked down him. "You're bleeding."

"It's just a graze." He smiled. "What a pair we make. Bloody and torn. Imagine what we'd be like if God *weren't* looking out for us."

"Don't jest." Her eyes sparked. "You could've been killed. I don't want to do this anymore."

His heart jolted. "What do you mean?"

"Every day is a trial." Her chin shook. "Every breath a blessing. I'm losing my faith with these day-to-day tribulations." She laid her head against the rock face. "I haven't even asked for a Bible reading in weeks."

"But I wasn't killed." He pulled her into a hug. "We're almost there. God never promises us life will be easy, just that our reward will be great. The others are waiting at the bottom of the hill for us. How about a piggy back ride? We'll be camped beside the Green River tonight with another ferry ride in the morning."

"It isn't good for the baby, Zeke."

23

"What baby?" His heart settled in his stomach like a rock slide.

Delly took a deep breath. "I'm pregnant. But don't worry. It's won't be born until we reach Oregon."

Don't worry? She was pregnant. With his brother's child. On the dangerous trail to Oregon Territory. Well, he'd squelch any romantic feelings growing for her. He couldn't do this either. Not with Delly's talent for getting herself in danger. His blood ran cold. Weekly, something happened to where he'd almost lose her. Now, with a baby to worry about, in addition to the nieces and nephews he already had … he couldn't do it. He was a strong man, but not that strong.

The stricken look on her face told him she understood the thoughts running rampant through his mind. She tilted her chin and squared her shoulders. "Please, help me back to the wagon. I'll ask Sadie to look at your side."

Without speaking, he hefted her in his arms and

carried her to the wagon. After setting her inside, he stormed away. He'd take care of his own wound. His heart hurt more than any scrape by an oxen's horn.

Delly woke to continuing chilly temperatures. Why bother getting out of bed? Cold, pain, and the stormy countenance of Zeke weren't reason enough. She glanced at the chubby cheeks of baby Sarah. There was her reason. Her and five more like her.

Junior ran by announcing the price of another ferry, and Delly crawled to peer out the front of the wagon. "Eight dollars! It ought to be a sin to charge so much."

It seemed the farther west they got, the more expensive the tolls. She crossed her arms and stared over Sadie's shoulders. Even with Junior playing poker, secretly he thought, they'd be lucky if their money lasted.

A white man and an Indian woman stood beside the river, donned in layers of calico and fur. Delly yearned to be able to get down and march over to reason with them. To top things off, the men planned to swim the livestock again. Well, she wouldn't watch. There was nothing she could do if disaster struck. She couldn't do anything but sit in the back like an old woman while Sadie did all the driving. She stroked the fur of the bear skin she sat on, and smiled sadly. At least they had a beautiful rug to adorn the floor in front of a fireplace in their new home. At the expensive price of her independence.

"What day is it, Sadie?"

"Close to the middle of August, I think I heard someone say." She flicked the reins to move the wagon onto the ferry.

"A little over halfway," Delly murmured. Could she continue the monotony, the daily dangers? According to the guidebook, which she was just about ready to chuck out the back of the wagon, they'd traveled the easy half of the journey. She laid her arms along the buckboard and rested her head on them. Her gaze fell on her Bible. That's her problem. She'd forgotten where her strength was supposed to come from. Pride caused her to fall. A sense of self-importance, thinking she could do it herself.

Another glance outside showed more of the same she'd seen day after day. Dirt, sand, and sage brush. A ridge of mountains lay a day or two travel ahead of them. She shivered against the cold wind and drew a quilt over her shoulders. The gentle pitch of the ferry carried them across the river without mishap and into air that stank of death.

Nausea rose, and Delly fumbled around her neck for her face rag. Cattle carcasses dotted the trail. Poor animals too tired and undernourished to go any farther. Vultures swooped in a macabre dance. Household items littered the ground. Chests, armoires, bed springs, mattresses, books, and tools lay among the dead animals.

For the first time in her life, Delly gave thanks for having so little. There'd be no need for her to discard a cherished possession to lighten the load.

When they camped that evening, Zeke announced that everyone needed to toss what wasn't absolutely necessary. She eyed the guidebook again. Stupid thing. Hadn't been right yet. Full of easy days and tranquil nights. She tossed it into the fire and derived satisfaction from the flames devouring the pages.

"Toss as little as possible, Sadie. You'll be setting up house in Oregon, don't forget." She held up a cast iron skillet.

Sadie shook her head. "You take it. I only cook with a dutch oven anyway, and I'd rather have this." She caressed the arm of a rocking chair. "Most of the widow's clothes are serviceable and can be used to make dresses for us and the girls. There're some shirts for the men from her husband's things. They're a bit worn, but still have some wear. Maybe we can keep more if we distribute stuff between us."

"That's a wonderful idea." Delly squealed with delight. "Here's a Bible for you. Oh, look, some novels." She sighed. "But those aren't a necessity." Neither were the few she'd brought with her. She'd already read them many times, but something about tossing books tore at her heart. She handed Sadie the Bible. She'd keep the books unless she absolutely had to toss them. "The clock will have to go, and those tools. Keep the hoe, and this sewing kit. Praise the Lord, there's two bolts of calico!"

"Do you have room for this?" Sadie held up a gorgeous blue and white flower patterned tea set. "I don't want it. Can you see Luke and his big hands holding something this delicate?"

"I'd love it. You can visit and have tea any time you want."

Zeke strolled by and frowned. "I hope you ladies are being sensible." The look on his face told Delly he thought her anything but.

She held the set to her chest. "We have so little. Surely, I can keep a few of these things."

He nodded. "Set aside what you want, and I'll check it over before we hit the high pass."

She'd make up her own mind. If she had to get rid of something later, then she would, but she wouldn't have a man that wasn't her husband dictate what she could and couldn't do.

Half an hour later, she straightened an aching back and glanced with pleasure at the small pile of new possessions. She'd taken the calico bolt of blue, and Sadie claimed the rose. The tea set had been repacked in a smaller crate and cushioned with bunches of dry grass. The iron skillet sat on top of the box. Sadie's pile sat in the seat of the rocking chair; dish towels, tin dishes, a dutch oven, and the Bible. Necessities for making a home in a new land.

"Go on to the wagon," Sadie said. "You've done enough for one day. I'll have Luke bring your share by later on."

Delly glanced at the sun setting over the mountains and leaned on her crutch. Streaks of crimson and purple painted a navy sky. She reached up and released her hair from its bun, allowing the curls to bounce against her shoulders and ward off a slight breeze.

The emigrants all seemed to be traversing a small hill. Their laughter and conversation gave the impression of a party. Delly hobbled after them, not wanting to be left out.

"Let me help, Ma." Junior put an arm around her. When had he grown taller than her?

"Thanks, Junior. You're quite the gentleman."

He beamed.

When they reached the top, another bear could've been next to her and she wouldn't have noticed as she gazed at the valley below them. The river, a silver ribbon, wound lazily through a prairie of moon-kissed shrubs. The sunset had changed to a panorama of red, orange, and yellow as vibrant as any artist's paint-splattered canvas.

"I've never seen anything like it. There's nothing to obstruct our view. It's like a dark ocean spread at our feet. How can something so desolate during the day be this magical at night?"

Zeke stepped beside her. "I stop here every time I travel through. I never tire of looking at this view. It is truly one of God's masterpieces."

Luke's eyes glistened. "I've seen so much ugliness in my life. Something this beautiful truly restores my soul."

"Wait until you see our land. The parcel you can farm is on the edge of our property." Zeke patted Luke's shoulder. "It'll be great having you close."

So he'd invited them to stay. The idea warmed Delly, although she wished he'd told her. She twisted her mouth. Why should he? They barely spoke anymore. Not since she'd told him she was expecting anyway.

Like the Israelites wandering in the desert, Delly feared the last couple of months had cast her into a wilderness of her own.

24

Delly rose from the pile of blankets and put most of her weight on her healing leg. She squatted, stretched, and smiled. Other than a slight twinge in her thigh, her wound appeared well enough to allow her to walk rather than ride any longer in the bumpy wagon. It's been a long month of recovery time.

She donned her britches, grabbed her crutch, and climbed outside to limp alongside the wagon as it traversed its first mountain. Her breath showed itself in puffs of white in the frigid air. The cold stung her lungs.

A steady rain the night before left the trail muddy, and Delly's crutch continuously got stuck. Despite a steely determination to make it to the mountain top, exhaustion forced her to the side of the road. The Johnson wagon rumbled past, and Dorcas left her friend's side to squat beside Delly.

Delly lifted a hand to ward off her daughter's protests. "I'm sorry, but I've got to rest." She propped her mud-caked crutch against a tree and closed her eyes. "I'm cold, I'm wet, and my leg hurts."

"I'm sorry to hear that, Mrs. Williams."

Her eyes flew open. Ira Bodine stood in front of her, a smirk on his handsome face. Dressed in black pants, an inky-colored duster that brushed the tops of his shiny boots, and a purple brocade vest over a blinding white shirt, he looked the epitome of wealth and good fortune. Not a speck of dirt dared marred his ensemble. Too bad his insides didn't appear as spotless.

Delly glanced at her own splattered pants and moccasins and pulled her tattered wool coat closer around her. "You're a fool for coming around here. Especially after the stunt you pulled the last time. Our wagon master would like nothing more than to shoot you."

"I've been called many things, but never a fool." The smile vanished from his face. His eyes hardened as he glanced at her crutch. "Seems you've been injured. Pity. I had such plans for you, my dear. Oh, well." He smoothed his moustache with his finger. "With your looks, I'm sure the men would overlook a little limp. And your daughter will still fetch me quite a price." He drew his hand down Dorcas's cheek. "If nothing else, I'll hold you ransom for the land deed."

Dorcas whimpered and pressed closer to Delly.

Delly straightened and struggled to her feet wishing she had a gun within reach. She forced her gaze to meet Bodine's lifeless snake eyes. "Leave. Our friends will come and fetch us soon."

He glanced up the trail where Zeke rode toward them. Bodine tipped his hat. "Until next time, ladies." He stepped back and disappeared into the trees.

"Was that Bodine?" Zeke held down a hand to help Delly climb up behind him.

"Yes." She swung a leg over. "I think he's following us. He's getting bolder. It's not just me he wants, but Dorcas too. I'm giving you the deed. I don't want to hold onto it any longer."

He lifted Dorcas and positioned her in front of him. "I'll shoot him if I see him again."

"That doesn't seem to be much of a deterrent."

"We'll see the next time we come face-to-face with that gambling scoundrel."

Delly wanted nothing more than to lay her cheek against his back, feel the wool warm from his skin on her face. Have her heart beat in time with his. But it couldn't be. Not with Zeke still suffering from his wife's death. Not since she carried another man's child.

But they did have something in common. Although she'd abhorred bloodshed, she'd violently defend her family if the need arose. With Ira Bodine shadowing them, she feared a confrontation between the man and Zeke only waited for the right time. She prayed this would be an instant when the good guy won.

She ought to shoot the man herself.

Zeke called a halt in a meadow half-way up the second mountain. Above them rose snow-covered peaks. Below, a green valley where a tribe of Indians had established a village. Wary of what had happened before, he had the travelers put the extra stock in the middle of the circle. The trail was quickly taking its toll on the animals, and they couldn't afford to lose any to thievery.

"Mr. Williams." A middle-aged man tethered his horse beside Cyclone. "We waited to leave Missouri with you because you told us we would cross these mountains before bad weather. We could've left with an earlier train, but were told you were the best. My children are crying because they're cold. Maybe we should've rethought our decision."

"This isn't bad, Mr. Robbins. Bad is what would be waiting if we'd left a month later." Zeke tried to move past him. The man blocked his way. "Look, no one stopped you from leaving with an earlier train. You wanted my expertise on this trail, and the experience of Hiram. Paid good money for it, too."

"My children are hungry. My wife's fingers are too cold to start a fire, and our rations are running low."

Zeke gritted his teeth. "I'm sorry about that, sir. If you followed the guidelines I gave you, you'd have plenty of rations to get you through. These woods are full of animals for hunting. Feel free to do so, and if your wife's fingers are too cold, why don't you start the fire for her?"

Other men crowded around, adding their opinions. Their voices steadily rose in volume. Zeke stilled his horse who skittered sideways at the crowding bodies. "We will be out of these mountains within the next day or two. Then it will be the heat and lack of water you'll be complaining about. We're all tired, folks. We need to make the best of things and keep moving."

Delly stood on the fringe of the crowd, her face pale beneath her bonnet. Did she think Zeke failed her too? Was she like the other doomsayers? He turned his head, not wanting to see any sign of condemnation on her face. Not that he didn't deserve it, especially after the way he avoided her after the breaking news of her pregnancy, but coming from a family member … well, he couldn't take losing her trust to lead her safely to Oregon.

"The Israelites complained against Moses when he was leading them to the Promised Land." Luke spoke up from behind them where he leaned against a tree with his arms crossed. "The Lord led them through, just as He promised to. Just as He will use Mr. Williams to lead you through." He marched to Zeke's side and stood as sturdy as an oak.

"This man is willing to go forward with an injured woman and a passel of children. Nothing more than any of you have to endure. We left our pasts behind for hope of a better future. Anything worthwhile requires work and hardship. Go on back to your wagons and let Mr. Williams be. Look around and count your blessings." Luke parted the way for Zeke to pass through the now silent men.

Zeke clapped Luke on the shoulder. "That was quite a speech, my friend."

"It's human nature to grumble when things are hard. Just as it is our nature to forget the bad when we come to finally see what we've been striving for. They'll come around."

"You ought to be a preacher. Are you a learned

man?"

"Can't read or write. Not even my own name." Luke slid the saddle from Zeke's horse. "But my daddy knew the Bible from his daddy, and my momma could read some. They wanted to raise me right. Even under the bondage of slavery."

"Well, they sure did, Luke. You're wiser than most educated people." Now, if only Luke's wisdom could bridge the valley wide gap between Zeke and Delly.

25

The next day they emerged from the mountains and stopped beside a soda spring. The children took Delly's face rag and let the water suck it into a hole then spit it back out. They shouted with laughter. Delly shot out her hand and confiscated the scrap of fabric. "What if it doesn't give it back? I'll be eating dust the rest of the way."

"Delly." Ben Johnson approached, twisting his hat in his hands. "Sadie says to come. It's Alice's time."

"It's too early." Her heart beat faster. What could she do? She didn't know a thing about birthing babies.

"Babies don't always wait. Sadie says get your medicine box and whatever clean towels you can find." He nodded and dashed back to his wagon.

Delly shoved her rag into her pocket. "Dorcas, boil some water and wait for me to call you. Keep an eye on the little ones." She retrieved the requested supplies and limped as quickly as possible to the Johnson's wagon. Alice's deep moans drifted across the camp.

"Alice?" Delly tossed the box up and climbed inside. "How are you doing?"

The woman's face glowed red with the effort of labor. Sweat ran in rivulets down her cheeks. "Slow…at first. They got…worse after…we stopped." She groaned and laid back against the quilts Sadie piled behind her for support. "I didn't want…to say anything…earlier."

"She's hurting," Sadie whispered. "I think the baby's turned wrong."

"What can we do?" Delly placed her hands on her softly growing stomach. This could be her in a few months. Earlier if she didn't take care of herself.

"There's nothing to do but pray and wait it out."

Alice screamed and bolted to a sitting position. Sadie placed her hands on the woman's shoulders and forced her back. "Try not to push, Miss Alice. It ain't time for that baby yet."

Delly dipped a rag into some water and wiped down Alice's neck and arms. Her fingers ached from Alice grabbing a hold with each contraction and grinding her knuckles together. *Please, God. I don't know what to do!*

The heat inside the wagon continued to rise, plastering Delly's and Sadies's dresses to their skin with perspiration. Alice had become too exhausted to do much more than writh and groan.

Delly sat back and glanced down. "Sadie!" Blood pooled beneath Alice's body. "I'm no expert but that seems like an awful lot of blood."

Sadie lit a lantern against the gathering dusk and held it to Alice's face. "We're going to lose her. Most likely the baby too." She set the lantern down and patted Alice's cheek. "Miss Alice? We've got to get this baby out now, you hear?"

Alice thrashed.

"I know you're hurting and we've been here all day, but if you don't push, we're going to lose you *and* this child." Sadie put her full weight on Alice's stomach and pressed. "Come on, Lord, turn this baby! Push, Miss Alice."

Delly twisted a rag and thrust it between Alice's lips, giving her something to bite down on. Mr. Johnson poked his head inside the tent. "Out, Ben. There's nothing for you to do here." While Sadie helped Alice push, Delly used rags to staunch the flow of blood covering the mattress under her friend. Tears obscured her vision. Her hands trembled.

One last push and she reached forward to grab a miniature baby girl. Alice shuddered and collapsed back onto the quilts. "The baby isn't breathing." Delly thrust the infant into Sadie's hands.

Sadie stuck a finger in the baby's mouth, felt around, then held her upside down and gave a firm smack on her bottom. A wail, no bigger than what a kitten might make, issued from the tiny girl. Sadie wrapped her in a small square of flannel and laid her on Alice's bosom. "It's a beautiful girl."

Alice gave a weak smile and tried reaching for her. Her arm fell to her side. Her eyes closed.

Delly shook her. What would Ben do if he lost

his beloved wife? There were few examples of a loving couple in Delly's world. She didn't want to lose half of one and a dear friend at that. "Wake up, Alice. See your new daughter. Please, wake up." Tears mingled with the sweat on her face. Please, God.

The stain of scarlet continued to spread beneath her. Delly fell to her knees and leaned over her friend. No breath escaped from her lips. "Oh, no. Please. Sadie, we've got to do something." Delly laid her head beside the baby and let the sobs she'd been struggling to hold in, escape.

"There ain't nothing we can do. She's gone." Sadie wiped her hands down her apron. "We'll try and keep the baby alive. Give her to me. I'll tell Mr. Johnson."

Delly shook her head. "No, I'll do it. You tend to Alice." She couldn't bear to see her lifeless friend. She folded the mewling infant close to her and climbed from the wagon.

Ben approached with a hopeful look on his face. His shoulders slumped when Delly stopped in front of him. "It's a gorgeous baby girl."

"And my Alice?"

"I'm sorry, Ben. We did all we could."

He dropped to his knees and covered his face. An unearthly howl burst from the man, and it took all the strength Delly possessed not to fall beside him and cry out herself.

Ben leaped to his feet and dashed for the wagon, springing inside. Sadie's murmurs drifted to those waiting outside. Zeke drew Delly and the baby into his arms. Delly sagged against him, welcoming his moment of compassion, no matter how brief.

"We tried so hard. The baby was turned wrong," Delly sobbed. "I felt so helpless. Sadie was wonderful, though." She held the baby up for him to see. "Isn't she beautiful? Alice would have been so proud."

"Like an angel."

Delly pulled away. "She needs her daddy now." She marched to the wagon and held up the baby for Sadie to take. Then, with the exhaustion of the world on her shoulders, Delly climbed into her own home on wheels.

Delly wrapped her arms around her stomach and rocked. Why, Lord? Alice hadn't even wanted to come. Love for her husband brought her this far. Delly thrust a fist to her mouth. What would the Johnsons do now? Alice was the glue holding the family together.

~

Ben approached their fire the next morning with the baby in one arm and leading the milk cow with the other. He thrust both at Delly. "I want you to have her. I can't care for her without Alice, and she would've wanted it this way. She cared a lot for you. Said you were like her little sister."

Stunned, Delly rose and took the baby. "But…"

"I named her Alice, after my wife." He trailed a finger down the baby's cheek. "She needs a woman to care for her. She's so tiny. Fits right in my big old hands. I'll be busy enough with little Abby. She misses her ma so much."

She nodded. "I consider this a great honor, Ben.

I'll love her as my own until you're ready to fetch her back."

He nodded, turned, then shuffled away.

"Oh, Sadie." Delly's legs refused to hold her any longer and she collapsed onto a nearby stool. "How can I do this with a child of my own on its way?"

"We do what we have to." Sadie laid a hand on her shoulder. "I'll help. For as long as you need me."

"I don't know much about babies." She glanced at the cow, noting the jutting hip bones. "I hope that animal holds up until we reach Oregon." Delly smoothed the downy fuzz on the baby's head, marveling at her perfection. "You poor dear."

The baby squirmed and cried. "I don't have any bottles. How am I going to feed her?"

Sadie smiled and tossed a glove into the pot hanging over the fire. "We improvise, until we can see whether someone has a bottle stashed in a crate somewhere." She fished the glove out with a stick, then, using a needle, poked holes in one of the fingers. "Luke, can you milk a cow?"

He rolled his eyes and grinned. "Of course I can." He grabbed a bucket and stalked away. "What simpleton do you take me for?"

"Will she live?" Delly stuck her finger in the baby's mouth.

"She's only a month early. There's a chance, God willing." Sadie smoothed her apron over her slightly protruding stomach. "I'd have plenty of milk if my own was here, but this child won't arrive until after we hit Oregon."

A laugh burst from Delly's lips. "I thought your pooch might have something more than to do with eating a lot of beans, but didn't want to pry. Seems like we're being over run by babies. Zeke must be pulling his hair out."

With baby Alice fed and clothed in a gown another emigrant generously gave them, Delly joined the others beside the grave of her friend. Clouds gathered overhead as thunder rolled in the distance. How fitting that the funeral of Alice Johnson should be overcast.

The Johnson family stood opposite her clustered in grief. They'd lost two family members while Delly gained one. She gazed into the baby's face. How unfair. What made her family different from the others? Tragedy often struck without warning, yet they'd been spared the heartache of death.

She choked back a cry, handed the baby to Sadie, then gathered her skirts and dashed for the wagon as the first thud of dirt fell on Alice's wooden casket.

Her lungs burned by the time she climbed into the wagon and collapsed on a pile of blankets. Tears left a fiery path down her cheeks, and she swiped them away with the back of her hand. No more crying. This land didn't allow for weakness. She'd started the journey optimistic and full of dreams. Half-way through, she sat in the back of a wagon smaller than the shack she'd lived in before, all her worldly possessions piled around her. She kicked the nearest crate and heard the tinkle of her new tea set.

"Delly?"

"I'm here, Zeke."

He climbed in beside her. "Are you all right?" He peered at her with such concern that Delly's sobs started anew.

"I'm just having a fit." She sniffed. "I'm not cut out for this life. I thought I was, but look at me. Crippled and whining; that's all I've done for the last few weeks."

"Your leg is getting stronger every day. You'll barely have a limp. We're past the half-way mark and luckier than most." He wiped her tears away with his thumbs.

"This trail is tough, I won't deny that, but God will see us through and give us the strength to endure. You whine all you want. When we get home, your smile will be so big, it'll block out the sun."

26

The emigrants reached the fork where the trail split for travelers to choose California or Oregon. Ten wagons took the turn toward California. Zeke's heart ached as they left. He'd tried dissuading them, letting them know they had no one qualified enough to lead them across the desert. But they'd heard the way was easier, and preferable, to climbing the mountains. Their determination won over his knowledge and reason. He shrugged. The way would be marked by the wagons that had gone before. Hopefully, they'd find the sparse water holes.

He turned to Luke. "That's it then. I tried giving them half of their money back. Some took it, a couple didn't. God be with them. They'll need Him." He glanced at the range of mountains ahead of them. His own train would have it hard, but there'd be grass and water for the stock. Something the desert couldn't provide.

Delly stood off to the side, her gaze fixed on the group that left. Zeke suspected she felt the same as he did. He'd get her to Oregon in one piece or die trying. Her lapses into crying fits of weakness bothered him. She seemed to have lost the spunk he'd admired from the first moment he saw her. He tugged on his hat brim and spurred his horse onward. She'd get that spark back. All she needed was rest. At least that's what he kept telling himself.

Now, she had a newborn and one on the way, not to mention Luke proudly told him Sadie was expecting. Whether Zeke wanted to be or not, he had a ready-made family to look out for and support. Only a scoundrel would walk away.

He'd tell Delly to hand over the deed. She could throw a fit if she wanted, but if Zeke was going to resume responsibility for the children, he'd need them under the same roof. Like it or not, Delly was going to have to marry him once they reached Oregon.

Ben Johnson shuffled by, his big hand latched onto his daughter's small one. What would he do now? Marry again or try raising Abby on his own? Zeke wouldn't want to try caring for a child without a woman's help. He'd be as lost as a kitten among wolves.

~

They camped on the banks of a small creek. Delly tried catching up on laundry, never-ending now with baby Alice, but the alkali deposits in the water didn't do much to get rid of the dinginess. Just like her spirits. Weighed down and stained.

The baby slept on a blanket beneath a tree. Delly stood on tip-toes so she could see over the rise where Sadie made supper. Scents of roasting meat drifted to her, and her stomach rumbled. She ought to help, but the ever present exhaustion weighed on her. She tossed the last shirt into the laundry basket then lay next to Alice and closed her eyes. Just for a moment.

A shadow fell across her face. She bolted up and smoothed the hair from her face. Ira Bodine scowled over her. She should never have fallen asleep or let down her guard. Not knowing Bodine had to still be out there somewhere.

"Another surprise?" His gaze roamed over her. "I'd hoped to catch you with your pretty little daughter, but babies fetch a good price too." He pulled a derringer from the pocket of his vest. "Let's go."

"Mr. Bodine…"

His expression hardened. "They'll be calling you to eat soon, and I'd rather not be found. I'm afraid your wagon master may feel the need to play gunfighter and call me out. Things could get ugly." He waved the gun toward the bushes. "Grab the child and let's go."

Heart pounding harder than a herd of stampeding cattle, Delly stooped to lift the baby. Should she cry for help? No, Bodine would have no qualms about pulling the trigger, and she didn't want to risk the baby's—her new daughter's—life. In the space of a few weeks, Alice had become very precious to her, gaining weight and strength, despite her early start in life. Delly sighed and stalked ahead of Bodine. She'd do what he ordered; until the opportunity to escape presented itself.

"I'm glad to see your limp has improved.

Barely noticeable now. And your hair has grown." He jabbed her in the back with his weapon. "You're still quite fetching, despite the rigors of living out here. Get on the smaller horse."

Using her apron, Delly made a sling to carry the baby across the front of her. Alice woke and cried as Delly swung herself onto the saddle.

"Shut the kid up or leave it here. The wolves won't mind."

Her mouth fell open at his crudeness. She thought of her crutch left beside the creek and wanted to bash him in the head with it. She rarely used it anymore, but Sadie insisted she keep it close in case her leg tired. Alice's cries increased in volume. Delly rocked and tried to shush her before Bodine made good on his threat.

He mounted his horse, grabbed the reins to the one Delly rode, and set off at a gallop. For an hour, the baby's wails reverberated against Delly's eardrums. What had started out as hunger cries turned into a full-outrage fest. "Shhh, Alice. Hush now."

Bodine halted and held out his hand. In the other he held a pistol. "I warned you. Now give the brat to me."

"No. You'll have to shoot me." Delly tightened her hold. "What did you expect? You took us with no way for me to feed her. She's less than a month old. She isn't mine so I have no milk for her. Let us down, and I'll try to pacify her with water."

"I don't think so. Hand her to me."

"No!" This could not be happening. Would there be a day out here where evil didn't intrude, intent on stealing every morsel of happiness from Delly's life?

"I'm warning…" He glanced over her head, cursed, then urged the horses on.

Delly glanced over her shoulder and smiled. A cloud of dust hovered on the horizon. Untying her face rag, she let it fall to the ground, a splash of sunshine among the darkness of the approaching night. Zeke might be unhappy with her, but there's no way he'd leave her in the hands of a man like Ira Bodine.

"Mr. Bodine." Delly hefted the baby more securely across her chest. "I can't continue at this pace."

"You have no choice."

"Unless you want to arrive with damaged merchandise, I need to rest. If we don't stop, I'm going to fall off this horse."

He swore and stopped. A valley lay to the right, the creek they'd left wound through it. Stiff rock faces rose on their left. "Give me the child's blanket."

"She'll be cold."

"Give me something of hers. I don't care what." He held out his hand. Delly untied her bonnet and gave it to him. He frowned. "Now give me the child."

"No." Her arms tightened around the sleeping infant.

"I will give her back. I'm just using her to insure that you don't leave." He wiggled his fingers. "If you weren't worth so much gold, I'd rethink my plan. I never figured you for a shrew."

"You don't know anything about me." She handed Alice to him, every nerve on end. She wanted nothing more than to keep the baby close and run away.

Bodine rode to where the path they followed divided, dropped the bonnet, then turned back to Delly. "Here." He handed her Alice, then headed down the hill and to the creek below them. Relief flooded through her, and she dropped a kiss on the baby's face.

When they stopped, Bodine slid from his horse and pulled a paper-wrapped parcel from his saddlebag. "You're disgustingly dirty, and the men's pants do nothing for you. Clean up in the creek and put this on." He tossed the package to her.

"What is it?"

"Strip down, wash up, and get dressed." He pulled her from the horse. "I advise you to do what I tell you at all times. Otherwise, this darling infant girl will be left behind." He crossed his arms.

"You're crazy." Delly refused to flinch beneath his stare. "Does it make you feel big to threaten a child? Strong to intimidate a woman?" She laid the baby on a patch of grass, stripped to her under garments, then waded into the frigid waters.

A muscle jumped in his jaw. His fists clenched. "Watch your tongue, woman, or you'll arrive at our destination sporting a few bruises."

Using the sand from the creek bottom, she scrubbed her body and scalp. How dare he threaten her and Alice? When Zeke showed up, he'd give the gambling man the what for. "Hand me the dress, Mr. Bodine."

He laughed. "It's silk. Not something that will hold up in water. Your undergarments are sufficient for now." He leaned against a tree and lit a cigar. "I can't believe you allowed yourself to get in a family way." His gaze flicked to her stomach. "Seems you're not the virtuous woman you claim to be."

Taking a deep breath, Delly marched from the creek, refusing to give him the satisfaction of seeing her cower beneath her clinging bloomers and bodice. A quarter moon and some cloud cover blocking the stars made full sight impossible, and for that she gave thanks. She lifted the garment he'd ordered her to wear, and grimaced.

Blood red silk, almost black beneath the moon light. She slipped it over her head.

"Now off with the wet undergarments."

She opened her mouth to protest and clamped her lips closed when he raised his eyebrows. She shimmied out of her under things.

The dress fit closer than anything she'd ever worn before and slid over her like warm water, then stuck to her damp skin in places she'd rather it wouldn't. Sheer lace trimmed an indecently low neckline. Her face heated as much from anger as embarrassment. "Readying me for my new job so soon, Mr. Bodine? It's a bit inappropriate for traveling out here, wouldn't you say? Besides, I'm cold."

He tossed her a black lace shawl. "You're as lovely as I imagined you would be. Once you got out of the slum clothes. I know a doctor that can take care of the temporary problem of another brat on its way." He reached out and tugged a curl. "Pity you cut your hair, but it's growing back quickly. Already past your shoulders." His eyes darkened.

"I can give you the world, Mrs. Williams. I've more money than you've dreamed of having or can hope to obtain as a rancher's wife. Be mine, and I'll spare you the degradation of working in a gambling hall. Men will flock from miles around to pluck gold at your feet."

"Dirty money doesn't excite me."

"Hand over the deed, I'll give it to the man who hired me, and we'll have enough money to live richer than you'd ever imagine."

The man who hired him? Poor Ezra hadn't really known where the real danger lay. Who had he spoken to during his last night of card playing?

"Why?" Bodine was crazy. "You don't know me, Mr. Bodine. You can't possibly be in love with me. Why am I so important to you?" She crossed her arms in front of her in a vain attempt to cover up. No undergarments and a silk dress left her feeling naked.

He pulled a cigar from his vest pocket and rolled it in his fingers. "At first I saw the value in selling you, but now … well, it would be nice to settle somewhere with a lovely woman by my side."

"It will never happen."

"You'd choose the hard life of a farmer over a wealthy lifestyle?

Delly squared her shoulders. "Given the chance? In a heart beat."

"Your choice. Grab the brat and get mounted." He stalked away.

She took her time tying Alice around her neck

and left her old clothing behind. *Lord, please let Zeke see through Bodine's trick of leading them in the wrong direction.* She adjusted the sling and climbed wearily on her horse.

The wind plastered the wet silk to her skin, and she shivered. She kept an eye on the rock outcroppings and thick brush. An opportunity for escape would present itself. It had too. She wrapped her arms tightly around the sling in front of her, drawing warmth from the baby. She should've shoved her out of sight the moment Bodine's shadow stretched across her.

Despite the fast pace the outlaw insisted they maintain, Delly's head drooped. She yelped as she started to slide from the horse. Bodine stopped, let loose a string of words that burned her ear drums, then stopped and helped her to the ground. "We'll camp here. No fire though, and keep that kid quiet."

Delly's legs buckled when she slid from the horse's back. She landed on her knees in hard dirt and dry grass. Bodine groaned, mumbled something about her ruining the dress, then marched a few feet away. Fatigue heavier than the horse she rode in on weighed her shoulders. She wanted to cry along with the waking infant.

A canteen landed at her feet. Grateful for the refreshment, she twisted the lid and took a gulp. Liquid fire poured down her throat and stole her breath. She gasped. "What is this?"

"Whiskey. It ought to give you some strength and warm you up. Be grateful, I shared." Bodine looped the reins to his horse over a tree branch. "Give some to the brat if it'll keep her quiet."

"I will not." Delly forced the words past her tortured throat.

"Bodine!" Zeke's voice rang from somewhere above them. Delly's heart leaped. "Let Delly and the baby go, and I won't have to kill you."

Bodine dove for cover, pulling a pistol from the saddlebag he'd removed from his horse. "You'll have to come and get her. Keep shooting and a ricochet might hit her or the child. Your gamble."

With one arm wrapped around Alice, Delly crawled into the bushes, drawing herself in as far as possible. He'd come for her. She knew he would.

What kind of a shot was the gambler? *Lord, let Zeke have the advantage.* Alice's whimpering erupted into a full-scale scream, stretching Delly's already taut nerves. Her stomach tightened, her throat burned, and she fought back tears.

Bodine approached at a running zig-zag crouch, dodging bullets that seemed to rain from the sky. It became obvious he searched for Delly, lured by the sound of Alice's screams. She refused to remain his captive. She tucked the dress into the waistband of her bloomers to allow more freedom of movement, and wincing against the rocks digging into her knees, headed as fast as she could toward the spot she thought Zeke would be.

"Mrs. Williams!" Bodine stepped out and blocked her path. He leveled his pistol at her head. She met his gaze as her blood ran cold. "You should have chosen me."

A shot rang out.

Bodine glanced at the spreading stain across his purple vest. His eyes widened. A drop of blood appeared at the corner of his mouth. His knees buckled and he fell to the ground. Delly stared for a moment at his lifeless body, then sprang to her feet.

~

No sooner had Bodine fallen, then Zeke slid down the rock face. "Delly!"

She ran full tilt into him. Wrapping his arms around her and the baby, he slid against the mountain. "You do keep a man on his toes, don't you?" His gaze flicked to her dress. "What are you wearing?"

"Something Bodine told me to wear. Is he dead?"

"I'll check." He smiled. "The dress is becoming, but I suggest you only wear it in your wagon."

"I'd rather burn it." She plucked it away from her and grimaced.

"That can be arranged too. Stay here." He released her then strode slowly to where Bodine lay. After rolling the man over, it was clear he no longer lived. Regardless of the circumstances, taking another man's life left a hole in Zeke, but he'd do it again if it meant the safety of his family.

He hefted the man over his shoulder then slung him on the back of his horse. The least they could do was bury him. If they didn't locate the man's family once they reached Oregon, they were now richer by two riding horses.

Taking the animal's reins in one hand, he slung the other arm over Delly's shoulders. "Woman, you do manage to find trouble. Life isn't boring with you around."

27

Delly sat in the wagon's driver's seat and stared dubiously at yet another rickety appearing wooden bridge. The oxen balked. She sighed and handed the reins to Sadie, then climbed down and grabbed their harness. "You guys pitch a fit every time we have to cross a bridge. Good thing it's our turn at the end of the line, 'cause they'd sure put us here if we weren't."

They tugged against her. "Forget pulling a plow. I'm going to shoot you when we get to Oregon and feed your meat to the Indians." Her muscles screamed as she tried pulling them behind her. That failing, she put her shoulder against one of the animal's flanks and pushed. How many more of these bridges did they have to cross?

"Get a switch and swat 'em," the oldest Oglesby boy yelled. "Show them who's boss."

Delly rolled her eyes. What did he think she was trying to do? "Dorcas, toss me one of the carrots we have left, then keep a tight hold on Alice and Sarah." Holding the orange vegetable in her hand, she dangled it in front of the animals. They snorted and took a step forward. "It's working!" The animals lunged forward. One snatched the carrot from her hand, ate it, then refused to move any further.

"Goodness." She peered over the bridge rail, fully expecting the structure to collapse beneath them. The creek ran rapidly over rounded pebbles and moss-covered rocks between two steep banks. The water didn't appear to be too deep. Maybe she should back up and try driving them across the stream. She shook her head. They'd never make it down one side and up the other without folding the wagon in half.

She dug her heels in and yanked on the reins. "Come on! Whip 'em, Sadie."

"I am." The crack of the whip snapped over her head. "It don't do any good with these stupid beasts."

The oxen tossed their heads and ripped the reins through Delly's gloved hands. A shot rang out from the Johnson wagon, startling the team who then dashed past Delly, slamming into her on their way.

Her heels flew over her head. She sailed over the split-rail of the bridge into icy water. She screamed and flailed against her fear of drowning before discovering the water only reached chest high. If the trip to Oregon didn't cure her from her fear of water nothing would.

Mortification heated her face. Her blood boiled. She glared at Joshua Oglesby who leaned over the railing.

"I'm sorry. I was only trying to help. Are you all right?"

"What were you thinking?" She grabbed hold of a protruding tree root to prevent herself from being swept downstream. "I could've been killed."

"I said I was sorry. You were holding everyone up. I thought the shot would startle the animals into moving, and it did. Do you want me to come down there and help you?"

"No, I do not!" Delly retied her sodden bonnet on her head. "I can climb out myself." Her feet slipped on the slippery bottom, and she disappeared beneath the water. Pushing clear, she coughed and sputtered. Zeke and Luke laughed from the riverbank. "Go ahead, gentlemen. Laugh until you're blue in the face for all I care. Serve you both right if I got washed downstream." She marched toward them and reached for a small bush to pull herself up.

~

Zeke's laugh cut off in mid-snort when Delly emerged from the creek, her flannel shirt and men's britches clinging to every wet curve. The Oglesby boys stared with open mouths, Luke turned his head, and Zeke's cheeks burned.

Sophia giggled from where she stood beside her wagon, arms crossed, a smirk on her face. Ben Johnson stood next to the woman, his eyes wide. Looked like Sophia might've hooked her attention on someone else.

Zeke cleared his throat. "You look like a drowned rat." An unclothed one.

"Don't bust a rib laughing." She bumped him

with her shoulder as she strode past.

"Uh, wait up." Zeke whipped his shirt off his back and wrapped it around her. She glanced down, her cheeks reddening.

"Still funny? Now that everyone on the train got a really good look?"

"If you wore a skirt like women are supposed to, you wouldn't be exposing yourself."

She crossed her arms. "No, I would've been dragged under the water and drowned. Now, you're the one standing there unclothed." High spots of color appeared on her cheeks and she turned her head. After pulling her soggy bonnet from her head, Delly smacked him with it before heading toward the wagon. Sadie stared with wide-eyes and one hand covering her mouth.

Zeke laughed. "Disaster follows my sister-in-law wherever she goes. Looks like I've found a new pet name for her."

Delly whirled. "Don't you dare call me that!"

"Okay." He held up his hands in surrender then called out to the other wagons. "Camp here tonight, folks."

Dried and wearing a calico dress, Delly joined Zeke beside the fire. She stuck her pert nose in the air and avoided his glance. He grinned and touched her arm. "Delly…"

"Well, well. Look what we got here, Roy. A pretty little quadroon." Two men approached Sadie, cutting her off from the wagon.

Zeke stood, keeping a hand on Delly's shoulder to make sure she stayed on the stump and didn't try anything foolish. With her dander up after her dousing, a man couldn't be too careful. "Once I go over there, find Luke and tell him to stay out of sight. Ask Hiram to come here."

"Where's your people, girl?" The larger of the men, wearing stained buckskins and his face hiding behind a scruffy, ink-colored beard, towered over Sadie.

"Over there." She motioned with her head toward Zeke.

"Can I help you two?" He sidled between Sadie and the strangers. "Go help with supper." She nodded and skittered away.

The man squared his shoulders. "We're looking for a runaway. Got reason to believe he's hitched up with one of these trains heading west."

"No slaves here. I'm sorry you've wasted your time." Zeke held out his hand. "I'm the wagon master, Ezekiel Williams."

"Hank." The man ignored the offered hand. "The one we're looking for is a big buck. At least six feet tall. A blacksmith by trade. There's a reward for his return. A good one."

"I've already told you he's not here."

"I don't believe you. The train that went to California said you had such a man with you. That he'd hooked up with a little light-skinned woman." Hank lifted his rifle.

Zeke reached for the pistol at his waist as the second man, Roy, stepped forward. "Look, you two…"

"He ain't here." Sadie joined them. "He did travel with us for a while. Got me with child and headed on." She wrapped her arms around her stomach and looked downtrodden.

Roy grinned, revealing tobacco-stained teeth. "Then I reckon we'll take you in trade."

"She's not for sale." Delly stepped beside Sadie and squared her shoulders. "She's been freed for a long time. Would you like to see her papers?"

"Can't read." He continued to eye Sadie. "You know what they do to runaways, don't you, girl?"

She nodded, keeping her head bowed.

"Well, then, reckon we'll be on our way. Probably meet up with y'all at Fort Boise." He nodded to his companion, and they disappeared into the trees.

Zeke reached forward and grabbed Sadie as her knees buckled. He lowered her to the ground. She buried her face in her hands. "It's best Luke stay out of sight for a while," Zeke told her.

She nodded. "How long?"

He shrugged. "Until we're sure those men have gone. He'll be all right." He glanced at Delly. "Take her to the wagon, will you?"

He watched them leave, Delly's arms around her friend. He'd suspected Luke of being a runaway. But seeing evidence of the fact caused his stomach to plummet faster than a waterfall and with as much force. He didn't condone slavery, and it wasn't practiced in the west, but what was he to do legally? Morally?

By hiding Luke, was he stealing or giving a life freedom? He shook his head, not understanding what Luke's hiding in the west might entail. But whatever it was, Zeke couldn't turn in his friend.

He whirled as a twig snapped and peered

through the gathering dusk at Luke's face. "What are you doing here?"

"Came to get some supplies and say bye to Sadie. I'll catch up to y'all before you hit those mountains. If something happens, and I ain't there, take care of Sadie and my baby, will you?" His eyes glistened.

Zeke clapped him on the shoulder, touched by his friend's trust. "They're family, Luke. I'll take good care of them. You'll be with us. Don't fear." In the span of a few months, he'd gained a sister-in-law, a passel of children, and an infant, with another on the way. Suddenly his cabin seemed mighty small. Amazing what time could do. He reached for his rifle. "Take this."

"No." Luke shook his head. "I'm a dead man if I get caught with a weapon. I'll make do with my knife. It'll be easier to toss away if I get caught." He wrapped a quilt around his shoulders, and slung another blanket, loaded with supplies, hobo style over his back. "See you." He blended into the shadows as footsteps approached.

"God speed, my friend."

28

"Ma, look." Junior pointed to the ridge above them.

The figures of several Indian braves stood outlined against the setting sun. A cold sweat formed on Delly's brow, and she spilled some of the coffee grounds she'd meant for the pot. Indians who hovered out of range didn't seem as friendly as the others they'd met. "Find your uncle and let him know, if he doesn't know already." They'd just pulled the wagons into a circle and started supper. As she stirred the rice, her attention reverted back to the ominous sight.

"That scares me." Sadie dumped in some greens she'd found growing along the trail. "Them just sitting there watching us. Makes my skin tingle. Why don't they come up and say howdy like the others have done?"

"I don't know." Delly shuddered. "They're like ghosts."

"Believe me, they're very human." Zeke pulled up a stool and poured himself a cup of coffee. "And we're in their territory."

"What do they want?" Delly moved the ring holding the pot away from the hottest part of the flames.

"I don't know."

"Can we shoot and scare them off?"

"That would most likely make them mad." He took a swig of his drink. "I know it's hot, but no one sleeps outside tonight. I've already got the men keeping watch in shifts. Junior and I will go first."

Delly served him a plate of beans and rice. Her hand trembled as she handed the food to him. What would they do if the Indians attacked? They'd lost over half their train at the split to California. With Luke gone, their number of able-bodied men numbered ten, counting Junior. Delly closed her eyes and prayed. *Lord, have your angels guard over us. If we have to fight, let your warriors fight alongside us.*

What would she do if something happened to Zeke? They might not be speaking to each other outside of good manners and practicality, but there was no denying her heart's yearning for more. Zeke Williams was everything Delly wanted in a man, and more. If sharing a homestead with him was all she'd get, she'd take even that small thing, God willing.

As the sun set over the mountain, she helped Sadie cleaned up after dinner, her gaze straying to the line of warriors. What were they waiting for?

Her gaze settled on the faces of her children. On Zeke's. The muscle tic in his jaw showed her he wasn't as relaxed as he tried to appear. She clenched her fist to keep from caressing the tension away.

~

Zeke jerked upright with the first shout as morning rose over the mountain. The second war cry spurred the others to action. Whoops, screams, and gunfire took the place of sizzling bacon and baking bread. Little Alice wailed from inside the wagon.

"Zeke?" Delly climbed from the buckboard.

"Stay inside." He tossed a rifle to Junior who crouched beside the wheel, and reached for his pistol.

"But…"

"Stay in the wagon!" He tried to soften the look he gave her, and judging by the stricken look on her face, failed. "Please. For once in your stubborn life, do as I ask."

"But I can shoot." Delly planted fists on her hips.

"Then shoot from inside." He grabbed Junior and pulled him down beside him as Delly darted under cover. "They're going for the stock."

The canvas parted over their heads when Delly poked out the barrel of another gun. Zeke smiled, relieved she'd listened for once. He couldn't worry about her *and* the others.

Men ran, ducked, shot, and were fired upon as war broke out between redskin and white man. The Indians rode past in a blur, making it difficult to get a head count. The dust kicked up by their horses hung in the air and decreased visibility. Zeke and Junior ran low to the ground and took cover behind some boulders.

"I'll shoot, you load." Zeke took the rifle from the boy's shaking hands. "You all right?"

Junior nodded, his face pale. "So scared I can't even spit."

"It's smart to be afraid at a time like this." As fast as he shot, Junior reloaded. The Indians hung off the side of their mounts, making themselves difficult to hit. Zeke stood, drew them from behind their shields, and fired before ducking again.

A scream rent the air. He glanced toward the wagon.

The side of the women's shelter resembled a pin cushion with arrows sticking from the sides. *Please, Lord, let them have taken cover behind the boxes.* A shot rang out, and a brave fell from his horse. *Good shot, Delly.* Continued gunfire coming from that direction let him know she was all right.

He stood to draw another brave out of hiding. An arrow took him in the shoulder and dropped him to his knees. Pain ripped through him.

Junior yelled his name, then grabbed the rifle and took his spot. Zeke shuffled closer to the rock and put a hand to his burning shoulder. Delly jumped from the wagon and dashed toward him, ridiculous in her britches and sunbonnet. A brave bore down on her and fear seized Zeke's heart. "Junior, watch out for your ma!"

The boy whirled and fired.

The brave fell at Delly's feet. Without pausing, she leaped over his body and knelt beside Zeke. "You're shot."

"I told you to stay in the wagon." He ground

the words through his pain.

"I can help."

"Not now." He shoved her down and turned back to the fight, shooting with his pistol.

The battle lasted close to an hour. Five Indians lay dead, and Zeke and another wounded. The other braves rode off, whooping, leaving behind their dead comrades. Zeke sagged with relief. His shirt stuck to him with blood and sweat. They'd been lucky.

"Wait here." Delly put a hand on his arm and raced back to the wagon, then returned with her medicine box. "This is going to hurt." She grasped the protruding arrow with both hands, and pulled.

Zeke gritted his teeth and groaned then fell back against the rock. His shoulder throbbed with a burning ache. "No kidding. You could have given me a minute to get my bearings."

She flashed him a shaky grin then poured whiskey over the wound, sending fire through his arm. She bandaged it with clean muslin. "I had to do it before I had a chance to think. Otherwise, I'm not sure I could've pulled it out. With a little rest, you'll be fine." She raised tear-filled eyes to his. Her chin quivered.

"What's wrong? You say it. I'll be fine. Especially with a pretty little gal like you taking care of me." Although her face so close to him, yet so unreachable hurt more than the hole in his shoulder.

"I thought we'd lost you. All I could think of when I saw you fall was getting to your side. We can't make it to Oregon without you."

He laughed. "Is that why you came running like a grizzly bear with a cub in trouble?" He had to be honest with himself. He wanted her to have come running because she loved him, not because he was their ticket to Oregon.

What if she did say she loved him? Would it take away his resolve not to care for another woman while traveling? Maybe. He was beginning to think his resolve with pure stupidity. So what if they were hitched? He was just as responsible for her and the children as if they were.

God, I've been a fool. He reached for her, fully intending to steal a kiss.

"Don't poke fun." She shoved against him, but he tightened his grip.

"You did good today. Shot like a real soldier. Junior too." He glanced to where the boy sat propped against the wagon wheel. Fatigue showed in every line of his body. "He did the work of a grown man."

"No twelve-year-old should have to shoot another man." Delly sniffed.

"Nobody should." Zeke's heart swelled with pride. Since Delly's encounter with the bear, the boy had done his best to walk the straight and narrow, only veering once to attend a poker game. The disappointed look on the faces of his sisters had put a stop to that once and for all.

"I once thought of joining the army," Junior spoke up. "But not any more. I don't take to killing. Whether it be it redskin or white." He struggled to his feet. "I'd best check on the stock. It's a heavy job with Luke gone. We've got the oxen, Zeke's horse, that scoundrel Bodine's horses, the goats, dogs, and a milk cow. We're getting richer by the day and it sure adds more work. Life was a mite easier when we were poor."

Thunder rumbled overhead. Rain fell in gentle drops, and Zeke pushed to his feet, chuckling. "Best I check on the others before I rest."

Junior's steps faltered and he turned, excitement making his eyes shine. "What about the Indian ponies? I've been hankering for a pony of my own. I was going to ask you for one of Bodine's, but I'd really like an Indian one."

Zeke shrugged. "If you can catch'em, they're yours."

The boy's exhaustion seemed to disappear, and Junior bolted past the wagon, lasso in hand, to where five pinto ponies left behind with their dead riders, grazed in a cluster.

Delly lifted her face to catch the welcome raindrops. A shadow moved beyond the perimeter of camp. Luke or Indians come back to retrieve their dead?

Zeke grabbed her arm. "Come on. Back to the wagon." What was taking Junior so long? Chances were good the Indians would be back to retrieve what they'd left, and no one should be out alone. He released the breath he held when Junior ran up, grasping the rope of a tan and white pony.

29

The next morning they crossed the Snake River into air so foul, Delly tried to hold her breath against the stench. Dead cattle, mules, and horses lay discarded beside the trail, providing a buffet for the circling buzzards.

By the time they stopped to camp, her stomach churned, and Sadie had already lost her breakfast. Zeke trotted his horse to their side.

"The train lost another mule. Ben Johnson lost an ox, so we've meat for another day or two. No telling how many more we'll lose before we're finished." A slow grin spread across his face. "Good news is, the scenery's about to improve—for Sadie that is." He inclined his head behind them.

A thinner, haggard, Luke sprinted toward them. Sadie climbed from the wagon and hitched her skirts to run. "Luke!" Tears streamed down her face as she threw herself into his arms.

Delly choked back a sob. "Should he be back?"

"Oh, I ain't leaving this woman's side no more," Luke stated, carrying his wife in his arms.

"Look how fat she's getting without me. Are you eating all the food?"

She hugged him. "I've saved a bit for you."

"I've scouted a head. Met up with Hiram and he stayed to see if he could find a better way, but tomorrow's going to be tough. No way to cross but over a rock ledge. Don't know how the animals are going to take to it."

Zeke removed his hat and ran a hand through his hair. "What happened to the bridge?"

"Fallen. The wagons will have to be taken apart and carried across in pieces."

Delly's shoulders sagged. *Would the hardship ever end? God, I'm losing hope and strength. Where's the Promise Land you said we'd receive?*

"I've done it before. It's a hard job, but doable." Zeke closed his eyes for a minute. "Instead of stopping here, we'll head on and stop there for the night. Get a head start on dismantling the wagons."

"I hid in the bushes during the Indian attack," Luke admitted hanging his head. "Couldn't do much more than watch and pray since I didn't have a gun."

Zeke clapped him on the shoulder. "You were there if we needed you."

"Yep, and that wagon train with them bounty hunters is a day or two ahead of us."

Delly's heart lifted. Her family was back together.

~

Delly stepped to the edge of the cliff and stared into a nightmare. A natural stone bridge, wide enough for one person, arced over a swift running creek. Fifteen feet below, water tumbled and roared over rocks, sending water spraying upward and washing over the bridge. More boulders towered around them. To her right, lay pieces of a wooden bridge, fallen and lying in the water. In the center of the creek, a flat rock, large enough to hold several people, jutted from the water. Occasionally, splashes covered the surface, wetting those standing there.

"Isn't there another way?" Her heart pounded in her throat.

"No," Zeke said. "This is the only way across."

Up and down the line others murmured, the sound washed away in the roar of the water. Delly trembled. "How do we get the stock across?"

"The wagons must be taken apart and carried across the rock island. Then the bottoms are put together, held in place with rope, and you cross to the other side using the wagon bed as a bridge. Lead the stock one at a time. Be glad we don't have to lower the stock by rope and pulley. We'll be doing that in a few days. Once we're across, we'll camp and reassemble the wagons. It's hard work. Anything you don't want to carry gets left here."

Zeke smiled and turned to the others. "This is the second time I've had to cross this way, folks. That wooden bridge never stands up against the current. Let's pull together and get across as quick as possible."

The women unloaded the wagons before putting together cold suppers for their families while the men did the heavy work of dismantling wagons. The sun began its descent as the last wagon and the larger stock crossed over, then the women began carrying gathering supplies.

With the sky tinted purple and grey above the mountain, and thunder rumbling in the distance, Delly took a deep shuddering breath and watched as the first woman shuffled her way across. When she reached the larger rock, she turned, grinned, and thrust her fist in the air.

Delly smiled and tied Alice across her chest. "Children, hold on to the back of my shirt. We'll make a chain." She felt her daughter's fist grip as they slid their feet across the wet rock. Her heart pounded in her ears.

Inch-by-inch she scooted one foot in front of the other. One of the children whimpered behind her. "We can do this," Delly said. "Keep your eyes on the opposite bank and pray. Look, others are waiting for us."

She followed her own advice, keeping her gaze glued to a stand of trees, and almost cried with relief upon reaching the other side. She untied the baby and handed her to Dorcas. "I'm going back for supplies. Have a seat by that tree and keep Alice on your lap."

The return trip was easier without the worry of a baby and children. Delly hopped onto the bank then loaded her arms as full as she could manage. "Sadie, balance the cymedicine box on top, would you?"

"Girl, you've piled too high. You can't see where to put your feet." Sadie set the box on the top quilt.

"All I have to do is put one foot in front of the other. Just point me in the right direction." Her moccasins rasped across the rock as she slid her feet.

Water cascaded over the bridge. She slipped and choked back a scream. Having lost her momentum, she didn't know where to step next. She froze, legs shaking, and tried to calm her rapid breathing. She glanced at the water rushing below her. The roar threatened to drown out all sound. People yelled for her to move forward. Adrenaline pricked her skin and stole her breath.

She shook her head. *I can't. I'll fall.* Her foolish pride had landed her in another predicament. Why hadn't she listened instead of piling her arms too high? Was she that lazy to cut her trips across? Waves of nausea pulsated through her abdomen and into her back. She closed her eyes against her dizziness and jerked when Zeke came up behind her and placed his good hand on her shoulders.

"Come on. I'm right behind you. Let me guide you." He pushed against her back, using his unwrapped arm to balance her.

"No. Stop it." She stiffened.

"You're holding everything up. You need to move." His breath tickled her ear. "It's raining upstream. The water will continue to rise until this rock is submerged."

"I can't." She forced the words through a tortured throat.

"If you don't, you'll have to toss everything you're carrying into the water, and I'll lift you in my arms."

"That would be wasteful. Besides, you're wounded."

He laughed. The sound warmed her. "One step at a time. Trust God, and trust me."

She nodded and took a step, secure in the fact that his strong hands wouldn't let her fall. One step led to another, and soon she collapsed on the opposite bank and let the supplies fall to the ground. "I could kiss your feet."

He laughed. "Later, if you're still so inclined. You stay here. Luke, Junior, and I will carry the rest."

"No problem." She fell backward onto the grass.

Dorcas handed her the baby. "You shouldn't have tried to carry so much, ma. You aren't a man, you know. You don't have to do everything."

Sufficiently chastised by a ten-year-old, Delly sat up to watch the others make their journey across. Dorcas was right. Delly didn't have to do everything herself. There were others, including God, willing to help. All she needed to do was accept. Could she give up a lifetime of habit to let someone else step in and lead the way once in a while? She didn't know, but knew she'd reached the point where she was willing to try.

One-by-one, the men carried across folded wagon bonnets, wheels, and tools. The creek continued to rise. Each wave sloshed higher on the rocks, splashing over their heads until the boys were drenched. Rain fell in a steady stream as the sky opened.

The younger of the two Oglesby boys slipped.

Luke shot out a hand to steady the boy, and Delly released the breath she hadn't been aware she held.

Delly noticed Zeke sitting against a tree. Worry and pain creased his face. She squatted beside him. "Your shoulder hurts, doesn't it? You did too much today. It won't heal if you don't rest it."

He waved away her words. "No help for it today. Every man was needed. Thank God, Luke came back when he did. I'm not sure we could've done it without him."

30

Fort Boise consisted of three fairly new buildings owned by the Hudson Bay Company. The only signs of life were a few company officials, some Frenchmen, and a lot of half-naked Indians. Delly didn't know what she'd expected, but it'd been more than this. Something that resembled civilization.

She sighed and stopped the wagon next to the small ferry beside a wooden dock. Zeke rode past and approached one of the company officials. He conversed with the man for a few minutes then returned.

"They do carry a small supply of foodstuffs, and the Indians are friendly and willing to trade." He grinned up at Delly. "The cost for the ferry is three dollars. The river is safe enough to swim the stock. We'll camp here tonight and leave in the morning. There's a squaw over there with fresh salmon to sell."

"Salmon!" She clamored over the side. "Maybe they've got vegetables too."

"Don't forget to buy as much dry foods as you can. Make sure it's enough for several months. We won't have time to put in a garden. Not before winter sets in."

Delly lifted the baby into her arms. "Come on, Sadie. Let's buy some of that fish before it's gone. Then we'll do an inventory of our supplies before we hit the store. Maybe they'll have some of the salmon smoked." Her spirits lifted for the first time in days. Amazing what a change in diet could do for a person.

"And eggs." Sadie shooed away a clucking chicken.

She turned as Zeke strode by with cages of chickens. "Are they ours?"

"Yep. Three hens and a rooster."

Delly laughed. "A milk cow and chickens. Why, we're positively rich."

He winked. "Yes, we are. You go on in and get what you need. I'll be back to settle the account."

Delly headed toward the trading post, then stopped. She and Zeke had spoken as if they were husband and wife. What was she thinking? Those were his chickens. Her cow. His oxen. Not theirs. The thought stung her throat. When had she grown so comfortable around him that he fit like a fine leather glove?

She pushed aside a worn buffalo robe serving as a door and stepped into the dim recesses of a smoke-filled room. Her eyes watered. Despite its less than savory appearance, the store carried any dry goods they might need, including a few bolts of calico.

She fingered the fabrics, relishing the bit of civilization the fort had to offer. The pink would look lovely on the little girls, and that blue almost made her salivate. Green for the boys. A bolt of brown wool would make pants for the men. She handed over almost the last of their coins, still refusing to use but very little of what Zeke insisted she use.

The grizzly bearded man behind the counter spit a wad of tobacco into a brass spittoon at his feet. The sound dinged through the room. "Y'all headed to Oregon, I hear."

"That's right." Delly glanced at Sadie who raised her eyebrows. Where else would they be headed?

"Pity. Heard tell a family died last month crossing the mountain. Another turned around and headed back east. Doubt they made it across the desert." He tallied Delly's purchases. "You'll have a rough time of it with that baby."

"We'll be fine." She straightened her shoulders. "My son will be by to get our supplies."

She stepped into the brightness of the summer day. Doomsayers gave her the creeps. "Sadie, what day is it?"

"I'm not sure. Sometime in August, I think."

"We're way overdue for a Bible reading. Zeke said we'd be here for the night. After supper, I'll be continuing our read in Genesis." She shuddered, thinking of what the storekeeper had said. "I need some comfort after that man's worrisome words."

She stared at the range of mountains looming a few days ahead of them. She wrapped her arms tighter around Alice, determined they'd all make it safely across if it took her last ounce of strength. Which it might, considering the hardships so far.

Ben Johnson strolled by, Sophia Miller clutching his arm. Delly sighed. Looked like there might be another wedding soon. Two people eager to find someone to share their burden with. Her heart ached with missing Alice. She'd looked forward to being neighbors with her dear friend. Could she befriend Sophia after all the animosity between the two? She'd try. That's all she could promise.

A shout echoed from camp, and two men darted past her, spurring Delly to increase her pace. "What in the world?"

Someone had constructed a make-shift corral from bent saplings and spare wood. Luke stood in the center with a blindfold over Junior's Indian pony, while Zeke whispered in the animal's twitching ear.

Luke motioned for Junior to climb onto the pony's back before he quickly whipped off the blindfold. A second later, Junior laid flat on his back in the pine needles. Delly's heart sprang to her throat.

She stepped forward and stopped when Zeke laid a hand on her shoulder. "Get up, son. Show him you're boss. Be consistent. He'll get used to the weight on his back." He strode forward to lift a saddle. "Use this."

Delly's heart froze.

~

"Hold the saddle under his nose." Zeke stepped

back as Junior followed his directions. "Let him get used to the smell." The pony snorted and drew back. "Be patient. He has to trust you."

After several minutes the pony no longer shied away from the strange object. "Now, put it on his back. Luke will hold him still."

Junior cast a wide-eyed glance in Zeke's direction and took a deep breath. The horse snorted and tried pulling away. "I don't understand. The Indian rode him. Maybe he doesn't like white men."

"You do smell different. He'll get use to you, and he's probably never had a saddle on before." Zeke leaned against a tree beside Delly. "Don't worry, he'll figure it out."

"I'm worried about injury."

"Let him grow up. Knowing how to break a horse is a valuable skill."

"That's easy for you to say. You didn't promise his father you'd take care of him."

"I'm the only father he's got now, and I say he can do this."

She hmmphed and crossed her arms.

Junior finally got a foot in the stirrup, held for a minute, then slung his leg over. The horse immediately bucked him off, landing the boy hard in a cloud of dirt. Zeke laughed. "Again."

"Are you trying to kill me?" Junior struggled to his feet.

"Persistence is what it takes to train an animal." Zeke moved forward to help him to his feet. "And this pony has a lot of spirit."

Junior grinned, and slapped his hat more firmly on his head. "You just gave him his name, uncle.

I'm calling this pony, Spirit."

The sun had set and campfires doused by the time, Zeke felt Spirit had accepted Junior enough to be ridden. He helped the bruised and aching boy into his bedroll then slid into his own under the wagon. His mind immediately moved on to the next few day's journey.

Soon, they'd be crossing the mountains. The most dangerous part of their journey. *Lord, help them.*

The last trip he'd taken, five people succumbed to the cold of the mountains. And they'd left only two weeks later. May God forgive him, but that wouldn't happen again. They'd keep moving no matter how tired the people were.

A bottle shattered. An Indian staggered through the wagon circle. Glass from the whiskey bottle winked from the fire pit. Zeke shook his head. Forts were an easy place to get the fire water, and unfortunately, too many of the natives succumbed to its liquid siren song. Often with fatal results.

31

Delly stared out the wagon bonnet at the towering Cascade Mountains. In one hand she held her tattered britches, so holey as to be almost indecent, in the other an equally ragged skirt. Around her shoulders, she'd draped a thick quilt against the chill of the morning.

"What are you looking at?" Zeke stopped by on his morning rounds.

"The mountain." She held up her worn pants. "I can't decide whether to wear these disgusting britches or throw them in the fire and be done with them."

"Let me help by telling you what to expect. You'll be walking. I'll be driving the wagon. These mountains are so steep the wagons are going to be sliding all over the place, especially with the recent rains. Anyone not driving will be walking and climbing over fallen trees and boulders. They'll be fighting their way through thick brush."

"Why can't we follow behind the wagons?" His words created an imagery that left dread in Delly.

The only good point was, once over these mountains, they were finished. Home.

Zeke shook his head. "Too much of a danger of the wagons sliding backwards. It's happened before; people crushed from a wagon sliding down the mountain. You stay out of the way."

Delly nodded. "I'll patch the pants the best I can."

An hour later, with drizzle wetting every available surface, the women and children stepped onto the poor excuse for a trail that cut through pine, fir, and cedar trees. Redwoods grew up and over, forming a canopy that almost shut out the weak light of the sun.

Delly craned her neck. She grew dizzy with the height of the trees and transferred her attention to the trail in front of her. *Thank you, God, I chose to wear pants.* How the wagons would ever make it across the muddy rock strewn trail, she could only guess.

Her feet slipped in the mud, and she fell to her knees. She grimaced as her hand plunged into a rotting log full of grubs and leaves. Wagons bounced and slammed over holes as they rolled slowly past.

She eyed a beautiful mirror in an ornate frame tossed carelessly into the bushes. Its weight too much to justify taking it along. Books with mildewed pages, rusted pots and pans, fancy dresses, and small furniture peeked through the thick brush, quickly being reclaimed by Mother Nature. Just as she would be if she collapsed here.

Pushing to her feet, she brushed against a tree.

It's water soaked branches dumped water down the neck of her slicker. Delly slapped the offending branch away and glanced over her shoulders. The others didn't seem to be faring much better. With Sadie's increasing bulk, she seemed to struggle the most. Delly slowed her speed and slipped an arm around her friend's waist. They might as well struggle together.

Someone shouted a warning from above them. Delly looked up and gasped.

~

The wagon in front of him slid backwards and picked up speed as Zeke watched, helpless to stop its disastrous descent. The driver cried out.

Zeke set the brake on the wagon he drove and leaped from the seat. He scoured the brush until he found two logs that would fit snugly behind the wheels. As he worked, he glanced continuously at the slipping wagon, praying the mules pulling it would grab a foothold.

His wagon as secure as he could make it, he dashed to try and prevent the catastrophe he knew would come. Luke obviously had the same idea. Together they tugged on the reins, yanking them out of the hysterical woman's hands.

"Get out of the wagon!" Zeke dug his booted feet into the mud. "Where's your husband? I told the men to drive today."

"It's his turn to help drive the stock. My kids are in the back!"

"Take them with you. Now!" The muscles in his arms groaned with agony. The healing arrow wound, flamed. The woman scrambled over the seat and into the wagon bed.

Luke strained with him, sweat pouring from his brow. "We can't hold this. It's going to crash into our own families."

Zeke peered around the bonnet. Delly's face stood out white against the brown of the mountain. Their gazes locked, and he nodded, hoping she'd understand his silent command and obey.

She wrapped her arms tighter around the sling carrying Alice and dashed to where the rest of their family waited. They slid down the hill and into the brush. Zeke closed his eyes for a moment, relieved, and the fear in his heart for his family's safety lessened.

The reins slipped as his feet dug deep furrows into the sodden earth. "You're right. Melvin! Back those wagons up."

Junior sprinted to their wagon and launched himself into the seat, taking Zeke's heart with him. Ben Johnson yelled and whipped his oxen to start their progress backward, while the older Oglesby boy did the same.

Zeke and Luke lost their battle to retain control and the reins slipped through their hands. Zeke felt the leather's lash through his gloves.

The wagon hurtled toward the others. The mules struggled to maintain a foothold and brayed in alarm as their legs were pulled out from under them. The whites of their eyes shone against their muddy coats.

The wagon teetered on the cliff. Caught on the trunks of young saplings. In what seemed like slow motion, it tottered and went over, dragging the mules with it where it once again stopped against a massive redwood tree.

Zeke and Luke whipped knives from their belts and dashed after it. With frantic sawing motions, they struggled to free the mules from their harness. By the time the third mule was free, the tree loosened itsr tenuous hold and the wagon barreled down the mountainside. The last mule screamed in pain as the wagon shattered against boulders before finally coming to a rest at the bottom.

The family who owned the wagon huddled at the top of the cliff. The woman moaned over the loss of their possessions.

Zeke replaced his knife in its holder and made his way to the grieving family. "Luke and I will go see what we can salvage once the others are safely across. Let's be thankful no lives were lost."

The man stuck out his hand. "There would've been if not for your quick thinking. We're indebted to you."

Zeke nodded. "I'm sorry I couldn't do more." He headed to relieve Junior of his wagon driving duties. "Once we cross over the Devil's Backbone, we're home free." Hopefully he could get the group safely there.

Later that evening, Zeke handed Delly a rump from the slaughtered mule. "Poor thing was still alive when we got down there. Scraped up and bloody with two broken legs. Seems we've been eating a lot of mule on this trip."

She accepted the meat. "Don't tell Dorcas what's in the stew. She won't touch it if you do." She dropped the chunk into the pot of broth boiling over the fire. "Were you able to save anything?"

"Most of their personal things. About half the food." He sat on a stool and removed his hat, letting the breeze blow the dust from his hair. "The Wilson's will be all right. They can pack their things on the three remaining mules. They won't have a wagon to live in until they're settled, but that's minor in comparison to losing a life. I'm sending Junior and a couple others ahead with the stock to better water. We'll be able to catch up with them in a day or two." He poured a cup of coffee and smiled. "Luke's going to be busy tonight. That road wrecked havoc on the wagons."

Zeke stared into his mug, seeing the faces of all they'd lost on the trail. Seth, Mr. Oglesby, the woman whose husband died of cholera. He lifted the coffee to his mouth. He wouldn't dwell on that. He'd focus on what he still had. Delly, and the children.

His gaze followed her as she fed the little ones. She might be young but she possessed a backbone of steel and was a natural mother and nurturer. He noticed the pooch beneath her apron and averted his eyes, wishing the child she carried was his. He tossed the remains of his drink into the fire.

It would be his. As soon as he convinced Delly to marry him.

By the time they caught up with the ones he'd sent ahead with the stock, they'd be setting foot on the beginning of his land. He felt tempted to tell Delly how close they really were, but the desire to surprise her won out.

He still hadn't asked her to hand over

possession of the deed, but God's Word seemed the best place for the precious slip of paper.

~

The Devil's Backbone consisted of three steep mountains covered with loose rocks. The walls of the trail cut so close to the wagons, they almost gave Delly an overwhelming sense of claustrophia. She wondered how anyone dared call it a trail to begin with. She could reach out and touch the rough stones. No one driving anything larger than a farm wagon could travel through.

"I can see why it's called the Devil's Backbone." The oxen's ears twitched as if in understanding. Sadie had taken to riding in their wagon with Luke, leaving Delly to manage by, and talk to, herself.

At least her friend would be close by. Zeke said he'd give Luke and Sadie a small plot of land to farm, and Luke expressed a desire to open a blacksmith shop to service the rapidly arriving pioneers to the new territory.

What would it be like starting a new life from the ground up?

She glanced at her gloved hands. Freckles dotted her arms, and she dreaded what her face looked like. Most likely like someone through a handful of mud at her and spots stuck to her face. Well, she'd never put too much prize on her looks anyway, despite Ezra's flowery words or Zeke's admiring glances. Looks didn't last and wouldn't build a roof over her childrens's heads. She smiled. But she did like the looks Zeke sent her way when he thought she wasn't looking. Made her feel all woman.

The trail slanted upward again, and Delly slapped the reins against the animal's backs. Something in the back of the wagon slid and banged against something else. She glanced over her shoulder to see Alice sleeping peacefully in her crib made from spare wood. Such a sweet baby. She would've been the joy of her mother.

Delly squared her shoulders. They'd had an adventure. No denying it. Something to talk about over a warm winter fire. She spotted Zeke's blue flannel shirt ahead. Would she do it all again? Definitely. For that man, she wouldn't hesitate. She loved him for sure and certain. No more denying the feelings rising within her. Seeing him day-after-day while they managed adjoining land, it's the closest she could get to marrying him.

Her spirit lifted as she realized God's hand in the trials and celebrations of the last six months. By His grace they'd made it. By His mercy, a healthy baby slept in a make-shift box in a weathered wagon.

Tears filled Delly's eyes as she looked on the trail ahead. She'd been ungrateful, full of whining and complaints. How had the others put up with her? She resolved to do better. To raise her children with the pioneering spirit.

One peak conquered; another begun. Rocks clattered beneath the oxens' hooves. The beasts strained, slipping on the loose ground, in their effort to pull the wagon. Their struggle reminded Delly of her own.

32

"Is that a house?" *Please, God, let it be so.* Delly straightened in the wagon seat, her gaze searching for Junior among the milling travelers. Surely they would've caught up with the herd by now.

The rest of the train had circled in front of a log cabin nestled in a meadow between two short mountains. Fields lay lush with hay and rippled in the slight breeze. Thick trees crowded the cleared areas. A garden grew behind a split-rail fence. Chickens clucked in the yard, running between the legs of mules and oxen. A pen held a sow and piglets. Junior's dogs barked and chased anything dumb enough to get in their path.

A woman stood in the doorway of the building and dried her hands on a starched apron before waving a greeting. Tears welled in Delly's eyes. A home. Civilization.

Zeke rode up, a grin splitting his tanned face and and crinkled the corner of his eyes. "This is it. The beginning of the end. Folks will branch off from here in the morning to claim their land."

We're that close?" Hope sprouted in her heart.

"Yes, ma'am. Climb on down. These folks sell beef, eggs, and vegetables to weary travelers. Go cook us up a feast." He winked and rode off.

"Dorcas, get Alice, would you?" Delly bundled her skirt in one hand and climbed from the wagon seat. Her spirits soared as high as the hawk circling above their heads. The scent of late blooming wildflowers and honeysuckle filled the air. She'd made it.

"Welcome. I'm Nora Lambert. My husband Hank will be along shortly. He's showing Zeke a stranger that showed up here after your drovers rode through." The woman stepped from the porch and bustled toward Delly. "Make yourselves at home. Times are long between folks visiting."

A stranger? "I'm Delly Williams." Delly held out her hand. "Zeke is my brother-in-law."

"Oh, everyone within a three day ride around here knows Mr. Williams. A fine man." She beamed.

Delly turned. "These are my children. My son, Ezra Junior, rode through a day ahead of us."

"On a painted pony. Rode out of here yesterday." Nora laughed. "Fancies himself a cowboy, that one."

"Yes, he does." A weight lifted from her shoulders. Junior had made it through. Almost a grown man, but it was still difficult for Delly to let him go. "This is a beautiful piece of land."

"Thank you. We got down off those mountains, I planted my feet here and refused to move. Decided

I wasn't going to tempt fate anymore. Poor Hank didn't have a choice but to settle here." She motioned toward a pair of straw-seated rocking chairs on the porch. "Come sit a spell. We've done all right for ourselves. Got us a few head of cattle, the Indians don't bother us much, and anything we plant in our garden thrives. Winters can be brutal sometimes, but I ain't complaining. There's plenty of wildlife to feed us if our smokehouse runs empty."

Delly settled in one of the chairs, set Alice on a blanket at her feet, and took Baby Sarah into her lap. "How long have you lived here?"

"About five years." The woman stared toward the horizon. "We've seen lots of folks move through here. Have a nice nest egg set aside because of it. By the time they reach us, folks are hungry for fresh beef." She sighed. "I've raised two sons, and buried three. It's been hard, but I wouldn't head back east for anything. No, this is God's land, plain and simple."

Delly's gaze followed Nora's. She'd love to settle close to the woman; have an older neighbor to show her the ropes. "How far away is my family's land?"

"You'll hit the beginning of it in the morning. The homestead will take another half of a day. It's real purty." Nora patted her hand. "A slice of heaven. Less than half a day's ride in the opposite direction is the town of Waterfall. Mr. Williams's got a lot of land, but still decided to settle close to the edge of it. Guess the land is half yours. Close enough for civilization if you wanted."

They wouldn't be isolated. Delly glanced around the wagon circle, thankful for the other emigrants. She'd have neighbors. Maybe even a church someday, and a school. Hope leaped in her chest.

She turned to Nora with a smile. "I'd like some of that beef. Fresh vegetables, too, if you've got them. And some eggs. Our hens haven't been laying."

"I've got all that, and your chickens will be all right once you get settled." Nora rose. "Come on out to the smokehouse." Delly called for Dorcas to come get the baby and keep an eye on the others, then followed the kind woman to the back of the house.

When she'd finished, Delly headed back to the wagon with smoked beef, a basket full of fresh vegetables, and a skip in her step that'd been missing for months. Across the circle, someone tuned a fiddle, and an older gentleman who Delly assumed was Hank, blew a few notes on a harmonica. She paused for a moment and stared into the darkening sky.

We did it, God. You brought us through, richer than I'd ever thought possible. She hugged the paper wrapped meat to her chest. Truly blessed. That's what she was. She hadn't lost a single family member. Instead, she'd gained two babies. Not to mention dear friends.

She tossed vegetables and meat into the stew and wished she'd had time to sew a new dress. Nothing to do now. Her faded blue calico would have to suffice. When was the last time she'd felt pretty? She stirred their dinner. And she definitely wanted to look good for Zeke.

Now that she'd admitted her feelings for Zeke to herself, how could she get him to propose again? She'd take getting hitched to him any way she could, business proposition or not. She barely limped anymore. Weight loss and hard work left her as thin as a rail, except for her growing stomach. Would he even find her desirable as a wife anymore?

~

"I found him in the trees, dead of a snake bite," Hank said, toeing the body with his boot. "He had this in his pocket." He pulled out a sheet of paper. "Has your name on it. Says you sold him your land. 'Cept I'm not believing it."

Zeke eyed the man lying beneath a juniper bush. "No, I didn't sell. For most of our trip, another outlaw followed us and kept trying to steal the deed. I'm thinking this is the man who hired him. When he couldn't get a hold of the land that way, he made his own deed." Zeke shook his head at the sadness of the man's greed. So close to the land he'd wanted to steal, now dead within a day's ride. "If you'll bury him, I'll let my sister-in-law know the danger is past."

"Sure thing. See you later at the party."

Zeke washed up in the water trough behind Hank's house and donned a clean shirt. He had plans for tonight, and they didn't involve him looking like he'd ridden the trail all day. After slicking his hair back, he made his way to the bonfire the travelers had made.

His heart stopped when Delly stepped into the firelight. She'd pinned her hair off her neck. Curly tendrils caressed her cheeks. Thank God, they'd be home soon. He planned on proposing again. Tonight. This time for love.

She approached him with a shy smile. "Good evening, Zeke."

"You look beautiful."

She blushed and lowered her eyes. "Thank you."

"I'll tell you every day for the rest of our lives if you want me to."

"What are you saying?"

His neck heated and his heart beat erratically. "I want to marry you. I want to raise that passel of children. Not as a business proposition this time, or out of a sense of duty, but because I can't imagine a life without you by my side." He grasped her hands. "What do you say, Delly? Will you be my bride?"

She leaned her forehead on his chest. "I can't believe this trip is almost over. So many times I thought I'd never make it."

Was she going to say no? His mouth filled with cotton.

"You're tougher then you think you are." He tightened his arms around her. Surprise that he could love another human being with such intensity shocked him. He'd always known he'd lay his life down for another, but this woman would, and had, caused him to take the life of someone who wanted to cause her harm. The knowledge left him short of breath.

This wasn't a responsibility of only a few

months. This was for a lifetime. Til death do they part. He planted a kiss on top of her head, inhaling the scent of her. "I'm proud to have you beside me, building a home, raising a family. It's the second greatest gift God could give me. If you'll say yes."

Tears shimmered in her eyes as she glanced up. "I didn't expect to marry on the trail. So many times I wanted to turn back. When Alice died, when Abby got the cholera. I'm so glad I didn't."

"You and me both. You are truly the most Delicious thing I've had the privilege to know." He pulled her head to nestle in the crook of his neck as they swayed to the music, oblivious to anyone around them. Her skin rippled beneath his touch. He smiled to know he affected her the same way she did him. "Tell me you want to marry me as much as I do you. I love you, Delicious Williams."

"Yes, Ezekial Williams. I'll marry you. Where's the preacher?"

~

After a brief ride to Waterfall, Delly stared into a small clearing as a married woman. Smoke rose from the rock chimney of a cabin. Her heart calmed at the homey scene. Two homesteads in as many days. The rigors of the trail continued to fall away with each sign of civilization.

This cabin was different than the Lambert's. Smaller, pigs rooting under the porch instead of a pen, and no porch graced the front. Would her new home be as humble?

She sighed. "I wish Alice was alive to see the end. She was so reluctant to come in the first place. Who's cabin is this?"

Zeke turned to her with a grin. He held out his hand and helped her down. "My uncle Rupert's."

She glanced questioningly up at him as he led her past Junior and the others.

"Hey, Ma!" Junior waved a cigar in her direction.

Delly clasped a hand to her throat. Not smoking! She'd just cured him of gambling.

Zeke laughed. "I'll talk to him. The way he's coughing, I don't think it's a habit he'll take up. He's done the work of a grown man on this journey. Let him reap the benefits. He'll suffer enough later today."

A short, wiry man marched around the corner. A smile split his bearded face.

"Zeke, my boy." He held out his arms. "Been wondering when I'd see your ugly face again. Who's the pretty girl?"

"Rupert, this is my wife. I assume you've met her son, Ezra Junior. That passel of children are my nieces and nephews. Delly was my brother's wife. We've got an adopted daughter, Alice, born on the trail, and those are our good friends, Luke and Sadie. Luke's one of the best farriers you'll ever meet."

Rupert clapped Zeke on the shoulder. "You've been busy. And this area could use a good blacksmith."

"How's the ranch?" Zeke moved his arm around Delly's shoulders.

She craned her neck to stare at him. Ranch?

"Better than fair to middlin'. I got in those turnips and potatoes you wanted, and that upper meadow is waist high with feed. I didn't have time to start cutting timber for a larger cabin, 'cause I had my own crops to get in, but with the three of us, we'll get one up in no time."

"You did fine. I've lots of help with me, and I appreciate what you did get done. I thought I'd be going without a garden this winter."

"Nope. All you got to do is harvest it. It's time."

Delly's head spun. A ready garden? An upper meadow? Who was this man she'd married? She fingered the tattered britches she wore and remembered the dead woman's clothes she and Sadie had salvaged. She should've kept on the dress she'd worn when they'd wed in Waterfall. "Are we rich?"

He tossed back his head and laughed, then lifted her and spun around. "Not yet, Darlin', but I plan on being someday. I told you not to worry about money at the trading posts. We've got hard work ahead of us, but money shouldn't be an issue. There's not many places to spend it around here." He set her back on her feet. His gaze bore into hers. "I wanted to surprise you, Delly. This here is our land. Over that rise is the prettiest valley you'll ever lay eyes on. Want to see it?"

She smiled and nodded. "More than anything."

He led her to Cyclone and mounted, lifting her to sit sideways in front of him. With a kick to his horse's flanks, they leaped away from the others and raced over the hill. With their speed, Delly tossed thanksgiving praises to heaven. They'd done it. They'd arrived, and except for a few scars, unharmed.

When they stopped, she gazed on an emerald valley covered with wildflowers in every hue of the rainbow. A clear stream meandered across the meadow. A small cabin nestled beneath tall cedars and pine. Horses grazed from a split-rail corral. Off in the distance, she could make out the shapes of several head of cattle. Overhead, a hawk soared, then swooped to capture a field mouse in its claws.

Tears coursed their way down her cheeks. "This is the best birthday present ever."

"You didn't tell me it was your birthday." He turned her to face him and wiped her tears with his thumbs. "I want only the best for you. We've the beginning of a grand life here. You can see where the garden is. Next year you can plant those seeds you carried in that gourd." He pointed to their right. "Over there is the field for feed. We've got chickens, two dogs, a cat, mules, a trained Indian pony, two that are as wild as the wilderness, oxen, and a milk cow. There's a handful of mustangs and fifty head of cattle. I'm saving to buy more horses. I'd like nothing more than to have a horse breeding ranch. Cattle too."

"I can't think of anyone I'd rather share this with." He crushed Delly close and captured her lips in a kiss. Her heart soared with the snowy clouds scattered across the scarlet and lavender sky. She'd found her love and he'd been worth the wait.

The End

ABOUT THE AUTHOR

www.cynthiahickey.com

Cynthia Hickey is a multi-published and best-selling author of cozy mysteries and romantic suspense. She has taught writing at many conferences and small writing retreats. She and her husband run the publishing press, Winged Publications. They live in Arizona and Arkansas, becoming snowbirds with three dogs. They have ten grandchildren who keep them busy and tell everyone they know that "Nana is a writer."